I0732746

HER HOCKEY STUDS

Power Players Hockey Series - Books 1 and 2

LARISSA LYNX

Contents

My Two-Stud Stand

Her Three Studs

Her Hockey Studs Copyright © 2021 by Larissa Lynx
Published by Literary Madness
Published May 2021

ISBN 978-1-949426-24-3 Large Print Edition
ISBN 978-1-949426-09-0 Paperback

This volume contains **My Two-Stud Stand** and **Her Three Studs**, both Copyright © 2020 by Larissa Lynx hard work of this author and only read authorized, purchased downloads. All characters are fictional creations; any resemblance to actual persons is unintentional and coincidental.

Proofread by Judy Zweifel at Judy's Proofreading. Cover by Literary Madness.

At Literary Madness, we strive to create a book free of typos. If you notice anything amiss, we're happy to fix it. litmadness@yahoo.com

My Two-Stud Stand

What shall I say? My emotions of fear
and surprise were instantly subdued by
those of the pleasure I bespoke in great
presence of mind from the turn this
adventure might take.

—John Cleland, *Fanny Hill: Memoirs of a
Woman of Pleasure*

ONE

The Encounter in Which They Meet

"PROMISE me you'll go out and get laid this weekend. You deserve it."

"*What?*" I stared at the colorful receptionist standing in the doorway of my glass-walled office, obsessively aligning the pile of loose papers in her arms.

"You heard me," she accused, abandoning all pretense of organization to look straight at me. "Go out, find yourself a hunk, and get laid." This from the woman who—when she wasn't proposing insane schemes—I considered my closest friend at work.

I scanned the well-appointed office to make sure no one else had been privy to Kathi's outrageous words. Thankfully the only other realtor still present had better things to do than eavesdrop in on my tidy, just-Windexed corner. Or so I hoped. "Would you keep it down? Or better yet"—I balled up the grocery list I'd started composing after scrubbing the panes so hard they squeaked and threw it at her smiling face —"put a sock in it."

"To celebrate your big sale, Carolina," she enthused, tapping her tongue stud against her front teeth with a *tsking* sound when my paper missile only grazed her shoulder.

The last few weeks had been, by turns, the most grueling and most exhilarating in my life. Yet with the ultimate goal realized, all my hard work culminating in a very satisfactory closing, an odd restlessness assailed me, kept me at the office far later than was typical on a Friday.

Dreading the return to my empty, lonely apartment?

Empty? my conscience screamed. *Empty!?* A mental picture of the leafy jungle my green thumb and I had created almost brought forth a smile, but a tepid one at best. A profusion of ferns and philodendrons did not good company make.

Knuckles rapped on one corner of my immaculate desk, bringing my head up, my thoughts back to the sterile office. Sterile except for Kathi, indigo hair punked out every which way, beaming down at me. "You've been majorly uptight since the deal almost fell apart, jumping through hoops to get everyone on the same page. I got all stressed just being around you." Kathi shrugged her shoulders, as if she were trying to loosen up, then she launched the wadded grocery list she'd picked up through the doorway, toward a trash can miles across the spacious workplace.

"Good arm," Trevor said with a grunt, which wasn't like him at all, as he walked over to pick it up from the floor and chunk it in File Thirteen before heading toward the conference room where he'd been sequestered with out-of-town buyers all afternoon.

"Bite me!" Kathi hollered in his direction. "On second thought, I wouldn't give you the chance, fucktard!"

"Ummm," I muttered, glad Trevor's clients had already left, giddy their counteroffer had been accepted. "Being a little harsh maybe?" Especially since I knew she'd harbored a crush on the rugged fellow since he'd joined our ranks earlier in the year.

She snorted. "The turd turned me down when I asked him out. Claimed it wasn't a woman's place. Whatever. Can I help it if he's a *loser! A loser whose socks don't match his sorry-ass sedate suit!*" This last part was projected loudly enough I knew the sedate, suit-wearing Trevor couldn't help but hear. "What kind of dickwipe wears a suit jacket these days? On a Friday! *In* the office?" Kathi grumped to herself.

Dickwipe? Firming my cheeks against the smile that threatened, I tried to commiserate. "He's too rough around the edges for you anyway." Bearded, handsome, and hovering forty, I thought he looked more like a lumberjack than a white-collar sales broker, but there was no denying his talent; he'd closed more transactions last month than anyone else. But lucky for me, not the big one I'd finally nailed down. "Maybe let it go?" I suggested. "Give the guy a break?"

Once she realized he wasn't going to respond to her verbal baiting, Kathi rounded on me again. "Now you!"

"Me?" Maybe I should've kept my mouth shut.

I'd assumed the topic of me was closed. Erroneously, it seemed.

"*Weeks* of haggling," she began, "*weeks* of worrying me to death over all the little details and you finally close the sale of the century, making the biggest commission of your life. And what do I find you doing?" She indicated my pristine desk, the sparkling glass walls. "Stalling! When you should be out celebrating! Cutting loose. Partying till the sun comes up."

It wasn't even down yet. But still...

"Celebrate? By having *sex*?" I practically squawked, unaccustomed to discussing it so blatantly. *It* being sex.

"Works for me. When's the last time you got any? This decade?"

Just barely. "Of course."

"You hesitated."

"I..." She was right.

My face flamed at the images conjured by her scandalous suggestion. Have sex with a stranger to celebrate the multimillion-dollar property sale I'd successfully brokered?

What a completely crazy notion. What a strangely tempting idea.

I shook the insane thought out of my head and tried to remember how I was the one with the common sense, not the wild libido. "I refuse to take sex advice from someone with a pierced eyebrow."

Crummers! Did I say that out loud?

But instead of taking offense, Kathi fairly gloated. She shimmied her hips, drawing my gaze to her crotch. "My eyebrow's not all that's pierced."

"You didn't!" She'd been *talking* clit piercing for weeks, but I couldn't believe... "You actually went through with it? Dang, Kath, I don't know whether to call you ballsy or brilliantly stupid." A flash of envy over her take-no-prisoners, damn-the-consequences ways speared through my conservative, chicken-hearted core. My clit buzzed, though, at the mere thought of a stranger putting his hands on me, spreading my folds to place icy metal— "No, thanks!"

"You're just jealous of my stylin' ways. Meet me at Twist tonight"—she mentioned the hottest nightclub around—"and I'll hook you up. Guaranteed."

Twist on the Town. Flashing strobe lights, lines of smack in the bathroom, and music blasting so loud my eardrums went on strike for a week— I'd gone to the skanky place once and swore never to return. I shuddered at the memory of being groped in blinking black light by stoned players just out for nameless nookie. "Twist isn't exactly *my* style, but thanks for asking. I do appreciate it, really, but I'm good." Good at selling properties and growing plants. Neither of which I thought counted. I flashed a smile, hoping it didn't look as fake as it felt. "Really. I'll head home, make brownies…"

Kathi leaned forward and braced both hands on my desk. "Carolina, Carolina, Carolina…" She sighed as if I were the most pitiful thing in the world.

Her straight arms pressed the swells of her abundant breasts together, the casual position creating cleavage worth being jealous over.

I thought of the Mentionables 34AA push-up she'd given me for my birthday—the Magic Marvel did its job plumping up my meager assets and was in an awesome purple tiger stripe, of all things—and reminded myself why I didn't absolutely hate her. The transplanted Texan was so comfortable in her own skin it would be easy to writhe with resentment if she wasn't so darn friendly. As it was, the closest I'd come to emulating her unselfconscious ways in the three years we'd been friends were the second piercings in my ears.

"I know you wanna get down and dirty, I can see it in your eyes. Pick somewhere else to go, then. A hotel. A fern bar. Hell, even Bennigan's. Anywhere. Doll up and go trawling for tight tush." Laughing, Kathi abandoned her artless stance and strolled away, heading toward her own desk —and the missed trash can—near the entrance. "Find yourself a sexy stud," she said over her shoulder, "and have your wicked way with him, that's an order. Come midnight, you'll thank me!"

I rushed to follow, stopping in the safety of my doorway. "Right. Because men are just lined up, waiting for me to crook my finger so they can bow down before me, kiss my feet, and hop into my bed." In my dreams, maybe. "Yeah, right. Like that's going to happen."

"Confidence, chickadee." Kathi grabbed the backpack that doubled as a purse and headed for the exit, walking backward. "After a big fat commission check like that? You should be riding high, girlfriend. Trust me on this, you're primed. Now go fix yourself up, buy a couple of drinks, and let yourself go."

"A drink or two and I'm ready for sex?" I forced another smile, even as my ears heated just hearing her absurd advice. "That's all it takes?"

Kathi rested against the doorframe and I caught the sidelong wistful glance she shot toward the conference room. "It doesn't take any if you're in the mood. Promise me you'll at least think about it."

I shook my head, perversely unable to think of anything else.

"Promise!" Squaring her shoulders and giving me a jaunty wave, Kathi was gone, leaving me alone with my turbulent thoughts. That and my twitchy, tingling crotch. Clit ring? Not in this lifetime.

Come to think on it, this part of Ohio didn't even have a Bennigan's, not anymore.

Wait a minute. I wasn't considering her outrageous suggestion, was I?

Go out, just for sex?

That was so not me.

SO WHY, three hours later, was I sitting at the swankiest bar I knew of in downtown Cincinnati, freshly washed, waxed, and plucked, ready to be…

Fucked!

My baser, braver side practically screamed what I was almost too inhibited to whisper.

Just thinking about it had my legs squeezing together, further mangling the pitiful scrap of lavender lace I wore that masqueraded as underwear. My fingers toyed with the flimsy napkin under the glass as I sipped my rum and Coke. And tried not to look desperate. Or pathetic. Or *virginal.*

God. Anything but that.

You've had sex before, I consoled myself.

Yeah, but it's been a loooooong time, my conscience insisted.

It hasn't been that long, I argued.

Oh yeah? And how many calendars have you changed out since?

I thought of my most recent less-than-impressive encounters with my former live-in boyfriend. On the whole, sex with him had sucked. *Exactly. More specifically, he said* you *sucked at it and you finally wised up and told the loser to get lost. That's why you haven't done it since.*

Lofty conscience, I thought. Why was it always right?

I swigged back the rest of my drink. So what if my meager sexual experiences hadn't been that great? If they'd soured me on wanting to jump back in the sack. Had made it easy to forgo men and concentrate on work?

I was older now, more mature. Curvier, thanks to my padded push-up.

Hornier!

Hmmm. My conscience was starting to sound an awful lot like Kathi, who had threatened more than once to get me drunk and pull the stick out of my ass.

One bubbly champagne and a second mixed drink later—I *was* here to celebrate, after all—I was halfway to drunk all on my own. And the stick was disintegrating faster than I could've imagined as visions of my impending sexual breakthrough filled my head.

A one-night stand. Physical intimacy with someone I didn't know touching me, stroking me… The lips of my vulva swelled, chafed by the lace thong. I couldn't remember ever being this aroused. Turned on by nothing more than naughty thoughts of being naughty.

"Cheers." I toasted myself, downing the last few swallows and savoring the sugary bite of rum and cola, wondering when I would garner the guts to make eye contact with one of the single studs out on the prowl. My newfound confidence had brought me to the door and enabled me to walk through, but old habits and insecurities overshadowed the desire to break out once I'd found my perch at the bar.

Holding the glass in front of me like a shield, I spun in a circle, whipping my legs around to twirl the barstool and peruse for new blood. "Fresh meat" Kathi would've said.

Just walking in, a striking, black-haired hunk caught my eye. So far out of my league, with his confident swagger and casual ease, I didn't try to catch his, wheeling back around before I wasted any time lusting for what I couldn't have.

The place had ambience, I'd give it that. Soft, glowing lights, overhead ceiling fans that circulated the occasional waft of illicit tobacco smoke, and if the background music was a bit loud, at least the songs boasted a melody and weren't nothing but nonstop drums banging around in my brain.

Noooo...all of the pounding was in my crotch, where my pulse beat a steady tattoo, eager for some action.

Here I was, primed for my first one-night stand and I hadn't yet managed to find anyone I wanted to stand next to, much less get horizontal with. I'd shyly scoped out everyone present upon my arrival and had been sorely disappointed when no one immediately made my juices *vroom!* If I was going to jeopardize my spectacular run of unintentional celibacy, then I at least wanted to do it with someone who revved my stalled engine and got me so raring to go, the little voice in my head would shut up.

"I have question." The deep words came from over my left shoulder and my stomach dipped in response. I was a sucker for a good accent. And this guy possessed a foreign one that indicated English wasn't what normally tripped off his tongue.

"Are you talking to me?" I whispered without moving, praying that he was.

"Why does beautiful American woman waste time drinking alone in crowded bar?"

I swiveled on the padded barstool and had to keep from swallowing my tongue as I angled my neck up, up, *up* to study the tall man who'd spoken. Holy Toledo, Batman—the hunk I'd noticed!

He smiled, crinkling the skin around his mouth and eyes. Taking note of the conspicuous glass tray the bartender slapped on the counter between us, he snubbed out his cigarette.

"Russian?" I hazarded a guess, inspecting the gorgeous creature towering above me. The bar's low lighting and the music's high volume had me sitting up straighter to get a better look.

"Chelyabinsk," he responded as if that answered everything. I wasn't sure whether Chel-whatever was his birthplace or a breed of poodle, but either way, I was hooked.

He nodded toward the empty space on my left, available only because someone had relocated the barstool that normally resided there. "May I join with you?"

This one could join with me any time he wanted. He looked to be in his mid-twenties and I could tell he worked out, the bulging muscles beneath his shirt causing an instant Pavlovian response. My rum-hazed mind wanted nothing more than to follow him home and listen to him talk all night long. My sex-starved body just wanted to hump his cock.

I guess I didn't answer soon enough because his smile dimmed. "Maybe another time, no?"

He started to turn away.

"No! Not another time. T-tonight!" I practically bellowed over the music, Frustrated with the stupid stammer that sometimes invaded my speech when I was nervous or in a hurry. At the moment, I was both. Afraid he was about to leave. And with him, my one chance at the dirty, spontaneous sex that now seemed so all-fired necessary to my self-esteem.

His smile returned and he leaned close, surrounding me with the scent of Old Spice.

"Tonight?" The timbre of his voice deepened, his accent thickening. He brushed my hair over my shoulder, his long fingers curving around my nape. The skin on my neck sizzled in response. "You would like being with Rurik tonight?"

In that moment I knew—I no longer wanted to be at the bar, paying ten dollars a pop for a few ounces of liquid. I wanted this man's lips on mine, his hands on my breasts. I wanted his tongue between my legs.

"If you're Rurik, then yes." I shouldered my purse and slid off the barstool, praying I hadn't left a wet spot on the cushion. Good Lord. I hadn't even known I could get this excited, but at the thought of having sex with this exotic foreigner, my insides burned so hot I was ready to melt—all over his cock.

"Yes." My voice was decisive. "Do you live nearby?" Had I just invited myself to this stranger's home? To his bed?

Damn straight I had! My conscience was ecstatic.

His white teeth flashed in the dim light. "Closer than you think. We go there now?"

Heck yes! I nodded, still amazed that he'd approached me at all. Granted, I wore the slinkiest outfit my closet possessed—a figure-hugging, sleeveless purple velvet dress, so short my ass almost fell out. I'd worn the micromini with white leather boots several years ago to a costume party. My own version of a go-go dancer.

For my seduce-a-stranger efforts, I'd exchanged the boots for a pair of three-inch-high sandals with ankle straps—in a deep plum color that didn't match anything I owned, save for the nail polish I'd bought on the way home. The heels were compliments of Kathi last Christmas. She'd called them "hooker shoes", and after our conversation at work, I'd known I couldn't wear anything else tonight.

Rurik pulled a twenty-dollar bill from his wallet, slapped it on the bar, and grabbed my hand. Did he have a condom stashed in there? Maybe two? *Stop thinking!* I ordered myself.

Easy to do as he guided me through the packed bar. His large hand dwarfed mine. His thumb swept little circles over my palm and my head spun. He had to be six foot three or better, and I could only imagine how the rest of him would compare.

We navigated through the crowd and I admired his broad back, shown to perfection in the long-sleeved black shirt he wore. Silk, if I wasn't mistaken. Above the collar, his inky hair, shorn in a casual, choppy style, tempted my fingers to explore. Every time he glanced down at me, a wicked grin curving his lips, I thought I'd faint. Either from nerves or longing, I wasn't sure which.

We emerged from the bar and he wrapped an arm around my waist, guiding me up the sporadically lit street. His fingers curved over my hip bone, and I wished he were touching naked skin. The juncture of my thighs dampened with every high-heeled step I took. "Are you parked close by?"

The glass fronts of several exclusive retail establishments, closed for the night, reflected our journey toward my, for once, non-repressed revelry. I couldn't wait to get started.

"I hope I am not disappointing my little American…" His hand lightly grazed one side of my bottom, snagging gently on the velvet nap. Sparks danced from his fingers and exploded near my clit. "But I stay here tonight."

He indicated the high-rise hotel we'd reached.

The Riviera? Goodness. Those rooms weren't cheap. I'd never set foot in the prestigious hotel, but now I knew. "You don't live here, do you?"

This was perfect. Sex with a total stranger. One I'd *never* see again. If I screwed up or didn't do it right, it wouldn't matter. Absolutely classic. Relief rushed through me and I relaxed, no longer quite as concerned about my potential performance.

Rurik ushered me through the revolving doors and past the tiled entry toward a large bank of elevators. Alabaster marble flanked every available space. The floor, walls, even the giant columns supporting the multistoried lobby all shone, sparkled. I stood a little taller and added a saucy swing to my hips. I was drowning in luxury and couldn't be happier about my willing descent into debauchery.

"I am on road much of year. But very happy my team staying here tonight." He gave me a sultry, seductive look that was easy to interpret. "Very happy."

That made two of us.

He pushed the elevator call button and a set of double doors slid open, accompanied by a soft *ping*. I preceded him inside the mirrored elevator, then turned around. And got my first really good look at him.

In the glow of the soft lights beaming down from the ceiling, I found myself staring at sin on a stick. The ends of his black hair were mostly dry but looked damp closer to his head, as though he'd recently showered. Scraped carelessly back, the longish strands just barely brushed his collar. A hint of a well-groomed beard shaded his jaw and bisected his chin, coming to a stop beneath his lower lip. No mustache adorned the upper.

The distinctive facial hair only enhanced the exotic vibe he gave off every time he spoke. "Ah, I see you spot hit I could not block." Keeping my hand captured in his, he raised our arms to finger the beginnings of a bruise on one side of his jaw.

I was too embarrassed to admit the rest of him snared my attention so fully I *hadn't* noticed. Not until he pointed it out. With little guidance, I grazed my fingertips over the flushed swell. "Ouch."

And hadn't I become the brilliant conversationalist?

"I trust you will kiss and make better." That sinful smile flashed again and his dark eyes seared right through me.

Behind him the doors hissed shut. We were alone in the private space. After reaching over to push the button for a floor near the top, he narrowed the gap between us, dropped a kiss on my palm and then placed my hand over his shirt buttons, anchoring it against solid muscle.

What manner of man sported a bruised jaw and resided at The Riviera? Boasted a big, strapping body with rock-hard abs?

The floor beneath our feet quivered and started ascending. He drew me closer.

I had trouble breathing. "Your..." I swallowed, my free hand tangling in the strap of my purse, the other sinking into the muscled ridges cording his stomach. I was breathing fast, so very lightheaded with excitement. Excitement that soared when my fingers dragged a couple inches lower, toward his groin, and sensed the firm heat of his erection just waiting to be released. "Your team of what? Russian sex gods?"

"Hockey," he whispered, and curved one hand around the back of my neck, touching my jaw with the other. "Tulsa Tornadoes." He leaned down, his thumb edging my lips apart. "And now, my beautiful American, Rurik is going to blow you away."

I didn't care that the line was as corny as a tub of popped and buttered kernels. Didn't care that he'd no doubt used it countless times before. Didn't much mind that he was so obviously a player the label could've been tattooed across his forehead. None of that mattered. All I wanted—

His tongue dove past my lips and swept away my thoughts, banished my internal dialogue. I moaned around the supple intrusion, loving his dark, smoky taste, reveling in the feel of his lips grinding against mine.

Hard, forceful kisses.

I decided there was nothing better.

Intensifying my contribution, I attacked him in kind, slanting my lips over his with voracious intent. He winced, an expletive I didn't recognize escaping from that talented mouth.

My head tilted back, eyes zeroing in on the bruise. "Too rough?" Darn. I'd just discovered I liked it a little rough. "I'll try to be more gentle."

Rurik chuckled. "Is sore, but the value of your kisses are worth it."

My kisses had value?

Taking in the bewildered look on my face, embarrassment tinged his. "Forgive me. My hold on English is not so good."

"Your *grasp* on English is exquisite," I said truthfully. "That means wonderfully good. Fantastic. Fabulous."

"I demonstrate fabulous." Renewing his seductive kisses, he cornered me into the mirrored wall and pressed against my body. The strength of him practically held me in place as his hands traversed from my nape and jaw to my shoulders where his calloused fingers snagged on the velvet.

Rurik released my mouth and leaned back. He stared into my eyes as he scraped his fingernails down, past my collarbone to the upper swells of my pushed-up breasts. He edged his big hands inside the padded cups and rubbed. My nipples instantly beaded and I inhaled, pushing them outward into his hands. He palmed both slight mounds and fiercely kneaded.

Nothing gentle in his touch—or in his eyes. A look of pure sin and hot sex blasted from his gaze. "Feels good, no?"

"Very good." I tried to pull his mouth back to mine, but he resisted, squeezing my breasts.

"I make guarantee it will feel more than good when you are naked on bed"—he rasped his thumbs over my nipples—"and I take you into my mouth."

How much longer was this elevator ride going to take? I clamped my thighs together, feeling the damp glide of my juices steaming the skin under my dress.

"Who says we need to wait for the bed? Touch me now," I said boldly, swinging my purse over one shoulder and attempting to push my dress off the other, to free my breasts from their unintentional confinement.

He blocked my efforts by settling one heavy hand on my shoulder. "No. We wait. Wait for no interruptions."

No? What did he mean *no?* In my own amateurish way, I was trying to be seductive here. Uninhibited. "But—"

His head swooped down and his tongue stalled my protest, spearing along mine, diving deep within my mouth. My fingers tightened around the corded muscles lining his neck and I sucked his tongue, pulling on the firm muscle until he groaned.

With one final squeeze to my breast and shoulder, his hands abandoned them for my legs. I gasped against his mouth when he skimmed his palms higher, raising my snug-fitting dress, digging his fingers into the bare skin of my hips.

I squirmed in his hold and he lifted me clear off the floor, bringing my center flush against his cock. Through the scrap of lace, his impressive erection nudged my flesh. With eager abandon I wrapped my legs around his waist and rode him through his clothes.

Glorious heavens. This was exactly what I'd needed tonight—for ages, actually—kisses that completely overwhelmed my every sense, that obliterated any remaining insecurity. I ground myself against him and thick cream dripped from my center, flooding the fabric between us.

Ding! The elevator lurched to a halt.

The doors opened with a whoosh, but I was too far gone to care if anyone saw us. Evidently, he was too. Without disconnecting our fused mouths, Rurik's hands molded securely beneath the bare cheeks of my ass and he whipped around to exit the elevator.

Yeah, okay. As his fingers scuffed over my skin, his groomed beard my lips, I was willing to admit there might be something to this waiting. I thought of the promise he'd made, of his tongue on my nipples once we reached the privacy of his room, and rocked my hips faster.

At the sound of applause, I pulled away from his questing tongue, swallowing as I stared into his cocoa eyes. My core ached. My clit cried out for attention. Every step he took bounced my slick lips over his denim-covered cock.

"Lookit that, Jace! Not here fifteen minutes and Rurik's gone and found himself a puck bunny!"

I tucked my face into his shoulder, squeezing him tighter with my legs, and avoided glancing at the enormous hallway he was striding down. With every step, my pelvis gyrated against him without my control. Heaven help me, I was about to come right there.

Me! The woman who had trouble letting go in intimate situations.

By taking emotion out of the equation—who cared if he *liked* me, if I was too tame or, conversely, too loud a lover—I felt free to simply experience every bit of sexual stimulus he wanted to deliver. Free to embrace my body's response without worrying.

Heck, I didn't need Rurik's tornado to blow me away. My own revelations were doing a fine job of it. That and his strong body surrounding mine.

Muted music and the rumble of multiple television shows spilled out from the rooms we passed. Deep voices echoed beyond the closed doors as he navigated the corridor, a couple of wolf whistles emanating from the open ones.

Rurik's powerful legs just kept eating up the hallway. A man on a mission, his hands squeezed my ass, rocking my sex over his cock.

Each long stride drove me closer to orgasm. When he finally paused before a door at the very end and didn't move, other than to slide me up and down his shaft, I wanted to scream. Why had he stopped?

"What is it?" I whispered into his ear, placing a kiss upon the lobe, then I drew it into my mouth and tongued the smooth flesh.

His long fingers tightened and pulled the globes of my bottom apart, digging farther toward the crevice of my ass. "One thing I forgot to tell you."

My sex sought his and I angled my hips, straining for relief. I released my hold on his ear-lobe. "As long as you haven't changed your mind, it doesn't matter. Just open the door. Take me inside." *Take me outside*. I wasn't particular. Not any longer.

"But I must... Need tell—"

"Rurik, please!" My lower body bumped against his, seeking an end to the intense arousal that held me in its grip. I was so wet I knew my juices had to be completely saturating the fly of his pants. Embarrassment vied with excitement over that realization. *What have you to be embarrassed about? He put you there.* True.

"Should ask…"

I dug my crossed feet into his thighs, every muscle in my legs tensing around him. "We're here. I'm ready." So dang ready, I'm close to mindless. "What are you waiting for?"

Giving a sharp nod, he ceased his fumbling explanation and, while holding me at an awkward angle with one hand, foraged in his pocket. The position pressed me even more intimately against his erection. I pumped against him, amazed that it no longer bothered me a whit whether I was ruining his jeans. They'd wash. Kathi had been right—with a new attitude and an ounce or two of liquor, I turned into a wanton.

It felt great.

After looking into my eyes for a second, he offered me a half grin, gave his card key a quick swipe, and turned the handle. Then he slammed his lips against mine and thrust his tongue deep.

Oh, could this man kiss.

The door swung open and Rurik crossed into the room, letting the door close behind us with a pneumonic *hiss-clank*.

The cooler air immediately assaulted my bare skin and recently exposed private regions. My purse slid from my shoulder and landed on the floor with a soft *thunk*, muffled by the thick carpet.

I heard another noise—running water?—but as if our newfound privacy unleashed his control, Rurik's hands were everywhere at once… grasping my ass, smoothing over my thighs, my calves, trailing up my torso to squeeze my breasts through my dress. My hips circled, abrading my clit against the hard ridge of his shaft.

His voracious kisses continued, giving me but mere glimpses of the well-appointed room in the glow from several lamps, still tidy, as though he'd just checked in. A kitchenette, sofa, and large television—blessedly silent—vaguely crossed my notice before a few determined strides brought us up to the second of the queen beds occupying one wall.

Keeping me anchored at his waist, he leaned over and stripped off the quilted comforter, revealing pristine white sheets for our encounter. With strong arms, he laid me in the center, following me down a scant second later where his lips and tongue commanded my full attention.

The weight of him was heavy. The taste of him divine. He kissed with such passion, an intensity I'd never experienced, hardly allowing me to breathe. I loved it.

My fingers went directly to his silk shirt and started unbuttoning. Heat poured from his skin and I delighted in the feel of rounded, muscled pecs worthy of any gym ad. My feet moved frantically over his jeans-clad legs, the pointy heels of my sandals preventing me from digging in as hard as I wanted.

Rurik raised my dress, gathering it at my waist. He released my mouth and aimed his potent kisses lower, lingering on one cheek, meandering over my jaw, sliding his hot tongue down my neck and past my collarbone. My nipples puckered with anticipation. His leisurely journey continued as he kissed his way to my chest, coming up against the dual fabrics of my dress and bra. Using that sultry, bearded chin of his, he plowed straight through the layers and sharply nipped the upper swell of one breast.

"Oh!" It startled me more than hurt. But all was forgiven when he blew a breath of hot air that streamed past my skin and heated me everywhere inside. The stupid fabrics of dress and bra were determined to regain their place and interrupted his next caress.

Dang, how I wanted the clothes off, so I could experience his tongue with nothing interfering. I wiggled beneath him.

A door clicked open.

My head swerved toward the sound. Even buffered by the mattress, I nearly gave myself whiplash.

In a daze of desire, I watched a muscular blond emerge from the bathroom, a white towel draped around his hips. "Hey, R, you forget someth—" When he saw me, his expression turned to ice. "Dammit. What'd I tell you about bringing them back here?"

"Jeff. Is not—"

"Shhht!" A hard look on his face, the newcomer sliced his hand through the air, calling for silence. He evaluated us for several long seconds.

I couldn't move, couldn't breathe. Couldn't scramble for safety, wasn't sure I wanted to. I just lay there, heart pounding triple time, my head angled toward the blond, Rurik tensed above me.

"Just will you look at her?" Rurik implored. "I think you approve."

TWO

The Encounter in Which They Connect

MY SEX CLENCHED. My mind grappled with the facts—two men!—and the possibilities. *Two men!*

"Jeff is roommate." I blinked and focused on Rurik, who hovered over my chest, trying to look conciliatory, his ragged breathing belying the effort. "He is team goalie." In a calming gesture, Rurik stroked one hand down my hair and the side of my face. Addressing Jeff, he said, "You like, no?"

"What is she?" At the harsh words, my attention zipped back to Jeff. A few years older than Rurik, he looked downright livid. "A peace offering for this?" He pointed to a huge greenish-yellow bruise splashed over one shoulder. A row of neat stitches marched down the center. "I told you to quit apologizing. Never thought you'd turn to pimping rides to—"

"No. She is good time for us both, I am thinking."

Jeff glared at me for a long moment.

Amazingly, given my past bedroom history, it wasn't *me* I worried he might find lacking. Might object to. It was the situation he'd unexpectedly found himself in.

That makes two of us, I wanted to chime in.

You can't be considering this.

What? Now *you* hesitate? *Hush up,* I ordered that nagging, pesky voice. *I'm trying to look alluring here.*

Not so easy to do when I was scared spitless. The lights were on, my dress half off. It might not be apparent yet that big-busted charms weren't mine to boast, but at the rate this was going, it would be soon.

Strangers you'll never see again, I reminded myself. So who gives a rat's rear what they think? As long as they get a stiffy and keep it till the job's done, that's all you need. And based on the protrusion growing beneath Jeff's towel, coupled with the one still solidly snugged between my thighs, that wouldn't pose a problem.

All things considered, I decided, I could handle being a peace offering.

As though he'd been engaging in a similar mental debate, and the side of a tango for three won out, Jeff's expression relaxed. His posture eased. Green eyes gleamed and a speculative smile curved his lips. "Rurik, buddy. I'm thinking you may have the right of it."

By the time he finished speaking, he'd already dropped the towel and was approaching the bed.

Oh Lord. Could a body be any more beautiful?

Fine golden hair covered a sun-tinted chest. Discounting the bruise, the words *sheer perfection* described his leanly muscled mass. The pale skin of his groin and white strip at the sides of his hips, combined with the thick strands of his bleached hair, would've marked him as a surfer if I hadn't just learned he blocked pucks for a living.

"Well now." His tone deliberated though his eyes conveyed pure conviction. "Mind if I join you two lustbirds for the next little while?" His voice was whiskey-smooth and it went straight to my head—and to my mound, every bit of slick, tender flesh welling open at the thought of having both men.

This is supposed to be a one-night stand, not a two-man orgy! my conscience had the audacity to protest again. For the uncharacteristic behavior, I ordered it to time-out.

Jeff hovered at the edge of the mattress, granting me an intimate close-up of his erection, already long and impressive. Trepidation of the torridly unknown aside, I wanted it inside me...any way I could get it.

"What's it to be, sweet thing? I sure would hate to be sent to the sin bin and—" At my confused *Huhmm?*, he clarified. "The penalty box. I'd hate to be expelled and miss out on such a tempting, fuckable sight." Jeff ended with a sigh, that gorgeous voice of his making even the crude word sound seductive. "But if three's a crowd, I'll take myself out of the game, find somewhere else to bunk for the night."

Awe at my wicked good fortune weakened my vocal cords. Since *unmhh* seemed the best I could muster, I remained silent.

Rurik dipped his head and nipped my neck. "Make decision. Or I make one for you."

Caveman tactics? To think, I'd never known what a turn-on they were.

In answer, I unwrapped my legs from their chokehold around Rurik's waist and held one foot out to Jeff. A devil grin lit his features as he cradled my calf and one-handedly set out to unfasten the ankle strap. "These're some sexy sandals, darlin', but lethal."

He slipped one finger between the sole and the bottom of my foot, tickling my arch. Lightning shimmied from my toes and lit up my crotch. "It's a damn shame," he commented, tossing the fancy sandal aside, "but lose them we must. Don't want any gouges in my back that aren't put there by your nails."

I whimpered at the loss of my "hooker shoes", more at the thought of scoring his muscular back with my touch, but I didn't have the heart to protest their loss, not when his fingertips were stretching my toes, caressing them. After disposing of the second sandal, he pointed my foot and took one toe into his mouth.

Game on! He was kissing my feet!

Sensation streaked up my leg from his warm mouth and the slide of his tongue flicking the responsive skin between two toes. When he sucked hard on several, flicking his tongue over the tips, I thought my foot would explode. The extra fifteen minutes I'd taken to paint my plain nails with two coats of Passion Plum had been worth every second.

Rurik wedged his erection more solidly against my mound. With my dress pushed up and only the narrow front placket of the flimsy thong shielding my inner lips from an all-out frontal strike, he felt downright *huge*. A satisfied grunt sounded in his chest and he returned to mine, stroking his fingers down and around the velvet covering my breasts, the swirling caress tapering on each revolution as he approached the summit.

Beneath the confining bra, my nipples strained upward as never before. Breathless with anticipation, I waited...

And dang if my foot didn't shoot a bolt of that tongue-triggered lightning straight to my belly-button. My stomach muscles seized in a fast contraction that shimmied my chest and jerked my toes from Jeff's mouth.

"So...despite your disinclination to chat," Jeff said with a smile as he smoothed his fingers over my well-adored foot, drying me off, "I guess this is working for you? The thought of us both?"

Not giving me time to marshal a comeback, he stepped around Rurik and possessed himself of my other foot to begin subjecting it to the same scorching kisses.

The amorous torture Jeff's hot mouth delivered tempted me to cut and run. I was so far out of my realm, if my brainpower hadn't been fogged back to the single-cell amoeban phase, I was sure I'd be terrified. At myself—for what I was doing. *For* myself—for where this was heading.

As it was, I thrived on every ardent pull his mouth made upon my toes. Loved the unrestrained way the raunchy caress made me want to respond. When my leg started shaking, I bit my tongue to keep from pleading with him to stop. Bit it harder to keep from urging him to greater liberties. Years of stifled sexuality weren't that quick to erase but I now knew, given the right situation and stimulation, I was well on my way.

"See now? You like this one." Upon reaching my nipple after his extended meander, Rurik purred with self-satisfaction. "When I spy her, I think we find perfect opportunity to bring us back on accord."

Jeff released my foot long enough to chide, "It's *in* accord, you big snipe," but with affection. "And I keep telling you we were never out of it, so quit wasting time congratulating yourself and strip that pretty purple dress the rest of the way off."

"Snipe?" I managed the one-word question and congratulated myself. Was that anything like Snape? Just because Rurik had longish black hair?

"Sniper," Jeff explained, maintaining eye contact with the other man. "It means he's a hell of a shooter on the ice." He stroked one hand up my just-shaved leg, smoothing his fingers over my shin and the back of my calf, fondling my knee, and finally settling warm, rousing fingers on my outer thigh. "But yeah…" He imitated Rurik's accent for the rest. "I am approving of this one."

Before I could protest the distant way they both kept referring to me *as if I weren't right there*, he twined his tongue over the top of my foot and back to my toes, strangling off any paltry thoughts of discontent.

Following "orders", Rurik tugged on my bunched dress, scooting it over my hips and higher. He didn't give me a chance to become self-conscious, for which I owed him my unwavering gratitude. As he worked the snug velvet up my torso and over my head, his lips followed the journey, taking tiny nips and nibbles until I emerged from the fabric, hair mussed, body barely covered. Lying there clad only in my push-'em-up-and-together bra and pathetic excuse for panties.

I should have been nervous. Concerned they found my form lacking. Regretful I wasn't some seductive siren who knew what she was doing. But no, all I could think was *Holy erogenous zones, Batman!* I mean, the point of my darn elbow was all stirred up by Jeff's kisses and Rurik's slow appraisal after he stripped me.

"Get on with it." Jeff lifted his mouth long enough to direct.

With a wink, Rurik leveraged to his feet, fingers working his remaining buttons. "You see, little one? He becomes impatient. Is happy I found you."

While he scanned my entire form, which included taking in the feast Jeff made of my toes, I marveled at the bulky, muscular chest he divulged by ridding himself of his shirt—impressive and all male yet without a speck of hair.

Made further intriguing by the detailed sun tattoo centered over his navel, orange and yellow rays arrowing outward…and downward.

Jeff suctioned harder on my toes, as if to regain my attention. A fresh gush of arousal coasted through my center, my body reacting as though I zoomed down a six-story slide at a water park, landing smack in a pool of passion. Blinking back the haze of desire that threatened to pull me under, I tried to focus.

But my dazed, lust-soaked brain couldn't decide where I should look. At the Golden Boy with the foot fetish—which I'd quickly learned to prize—or at the dark European beside him. Or maybe at the tiny swells plumped up on my chest.

Dang. For once in my life, I felt sexy all over.

After depositing one last lingering kiss on my toes, Jeff bent my legs, placed my tingling feet on the mattress and widened my thighs. Once my lower half was arranged to his satisfaction, he crawled up on the bed beside me, propped the side of his head on the heel of one palm and leaned toward my chest. His free hand traced the border of the bra as he stared at me, something I couldn't quite identify shining from his eyes.

Interest? Admiration? Simply awareness? I'd take any of the three.

My breasts quivered beneath his whisper-soft attentions. My feet quivered too. I wondered if I could get away with never washing them again.

He skimmed one finger beneath the bra's edge, just barely grazing my areola. Then two fingers snuck past the shielding fabric. He widened them, then brought them up and together, scissoring the soft tissue from base to tip, lingering over the puckered flesh at the top. "Feel this?" *Every sensual glide.* "I'm gonna lick here next. Just like I did your sweet little toes. Like I think Rurik's about to do to your pussy. He's gonna drink from you while I ply my thirsty tongue *right here.*" He ground his fingertip into the hard knot of my nipple, drawing a whimper from my parched throat.

When I thought of reciprocating and quenching my thirst—and curiosity—on the length of his erection, saliva flooded my tongue.

I wanted to floor him with a pithy reply, but sexually laced zingers weren't yet part of my repertoire. Salient sallies aside, I couldn't decide what I liked better—the way he touched me or the composition of his face.

A subtle citrus scent wafted from his squared-off jaw, indicating the scrape of a razor had recently met the smooth skin. Flared sideburns dipped below his ears. It was clear the deceptively casual angle had been crafted with care. More than a tad retro, he totally rocked it. Owned the look—and my complete surrender after the way he paid deliberate homage to the one part of my anatomy I'd always struggled with feelings of inadequacy over.

Causing a slight creak of bedsprings, Rurik knelt between my legs. He used his shoulders to hold my thighs apart and brought his face right up to my core. Assailed by a stab of unease, I considered the "view" he was now privy to. Couldn't get much closer than this. Just when my newly stifled inhibitions threatened to surface, leading me to wonder and worry, to question how I might compare and be found wanting, Rurik again put any fears to rest.

"Ahh, is pink and puffy. Shiny with exciting," he breathed over my engorged flesh, obviously pleased. As though preening under his notice, the compliment enticed my cream to run thicker. I tensed my thighs to hide their trembling.

"Excite*ment*." Jeff made the correction with the ease of long acquaintance.

"Yes. It is excitement I am feeling—and seeing." Splaying his hands on my inner thighs, Rurik leaned in and directed another puff of air over my "shiny" folds.

Jeff edged the lacy trim away from one nipple. The stretchy fabric scraped over the sensitive bud he'd just primed to erect attention and I flinched. "Are you always this quiet?" he pondered out loud, as if he didn't really expect an answer.

"Just taking it all in," I whispered back. Regular volume might be beyond me, but I no longer wanted to hold my tongue. Not when there were so many other things I could do with it. "If you're so inclined, we can debate politics and religion postcoitus."

He gave a bark of laughter. "We could always add in finances and immigration laws while we're at it."

"Don't forget sexual histories and gun control." I smiled back, stunned at the easy, reciprocal exchange. Since when did I possess flirting skills in the company of a total stranger—make that two —and exhibit them with such aplomb? Especially while lying naked on a bed, about to be…

Fucked, darling. That's the word you're after. Think it. Say it. Do it already!

A tremor ran through me, the reality of what was about to happen thrilling me senseless.

"Fair enough. But that's for after. For now, I want you to watch what he's doing." The note of command was unmistakable, the humor sliding from his gaze. As the tips of his fingers fluttered over my breast, barely connecting with my skin, I told my eyes to look downward. But they refused to budge, remaining locked on Jeff's.

Even as I felt Rurik work a finger under the strap of my thong.

Eek-mmm, I almost squealed it was such a turn-on.

Instead, I somehow managed to ask, "What made Rurik think you'd approve of me?"

He glanced at my bra. "I sort of have a thing for purple."

My toes curled. "Don't forget feet."

"No. Just purple. And *your* feet. Must've been the killer heels. Now look at him," Jeff ordered. "I want to see your face while you watch him eat you out."

Good Lord. Two cavemen?

My arousal skyrocketed. Obeying, I glanced at my bent legs where Rurik was easing the soaked fabric from between my inflamed labia. Red-hot desire flared along my cleft as any token hesitation disappeared. I moaned, past caring about my sexual resume—or lack thereof—and lifted my pelvis toward his mouth, but Rurik backed away and only blew up and down my flesh. I told him, "Stop teasing me. Touch me. *Lick* me."

Reaching behind my back, Jeff released the clasp on my bra. I didn't have time to regret losing the added plump factor, not when he *mmmmmd* deep in his throat and covered both breasts, massaging them with his palms. Glorious relief shot from my nipples through my chest. "I like this all-natural thing you've got going on."

I had a thing? "I'm wearing a month's worth of makeup."

A look of pure indulgence suffused his features. "Sure you are."

I was! But didn't care enough to argue over it. My clit burned for attention. Worse than before, now that Rurik had moved the thong strap to the side. I gestured toward my weeping center. "Hot air caresses are just that—hot air. I need you to touch me like you mean it."

"Ah, so the sweet thing flares to life," Jeff drawled, leaning on his side to trace circles around my bared nipples. "Rurik, do you think we should give the little lady what she's asking for? Appears to me we have a clear breakaway shot."

"I aim for goal now."

When both men put their lips on me, I stopped trying to muddle through their code speak. Practically stopped thinking altogether.

I'd been wrong earlier. There was something better than Rurik's kisses—having *two* men worship my body with their complete and undivided focus. And their hot lips and eager tongues.

Rurik licked the inside of my thigh and Jeff sucked one breast into his mouth, drawing on my nipple as he had my toes, granting the tight, aching bud with extreme suction I felt all the way to the thrumming soles of my feet.

Rurik's velvety tongue treated the folds of my sex to long, slow licks. Sensation battered me from every direction and my hips thrust against his mouth, seeking firmer contact. His tongue darted and delved, diving deep into my innermost flesh. Then it retreated to slide sinuously around my opening. I felt the liquid of my desire dripping down the crevice, toward my anus.

Jeff's lips encircled my nipple and his teeth brushed against me.

"Harder," I implored. He bit down, pinching my breast with the tips of his teeth.

Rurik lifted my hips clear off the mattress and brought my core higher toward his face as his hands slid over the halves of my butt. He fondled each cheek, pulling them gently apart, exposing my ass to the air.

My fingers tangled in Jeff's hair, keeping his mouth pressed against my breast. My sex flexed, riding along Rurik's chin. His tongue was doing wondrous things, flicking over my clit, then plunging inside my tunnel. He groaned and lowered me to the bed. I whimpered at the loss of contact when he straightened. Whimpered again when his hands went to his belt, and he quickly unfastened his jeans and pushed them off.

More of that impressive maleness. Lots more.

"I am ready now," he announced, fisting his erection as he leaned over me.

"Thank God. I can't wait." My pelvis floundered, rocking in the air, edging closer to his flushed penis, so thick and hard, I thought I'd die from want.

"Hold up, cowboy." Jeff released my breast with a small *smack* and moved to straddle my face, his long cock dangling near my chin. "Can't go blasting off quite yet."

He leaned over and retrieved his wallet from the nightstand, then flicked a condom packet toward Rurik, withdrawing a second one for himself, which he tossed near my head. When he rose above me and centered his erection over my face, I arched up and took the crown into my mouth. Securing my lips behind the raised ridge, I sucked hard. Then harder still.

I hadn't known what to expect, but the past few minutes my mouth had craved his cock, my tongue frantically swiping over my lips, needing to suckle him.

To my extreme gratitude, he didn't try to shove inside, just balanced on bent knees over my torso, his elongated penis looming near my face, allowing me to come forward and take in what I wanted. His crest alone occupied a lot of my mouth. The hinge of my jaw worked, opened extra-wide as I tested positions, tilting my head to find the right angle.

In no apparent hurry, Rurik just kept massaging my entrance with his cock. His hand swept all over my thighs and hips, occasionally pinching or squeezing, before moving on to fondle another part of my intimate anatomy.

I peeked up at Jeff and took in the sight of his long erection disappearing beneath my nose. I observed the fine golden hair on his groin, the ridged muscles of his abs above and, higher still, the flat line of his lips just below the serious look now shading his gaze. Trying to process it all staggered my mind. To be here, like this, with both these men? Surprising didn't quite cover it. Stupefying came closer.

I slammed my eyes shut against the visual stimuli and concentrated on the new tactile world surrounding me, swamping me.

Hard, muscular thighs searing along either side of my torso. Crisp sheets beneath my fingers. Insistent cock parading up and down my pussy. *Put it in*, I needed to holler, but the one occupying my mouth swelled, lurched.

Jeff's hands came to my head and forcefully held me still. "Ease up, darlin'," he said on a gasp. "You keep on and I'm liable to blow."

I blinked up at him. Wasn't that the point?

He gave me the semblance of a smile and smoothed a strand of damp hair from my temple. When had I started to sweat?

Still ensconced within the confines of my mouth, his cock twitched and he rolled his hips, a languid, controlled motion that pushed him in a little more. Then he pulled out a fraction. Then back again. *In. Out. In.* "Slow and steady for a bit, hmmm?"

Mouth full, tongue busy, I nodded around him, exploring...tasting.

As though he'd been waiting for a signal, when I moaned at the salty ooze of Jeff's essence greeting my tongue, Rurik gripped my hips and tugged me to the edge of the bed. Jeff scrambled backward to stay lodged in my mouth but he needn't have worried. After finally getting a cock in there, a squeaky clean one at that, no way was I letting go.

Rurik placed his sheathed erection at my opening, rubbed himself up and down and along my center. The action tugged on the thong, abraded my saturated slit all the way to my anus.

After Rurik taunted me a few more seconds, he used his fingers to spread my folds. I felt every nuance as he nudged right up where I wanted him most and settled in place, against my opening. A heartbeat later he buried his shaft all the way inside, filling me in one smooth stroke.

My lower body shuddered around him and I came, squealing my pleasure against Jeff's cock and shocking myself with the intensity of my orgasm. Nothing slow or controlled here, Rurik hauled out, then plunged in again, thrusting deeper.

Spasms and sparks seized my loins. My fingernails scratched the sheets until Jeff captured my hands and interlaced our fingers. My tongue delved hard over the tip of his cock, seeking more of his shape and taste. He leaned forward and trapped both my wrists overhead in one of his hands, bringing the other between us to palm my breast, pinch my nipple and cause me to instinctively bite down on his shaft. He grunted and pushed farther into my mouth.

Rurik started a rocking tempo, smoother now, sliding in and out of my passage. His fingers curved around my ass and the tip of one teased my anus. The foreign contact had my tunnel clasping his rod harder, trying to hold him deep. I couldn't stand it. Everything they did felt so spectacularly wonderful. Another orgasm was building, tightening every muscle in my body. I wanted to scream. To vocally liberate every bit of restraint I'd reluctantly held on to for years. But I knew better.

So I swallowed the urge, instead let my tongue stroke and slide over the man in my mouth.

"She is beautiful girl," Rurik said, lunging faster.

Scooching back, Jeff eased his erect cock past my lips and stared into my eyes. "That she is. Quieter than your usual sort. Softer."

Protesting the unexpected criticism, I licked my lips, now swollen and sensitive. "I can be loud."

Jeff chuckled and plucked my nipple. "Let me hear it, sweet. Loose that ragged cry I see brimming in your eyes. Free the passion."

Feel the pain, I could almost hear the unspoken sentiment. Then Rurik's voice, "I come now."

While Jeff held my gaze, Rurik pumped, his thick cock massaging the inside of my passage. I wanted to climax again, wanted to howl out my release just to prove I could, but I resisted the temptation. I needed this experience, this fabulous feeling of decadence, of freedom, to last. Knew better than to do *anything* that might interfere.

One of Rurik's fingers edged inside my rectum.

Eyebrows soaring, I avoided screeching at him to get the hell out—because in a weird way it felt intriguing and maybe even totally good—and instead concentrated on constricting every muscle in my pelvis, holding him tight.

"You just hang in there," Jeff encouraged. As if I needed any encouragement. "I'll make you scream."

Releasing my hands, he moved to the side and licked my breast again, then he headed toward my abdomen, gliding his tongue along my skin, down the center of my chest, leaving a trail of liquid fire in his wake, staring up at me all the while, that heavy-lidded, focused gaze the stuff of fantasies. Mine, for certain.

The thought of having his tongue on my clit made me wild. My hips thrust upward, trying to meet his mouth. The action forced Rurik's iron rod deeper. Two quick driving plunges later, Rurik squeezed my ass and climaxed with a shout. He slipped his backdoor finger free but kept driving his cock inside. "It is time, Jeff. We change on fly, no?"

Rurik's words halted Jeff just as he arrived at my mons.

"I thought you'd never ask." He stood with a grin and curved his fingers around his long erection, stroking himself. I watched in silence as Jeff stretched over me to reach the foil packet he'd dropped. He made quick work covering himself.

Then he angled his body between my legs, alongside Rurik, gave one plum-tipped toenail a tweak and ran his hand up my thigh. "I think I'll have to tell you *no* more often"—he cut a quick glance at his roommate—"if this is the type you bring back to tempt me." Jeff turned to me. "Let me know you're having fun, now. Let me hear it."

Faster than I could blink, Rurik pulled out and left me empty, and Jeff invaded the hollowed space with his thick shaft. I gasped. My lower body convulsed, acclimating to his size. He was wide, filling me to overflowing. My eyelids slammed back down as he began to move.

I clutched his erection with my inner muscles, embracing him with all I had. Could this get any better? Awash on a sea of sensual bliss, I gripped my breasts. The hard knot of my nipples pressed into my palms, so tight and achy I wondered if I'd ever find relief. Bracing my heels on the bed, I rotated around Jeff's shaft, squirming to get closer. I bit my lip, luxuriating in the long, slow drives of his cock as he plundered me so thoroughly I couldn't imagine a more spectacular way to celebrate.

"What's your name?" He asked the question and increased his rhythm, pistoning inside me so fast I was jolted backward on the bed.

"Car-o— Oh!" Sudden warmth brushed over my clit, then enveloped it in slick heat. My eyelids popped open and I jerked forward, braced on my elbows.

Rurik had his mouth fused to my inner lips. His dark head was nestled at the juncture of my legs and he licked and sucked, directly above Jeff's plunging cock. At the sight, my anus and vagina spasmed in response. I strangled off the keening shout that threatened to break free, mashed my lips together as the walls of my sheath rippled around Jeff, who was grinning like a demon. "Sorry." He sounded anything but. "I didn't quite catch that."

"Crlna," I said in a rush as Rurik angled his head and winked. He rose above the folds of my sex and gently pulled them apart, exposing my needy clit. His tongue snaked from his lips and danced over the delicate nerves.

"What, darlin'?" Jeff asked, his hands braced on my hips, lifting them higher, bringing us closer.

He swung from side to side, his cock ratcheting deeply inside my body. With two fingers he snagged one side of my pitiful panties. Twisting, he caused the strained fabric to cut into my ass. My anus fluttered against the added stimulus.

"Carolinaaaa," I said on a long exhale as the turbulent sensations wound me so tight I was ready to burst.

He gave a rough laugh. "Still not sure I caught that." Releasing his hold on panties and hips, Jeff lowered me back to the mattress, Rurik following the change in altitude without a hitch, his lips staying glued to my core. "But no matter, I'm just glad Rurik caught you tonight."

On straight arms, Jeff bent forward and propped himself over my torso, increasing the speed of his thrusts. I couldn't stop the small, muted cries that escaped every time he plowed deeper.

Rurik hummed his agreement and changed the pressure of his tongue by sliding the flat of it over my clit.

Jeff strummed several fingertips over one nipple and I nearly came full-out, wished I could announce it to the world.

My own personal sexual revolution. For one.

Make that three!

Take that! I wanted to tell my former, soul-and-self-confidence-crushing lover. The one who'd told me I was so pathetic in the sack that no man could get his rocks off on the same mattress.

Ha!

I'd already seen to one and was nearly ready to discharge the other.

But first—my own. The most powerful orgasm I was sure I'd ever experience.

Stop analyzing! Enjoy it already.

I am! Can I help it if I want this to last? If I wished I could stop time and stay in this moment for—

Thwack! A palm to the outside of one thigh startled me from the introspective self-congratulations. Another two quickly returned my concentration to the man between my legs.

My middle shimmered, electrified by the ever-tightening sensations. I—

Thwack!

Thought blurred. I stared at Jeff, whose emerald gaze was narrowing on my face, even as one hand fluttered lightly over a nipple and the other—

Thwack. Thwack!

Mmm. "Are you spanking me?"

Not accusing, just incredulous.

"No, sweetheart. These are just little taps." His fingers firmed on my nipple. "There wouldn't be any doubt if this was a spanking."

Oh.

Curious, ducks?

Was I? Two more slaps—or should I say "taps"? —to my hip and I didn't care. Would've submitted to just about anything he suggested at that point.

"You with me?" Some of the control left his features as his rhythm became less precise, a little more jerky.

"All the way." How did I answer so bravely?

I guess it was the right choice because the tension smoothed from his face, a curious sort of pride taking its place.

"Good girl. Hang on now."

Jeff nodded as if to himself, stopped slapping my thigh and brought both hands to bracket my hips, his thumbs sliding inward on my abdomen, supercharging everything. My response. My awareness.

He was in me!

This hot stranger! His dick thrusting me to paradise while Sexy Stranger #2 licked me to heaven.

My naughty foray over to the wild side had gone better than my wildest dreams. Mr. Surfer Bod with the green glimmer and intense personality —and the thick, wide dick that I liked very much—and my English-challenged Russian with the very talented tongue… Both of them at times licking, sucking, staring, smiling—

At the odd combination of praise and pride I sensed from Jeff, mixed with the even more perplexing flashes of anger—arousing anger if I was honest—coming off him, my pelvis rocked violently between their attentions. Too much! It was too much. I couldn't—

You can. You will!

Too much. But my internal protest was half-hearted this time, battered down by the pure bliss filling every cell.

It will *never* be too much; I could do this forever.

The errant thought blipped through my brain and the spring inside me uncoiled with a snap.

My release erupted around Jeff's shaft and my entire body shook, vibrated from the force of it. Rurik's tongue kept licking, driving me higher and I exploded again.

With a primal yell, Jeff drove in deep and froze. His cock pulsed within my tunnel, surrounded by the quivering aftershocks of my body.

Someone in the next room pounded on the wall.

Rurik plucked at the thong strap by his cheek.

"Certainly don't need this, anymore, do we?" Still embedded and without taking his gaze off mine, Jeff wrenched the threads apart, disposing of the abused panties. "Well, miss, Rurik and I have enjoyed fucking you tonight." His spent cock gave a lurch within the confines of my body. "Immensely."

Too sated to be self-conscious, even knowing we'd been overheard, I simply lay there, exhausted and staring at his captivating green eyes. "I enjoyed..." I was panting. Energy thrummed through me unlike anything I'd ever experienced. "Enjoyed...myself immensely...too. Can't imagine anything...better."

And I couldn't. These two hot hockey players had restored my faith in my own sexuality, had kindled my desire to keep on exploring. Kathi would be thrilled.

"You can't?" Jeff sounded dismayed. "What's wrong with these Midwestern boys? That was only the first period. There's two to go. And didn't you notice—you've yet to scratch my back."

"We're not...not finished?"

"Not by a long shot." Jeff grinned at me. "Or as our friend says, 'Not by a slap shot'."

Rurik raised his head, his bearded chin shiny with my dew. "Want me to call rest of team?"

Oh God.

"You're...j-joking." My breath caught on the words.

He had to be joking. Right?

Yippee!!!!!!!!!!!! that little voice hollered. The one I'd finally let out to play.

Her Three Studs

Encouraged by this, her hands became
extremely free, and wandered over my
whole body, with touches, squeezes,
pressures, that rather warmed and
surprised me with their novelty, than
they either shocked or alarmed me.

–John Cleland, *Fanny Hill: Memoirs of a
Woman of Pleasure*

When Her Contradictions Rouse His Curiosity

"WHAT? THE T-TEAM?" The naked female sprawled across his hotel bed practically squeaked, her startled gaze zipping between Jeff and his roommate Rurik, where it stalled. Her face, already a smooth porcelain beneath the "month's worth" of makeup she claimed to have applied, paled to the point he thought she might faint. "D-did you just say…? Did I hear y-you offer to…to *invite the whole team in here?*"

"Don't say things like that." Jeff punched Rurik in the shoulder hard enough to hurt a weaker man. The muscled Russian barely reacted to the blow, but he did rise from his position between her splayed legs. The finest pair of legs Jeff had seen in—

Forever, it seemed.

But he'd been done with screwing around, dammit. Hadn't in over a year. But with *this* one?

Hell.

Why had he joined in? The two of them could have tangoed without him.

Staring at her told him why. She wasn't like the others. His other, countless, one-night partners had never seemed so very alluring *after* the deed was done.

Jeff stepped back, away from temptation. "Look at her, R. You scared ten years off her life." Because it was easier to blame the fast-moving forward of the Tulsa Tornadoes, the team Jeff played goalie for, than to admit his own control had crumbled at the first sight of her, he socked Rurik again. "Asshole. You don't say shit like that to ladies you've just met."

"He's kidding?" Her voice quavered and drew his attention back to her face. The tip of her pink tongue swept hurriedly over trembling lips. "He won't call the rest of the team? Invite them in here to-to...*have sex*?"

Hell. She couldn't even say it, had to whisper the last two words. How'd she end up in bed with the two of them? And how soon could he get her out?

Jeff didn't give Rurik a chance to answer. Shoving the other man aside, he leaned in between her legs and stared down at her, trying to forget how great she'd just felt snugged around him, all slick and swollen. "He's just yanking your chain, darlin'."

"I..." She wrenched her gaze from his and sought Rurik's.

Pissed that she hadn't believed him, Jeff applied two fingers to her jaw and turned her head until their eyes met. "Despite my cock's desire for another round or two…we're done for tonight. Scout's honor."

His words had the desired effect of dousing her interest in anything that Rurik might say. Jeff took perverse pleasure when her gaze automatically zoomed to his just-spent, still-erect penis. Damn. All the time he'd booked away from the bedroom and bunnies hadn't been worth shit. Like a junkie, one hit and he wanted another. Craved her slender body.

What was wrong with him?

Getting laid and blocking pucks. Having a good time. *That*'s what he'd lived for, all Jeff cared about until his sister's accident. Then right after she died, he'd fucked everything in sight, sometimes recklessly, always with a vengeance. Trying to drive out the guilt shredding his insides like a piranha.

It took a scare with gonorrhea—a teammate's scare, not his own, thank God—to straighten him from that downward spiral.

And one look from a startled, purple-shrouded beauty to plunge him back in.

Fuck. At least this time he'd remembered condoms. Wasn't about to forgo that necessity, not with how Coach had taken to passing them out before every game. The two he and Rurik just used had been in his wallet since the end of last season, not quite a year ago. Because since he'd been tested, after being shaken from his guilt-driven, unsafe-sex-riddled grieving, he hadn't bumped up against anything more intimate than his palm. Hadn't been tempted overly much either. Not until tonight.

With this one.

He tore the used rubber off his prick and pretended he didn't hear the stifled mew of longing she couldn't completely suppress.

It only made guilt eat at him. Because he still wanted her too.

Dammit. What did he have to feel guilty over? The way she pressed her thighs together and shielded her breasts as she came onto one elbow? The little-girl-lost look in her eyes? The one she tried so valiantly to disguise with a show of confidence more contrived than convincing? "It's been fun, guys. Tremendous really, but I need to go."

She managed to impart that with only a slight tremor. One that confirmed his suspicions. This little gal, the quiet female who'd jumped in their bed without a single introduction between them, hadn't a clue how to go on from here. He'd bet his next trip home she'd never been in this position before.

"You've got that right," he confirmed, reminding himself as well as her, "it's past time for sleep. In *separate* beds."

"Come." Unusually quiet the past few moments, Rurik approached, still naked, and held out his hand. "Rurik will escort his pretty American to her automobile. Ensure she is getting there safety."

"Safe*ly*." Sliding into his jeans, Jeff elbowed Rurik away. "And no, you won't, I'll take care of it."

Jeff knew what would happen if Rurik rushed her out the door. He'd light a cigarette in the elevator, despite the non-smoking signs, grope her bottom with a condescending little pat once the doors slid open on the first floor and, with his next illicit puff, blithely send her on her way. Now that Rurik had gotten what he wanted and could sleep like the well-fucked dead, she'd drop from his memory faster than he sliced a puck across the ice.

No matter that she'd been the "present" Jeff hadn't asked for, he had unwrapped the pretty purple package and played with it. Lustily. Now he needed to see it safely returned. Before his unforeseen shot of guilt expired.

He hated feeling guilty. Usually didn't, not anymore. But there was something glittering behind those unusual pewter eyes—and it wasn't tears.

A not-quite wounded vulnerability he had to shore up fast. For his own sake.

"You will not," Rurik protested, lowering the arm she'd ignored and reaching for his shirt. "I brought her to you. I will take her out."

"She's not trash to be discarded."

"Who says she is trashed?"

"Snipe!" Every speck of aggravation welling up from his depths came through as Rurik's nick-name exploded from his lips. "*Trash*, as in garbage, not trash*ed* as in drunk. Don't give me grief over this."

CHOOSING to let the two cavemen debate amongst themselves, I took the easy way out. The coward's way.

Too chicken to do anything else, I scuttled toward the bathroom.

"I said I will be walking her." Rurik's distinct, heavily accented English reached my retreating form.

"No, I will." Jeff sounded implacable. Which I found ironic given how it was obvious he couldn't wait to be rid of me.

"I found her. Is my responsibility."

"I'm relieving you of it."

Almost hysterical at the thought of these two studliest of studs arguing over who would, in theory, carry my books to class, I shut the heavy door with a solid *clunk* and pushed in the lock on the handle. As if that would keep them out if they wanted to break in.

And why would they? It wasn't as though all three of us hadn't just gotten what we'd wanted. *And then some*, my conscience snickered.

Prodded into the single reckless act of my uninspired life by my wise-ass conscience and wise-cracking friend Kathi, I wanted to laugh at the absurdity of it all.

I wanted to melt, right into the big sunken tub commanding their oversized bathroom. Who knew professional sports teams traveled in such style?

Idly curious when self-recriminations and regret might set in—they hadn't yet—I snagged one of the smaller hand towels and turned the sink tap on full blast. All the way to hot. Seconds later, the thick towel was drenched. I couldn't stop my groan when the wet material met my inner thighs. I stroked it higher, flinching when I pressed it deep.

My legs wouldn't stop quivering.

In one amazing swoop, I'd just doubled the number of men I'd slept with in my lifetime, going from two to four.

Above the black-speckled granite counter, the giant mirror reflected a ghost. One with a sheet-white face, enormous eyes, and lips—

Ah. My lips. They'd never looked so naughty. So glamorous and full. Swollen and red from sliding over his cock. Jeff's cock. From kissing Rurik.

Holding the damp towel in place with a squeeze of my shaking thighs, I grabbed a washcloth off the rack, heated it just as fast and clamped the steaming square to my face. Blotting out my reflection.

My very first one-night, two-stud stand.

How magnificent it'd been.

How awkward, now that it was time to leave.

When I could no longer hold my breath, I peeled the soggy cloth away, doused it again and quickly washed my face, scrubbing off the smudges of mascara. I needed to erase the raccoon reminder and ratchet up the courage to open the door.

Because not only did the way home lie beyond it —the way to my quiet, plant-filled abode—but so did my dress and underwear.

Delaying, I scanned the luxurious bathroom, spotting a contact case and a bottle of solution on the counter along with two toiletry bags.

"Hey..." A single knock sounded and Jeff's voice carried through the door. So he'd won the testosterone-laden battle? "You all right in there?"

Still staring at the stranger in the mirror, I eased the towel from between my legs and answered. "I'm grand. Just grand." And I was. Astonishingly so. "Ummm…"

My normally sedate hair—a blah color somewhere in the middle of brown, blond, and boring, and usually tamed in a ponytail or neat coil for work—was wild. Disarrayed and sexy-looking. So not me.

Turning away from the sight, I opened the door just enough to slide my arm through. "Could you hand me my dress please? My underwear and sandals?"

"You got it. One pretty purple ensemble coming right up." A couple steps, the rustle of fabric and then soft velvet met my outstretched hand. "Here you go."

My fingers clutched at the dress, crushed the fabric and intertwined within it, almost as if they sought refuge from his knowing gaze. Who would've thought hands could feel so naked and exposed? *Hands.*

I squeezed out a muffled thanks.

"Welcome. Put it on, then come out."

Swiftly trading the dress to my other hand, I thrust my arm out again, empty fingers opening and closing. "The rest?"

"Not yet."

"*What?*" I wrenched the door open a few inches, swinging the eight-foot barrier in front of my nude body like a shield. I glared at him. "What do you mean 'Not yet'? You're holding my panties and bra hostage?" I took in the empty room. "And where's Rurik? Not-not-not," I stupidly stuttered in my haste, "*not* getting the other guys—"

"No! No." Jeff chuckled and eased closer. He smoothed one finger over my white-knuckled grip on the door. "I sent him away. Thought you'd be less skittish with only one of us to deal with."

That was thoughtful. Especially for a guy. "But I didn't get to thank him."

"Thank *him*?" The thoughtful rat bit his lips against another laugh, then loosed it anyway. "You're priceless."

My darn face burned like a campfire. "Lucky for you, that's the case. I'm sure a *paid* hooker wouldn't tolerate you laughing at her."

He sobered, his features hardening into the expression he'd worn when he first caught sight of me earlier tonight, before he'd morphed into the patient seducer. "I wouldn't know. Haven't had to pay for it before."

Of course he hadn't. Not someone who looked like him. Who could smile and charm as he did —when he chose. Not someone who fucked like him.

Releasing the stranglehold on the door, I firmed my palm under his nose. "My bra and panties, please."

He stayed where he was. "Hey, if it'll ease your mind, I'll be sure and pass your thanks along to Rurik. I'm sure he'll appreciate the humor."

"That makes one of us. How'd you get him to leave? I heard you guys arguing."

Jeff pointed to the stitches marching across one shoulder. The injury I gathered Rurik had accidentally caused. "I stooped to using guilt, that's how. Feel flattered, sweetheart, that's not like me."

"Aren't mornings—I mean *minutes*—after supposed to be over quickly? Why are you prolonging this by withholding my undergarments?" I wasn't about to say *bra* and *panties*.

He leaned in and stole my breath. "Why are you prolonging it by standing there pretzeled up behind that door so all I can see is your face? Except in the mirror behind you, where every lush, feminine curve is temptingly displayed."

"*EEK!*" I whipped back and snapped the door shut.

Two minutes later, dress smoothed in place—smoothing my hair abandoned as a useless effort—I opened the door and emerged into the room, my sensitized thighs rubbing together with every slow, deliberate step. *Why is it I feel more naked now than I did earlier—when I was naked?*

The thought streaked through me, causing—

"Because the edge is off," Jeff answered.

Before I could process how my lips had betrayed me, he advanced and wrapped one hand solidly around my nape. His thumb stroked sweetly down my neck, the gesture at odds with the sour expression curling one side of his mouth.

"Why do you keep doing that?"

"Doing what?"

I stiffened to pull away but his fingers firmed, held me in place. "Frown at me one minute and then act nice the next? Why won't you just give me my clothes so I can leave?"

I thought he wasn't going to answer, was just going to keep dragging his thumb up and down my neck until he tired of it and released me. So it was a shock to hear him admit, "Because I like puzzles and you intrigue me. Because I still want you and I wish to hell I didn't."

How did I respond to that? "Um...sorry?"

His hand tightened and slid around to the front of my neck, his fingers bracketing my throat just beneath my jaw. Not hard or threatening, just enough to make me *aware*. Of him. Of his strength. As if I could forget for one second.

I swallowed against the slight pressure, so far out of my element the periodic table resided on another planet. "Hell, sweetheart—what was your name again?"

"Carolina," I spoke past the nerves constricting my throat, his touch now feeling like a balm, comforting in a weirdly stimulating way.

"Carolina. Right. I'll try to remember. Don't go apologizing. These are my fucked-up demons, not yours. Don't take them on or assume responsibility for my feelings."

"That's shrink talk if I ever heard i-*umptht*!"

Now it *was* his fingers tightening as they slid from my neck to grasp my chin. He whispered hoarsely, "Shut up. Just shut the fuck up."

My throat made some wounded-animal type of noise, one that sounded suspiciously like yearning.

I didn't know how to deal with this! Fast, fun sex—that's all I'd been after tonight. This wasn't fun—standing under the command of a six-foot-plus growling man while my underwear played hide-and-seek, and my common sense seemed reluctant to jump in the game.

Not fun? my conscience screamed. *Who are you kidding? This is a blast! It's arousing and scary and so darn exhilarating.*

"You're just..." Jeff took a breath and both his fingers and posture softened. "You're just making me face them in ways I hadn't expected."

Them? His demons? "Me?"

The click of the hotel door unlocking sounded like a sonic boom. Jeff didn't wait for the handle to rotate, "Not yet, R!" Keeping his gaze on mine, he ordered, "Come back in ten. Not a second sooner."

"I need to leave." Suiting action to words, I twisted from his grasp.

"Wait." Strong hands clamped on my shoulders. "Please."

That tacked-on please zapped my instinctive protest. "What?"

"Only this." With a deliberate pause, as though weighing his actions and my reaction—or lack of one, he slid his palms to my upper arms and tugged me forward and bent his head.

Though I'd been expecting it, oh say, for two seconds, his kiss still caught me off guard. The sure, firm press of his mouth, the tiny nibbles his lips took from mine, the casual, unhurried glide of his tongue...

A whimper escaped my throat when he slanted his head, moved his mouth to a different angle. His fingers kneaded the flesh of my arms with growing fervor but his lips stayed light, playful almost.

It hit me then—he was taking his time.

Kissing me thoroughly and rousing me right back on top of that edge faster than I would have believed possible.

How could I feel the insistent thrum of desire, the hot thrill of sexual want spiking through my core so soon? After all we'd just done?

His hand skated over my shoulder and up my neck, threaded into my hair above my nape and tugged. The pressure revived every previously sated cell. I muffled a groan. Then another as his tongue teased my lips.

Teased. That's what he was doing, the rat. Keeping me on edge and confused.

I spit out his exploring tongue. Blinking fast, feeling more and more off-kilter from his unexpectedly sensual approach, I jerked back against his hold, scalp tingling. Will threatening to wilt when he held firm. "Puzzle or not, this is one game I'm tired of playing."

I was going to shoot Kathi with a gazillion rubber bands for encouraging my strut on the wild side. She'd forgotten to divulge the rules of this game she played so well. Slutty behavior, strangers, and me just plain didn't mix. I was foolish to think they might. "You've had your fun. Now I want to go home."

"You saying you didn't have fun?"

"I did, but now I'm not." *Liar!* "Jeff…" His name was a one-word plea. To release me or throw me on the bed, I wasn't sure. "I need to call a cab."

"A cab?" Surprise loosened his fingers and I slipped free.

"Cab. Uber. Whatever." So accomplished at trolling for cock—not hardly—I'd stupidly left my phone at home, plugged in and charging. Where it did me so much good now.

On bare feet, I rushed to the desk on the opposite side of the room. No time for second thoughts. I palmed the receiver and hit zero.

"Riviera front desk. How can I improve your stay?"

"Hi. I need—"

Jeff reached around me and pried the receiver from my grip. "Sorry, wrong number." He slammed it down and pulled me back against his chest. "Soooo," he breathed over my ear, stroking one thumb up the side of my neck. "You didn't drive here, then."

Just as I started to lean into him, he released me and stepped away. "Come on, Purple Princess, I'm taking you home."

"But—" I whirled around to do battle over his commanding ways. The urge faltered when I saw he held my sandals. They dangled from his index finger by their thin purple straps.

"I can be a nice guy. Let me prove it to you." A boyish grin softened his expression. "Truce?"

Boyish?

Ain't nothing about this man childish, sweetcakes.

My dang conscience again. Heck, I'd thought the multiple orgasms had finally shut it up.

Jump him for another and I'll go to time-out. Promise!

Ready to strangle something—my conscience, Kathi, maybe my own reluctance—I took possession of the shoes. "Thank you."

I retreated to one corner of the mattress on the still-made, neat-as-a-pin bed, to slide my feet in, wind the straps around my ankles, and hook back on my "hooker shoes".

I laughed at the thought. How could I have known what Kathi called these beauties would —practically—come to pass?

"Care to share the joke?" Jeff knelt to finish fastening the second sandal.

"I think not. It's at my own expense." My shaky self-confidence was turning to ash, burning to cinders with every second I stayed. Still feeling the lack of panties and bra, I pushed him back and stood. "My purse? Where— Oh, there it is."

On the floor where I'd dropped it. A lifetime ago.

Jeff jumped to his feet and snatched it off the plush carpet before my sky-high shoes and I made it halfway. He tucked my purse under one of his arms and offered me his other. "All set?"

"This isn't prom." I nudged his hand away. "Stop acting so gallant. We, uh…" Fuck, *darling. The word you want is* fucked. I growled back silently. "Had sex. You're not required to take me home." I attempted a grin. "I put out already. Hard part's over."

When I tugged at my purse, he held on tight, drawing me closer.

"Carolina." He gave my name an extra fourteen syllables. And every one of those vibrated through me.

"What?"

"It's late. It's dark outside." He stated the obvious. "We're in a big city. *Downtown.*" Said as though it equated with *toxic sludge.* "I am seeing you home and that's the end of it."

"But I live twenty miles from here." Why had I listened to my sensible side and arranged a ride, thinking I might imbibe enough to warrant not driving? I was stone-cold sober. *You're drunk on lust, though, head and crotch are swirling with it.*

Hush up, I wanted to scream. At my conscience or Jeff, I wasn't sure. Either, maybe both. This wasn't how I planned it! Maybe because I'd only planned the *before* portion, having no inkling the *after* would prove so difficult to navigate.

"Hush up?" Jeff looked at me in surprise and his eyes flashed like faceted emeralds when he smiled.

"Not you. Me," I babbled. Then groaned. "It'll take thirty minutes. I'll be fine. The front desk can order—"

"Won't be necessary." Retaining his claim on my purse, he swiped a set of keys off the credenza and snagged my hand. "Thirty minutes, hmmm? I think I can manage to stay awake that long. If I get sleepy on the drive, you can entertain me."

"Entertain you?" He escorted me out of the room and curved his non-purse-carrying hand around my waist. I was relieved the hall was substantially quieter than it'd been when I'd arrived with Rurik. Doors were shut. Televisions and conversations muted. "Oh, I bet."

I could just envision what "entertainment" he expected me to perform for an encore.

His hand patted my hip. "Come now, Carolina, what's going on in that pretty head of yours?"

His velvet-over-steel voice told me *exactly* what was going on in his. "Why don't you tell me?"

"I don't know what *you* were thinking, missy..." Dragging his hand down one buttock, he drew me to a halt in front of the elevator. He pressed the call button, then tipped his head toward mine and winked. "But I was thinking we could play word games."

When What She Believes About Him Matters

THE KEYS WERE to a clean but older-model vehicle stashed in a corner of the parking garage. A team rental? If so, it had certainly seen younger days. A big SUV with vinyl bench seats. After guiding me to the underground garage, Jeff opened the driver's door and lifted me up, halting my progress before I'd scooted all the way over.

"That's far enough." Keeping me in the middle, he tossed the old-style seat belt over my lap. "Stay put and buckle up."

He climbed in after me, buckling his lap belt in place as I glanced at the dash long enough to notice a stack of Riviera business cards and several cellophane-wrapped peppermints.

He put the keys in the ignition but didn't turn them, instead crossing his arms at the wrists on top of the steering wheel and angling his head until he was looking at me. "Well now."

"Well." This was odd. It felt...like a date. Impossible. "This is weird," I said into the thick silence. "Too weird."

"Not if we don't want it to be."

In the artificial-hazed glow from the overhead parking lights, I stared at his full, kissable lips. Admired his chiseled jawline and about flipped over when he shot me a grimace before reaching into his shirt pocket to pull out a pair of eyeglasses which he promptly slid in place.

Old-fashioned, black-rimmed Wayfarers.

Jeff saw me staring and his face reddened. "You caught me. My geekdom is showing."

"Why? Because you wear glasses reminiscent of Buddy Holly's, or because you're hot enough to pull it off?" And still look so cool I could drown in my own drool?

Talk about geeky! Are you listening to yourself?

His grin turned rueful. "I normally wear contacts, all day every day."

"I know. I saw the solution on the counter." There. That sounded suitably observant. Without being stalkerish, I hoped. "Ah, what about my panties? My bra? Do I get those back now or do you guys have some sort of trophy room they get enshrined in?"

He snapped his fingers. "Knew I forgot something."

"You forgot," I repeated dully, not sure what to make of that.

Jeff looked pointedly at my breasts, then lower, at my pelvis, both of which instantly responded to the heat he exuded, growing warm and languid. My pelvis, that is. My breasts just grew heavy. He started the engine and followed the giant arrows navigating the underground lot. "No trophy room but that's not a bad idea. I'll have to bring that up at our next team meeting."

I slugged my fist into his thigh.

"*Umpf.*" Turning the wheel to spiral up the maze of concrete with his left hand, he lowered his right to my leg and kept it there, where I felt the impression of every single finger. "I did forget your scrappy panties, sorry about that. But I remembered your sexy bra."

I tore my gaze from where his hand rested on my thigh and inspected him, critically analyzing where he might have stashed it. The expensive push-up was padded out the wazoo, giving a semblance of cleavage to my modest—actually, minimal—bosom, not an easy piece of man-hunting machinery to hide. Jeff wore a casual short-sleeve button-down in a subtle red plaid untucked over jeans. Decent-fitting jeans, not those expose-half-your-butt-crack jeans a lot of guys wore these days. There was no way he could have stuffed that bra in a pocket, not without creating a lump the size of Kentucky.

"Where is it?" Oh, hell no! Inspecting his smug form, I had a flash of something Kathi had shared, one of those sexual tidbits you really wished you didn't know but once it was in your brain, you couldn't seem to erase it. Something about one of her former bed buddies availing himself of her underwear. She'd caught him in her silky lingerie one time too many and gave his ass the boot. But not before telling me how he'd turned one of her bras into a garter belt, fastening it around his hips and—

And *barf*! Just the idea of Jeff wearing my prized push-up made me cringe. "You're not wearing it! Not on your—"

He laughed so hard the wheel shimmied and rocked the tires. "No! It's on me, yes. But not *on* me. Never fear, you'll get it."

"Hmmm."

We emerged into the dark night and he braked, pausing before pulling onto the street. "Which way, Miss Carolina? Where am I taking you?"

So far beyond anything I've ever known.

I shook myself and gave him directions. Then I tried to relax. To make the muscles in my leg not flex and tense beneath the hard warmth of his hand. Tried not to constantly recall the unexpected pleasures the night had yielded. Tried to forget this was the last time I'd ever go gunning for a one-night stand.

Sex with a stranger.

Why? Because it had gone so spectacularly well, so far beyond my wildest hopes, and I wasn't naïve enough to think any other encounter could ever live up to this one.

But the strangest part? The thing I kept having to remind myself as we merged onto the freeway and melded into place behind hundreds of other red taillights creeping ahead, was how Jeff certainly didn't seem like a stranger.

And I wasn't sure he ever had.

I also couldn't quit thinking about my missing panties. And how my sensitized thighs rubbed against the slick vinyl, pressed against each other...so close to the heat of his hand.

"TELL me what you were doing out tonight," Jeff asked me out of the blue after several minutes of silence. "What prompted you to go on the prowl?"

Huh? "On the prowl?"

That sea of red taillights made sense now. A multi-car pileup had closed the freeway and forced everyone on to side roads. So the drive that should have taken half an hour was now twice that. At a minimum.

You complaining? Take advantage, my subconscious prodded. *He's hot, being next to him makes you hot, so boink him already!*

I already did, I argued back. *And his friend too!*

"Uh..." I stammered. "What makes you think something had to happen?" *Right-o, because you go on tush patrol every night.*

Grrrrr.

"Some stranger picks you up in a bar and mere minutes later splays you out before his roommate, no questions asked, no protests uttered?"

Put like that, I sounded like a tramp. Like a Grade A sleaze.

Funny how it didn't really bother me. Not now, not with his long fingers twitching on my thigh, snagging over the velvet and coming *this close* to skin. How I wanted him to touch me again. All over.

Unlike boyfriends or coworkers, I wouldn't see him again. I still had the freedom to "play", all night long if I wanted. But maybe he didn't. "Don't you have a curfew? Won't you get in trouble if you aren't in your room tonight?"

"Nah. R will cover for me if it comes to that. As long as I'm at the airport tomorrow morning, I'm good. And don't think to change the subject. You aren't the usual type, so I'm asking what made tonight special."

How did he know? It wasn't as though I had *Nearly a Virgin* tattooed across my forehead. Was it? "What do you mean 'usual type'?"

In the glow from the dash, I caught the knowing look he sliced my direction before returning his gaze to the store-lined street we tiptoed along. "There are two kinds of women who engage in threesomes. The first are the ones who want it even if they play like they don't. But it's in their eyes—the experience, the thrill of the chase. And the capture, when they snare what they want. That was missing from you."

"Experience?" Well shoot. I hadn't thought it was so noticeable. And I could've severed my tongue when I heard it ask, "So I didn't do it right after all?"

"That's *not* what I said, so stop giving me that hangdog expression like I ran over your killer purple heels." His fingers firmed and scooted toward my knee until they rested on my skin, no purple minidress in the way. He gave my bare leg a squeeze. "Now the other kind of filly to romp in bed with two guys is the one who has to be coaxed. She's usually dating the same guy for a while and he's the one pushing for it. So she does it for him, sometimes in exchange for letting him bring another woman into bed with them. Tit-for-tat, that sort of thing."

"T-turn here," I choked out, practically losing the ability to speak the more he shared. The more inept I felt.

"That's not you either. Not by a slap shot." He tried to make me smile.

The one I gave him faltered, then fizzled. "So it was obvious, um, that I'd never done this before?"

"Hell yeah, it was obvious. I wouldn't have joined in otherwise."

I found that hard to believe. Voluntarily turn down free and easy sex? That didn't mesh with what I knew of guys, much less professional sports players. "Rurik. So the plan is, he lures them in and you, uh"—*you just* did *it, ducks, might as well* say *it*—"ah, fuck them?"

"Something like that." His voice was tight. "But I haven't wanted to play in a long, long time."

"Like I'm going to believe that."

"And I'm gonna bother lying? When I've already had you?"

Faced with the irrefutable truth, I had no choice but to believe him. But what did it matter? Why was I suddenly flattered to learn that he didn't do this all the time?

You aren't. No emotion, remember?

Why me? Why tonight? Why break your spectacular string of no sex with *me*?

The big vehicle idled at a backed-up stoplight, my unvoiced questions blaring in my brain.

As if he heard all I wanted to say, Jeff exhaled loudly. "You aren't gonna ask?"

Not sure I want to know. So I asked something different. "Why were you so angry when you first saw me?"

His foot tapped impatiently on the brake pedal, causing the SUV to bounce in place, but the hand on my leg remained gentle, soothing almost. "Because I felt like my personal space had been violated. I've told Rurik I wasn't doing that anymore and to stop bringing his conquests back to the room. Actually, he and I haven't roomed together for over a year. We used to. Don't get me wrong, I've done it and enjoyed it. I'm just, I don't know, at a different place in my life now. Got a few years on him, some stuff's gone down. So when Brandon—he's one of the other guys—got married, he and I started rooming together and I haven't had to worry about any of that. But his wife just had their first baby and he took off a couple of games to be with her, hence me and Rurik."

"The Riviera," I commented neutrally, absorbing what he'd just shared. "It's a pretty posh place for a bunch of…"

"Sweaty guys to crash?"

"Well, yeah."

"That it is. But we've got a personal in with the owner."

"You mean of the hotel?"

"Yep. That and the Sidewinders."

The what? Before I could ask, Jeff added, "He's my uncle."

"Get out of town."

Jeff clicked his tongue and eased off the brake when the light turned green. "Hate to hear you're so eager to get rid of me."

I so wasn't. "I'm not."

"Too bad because we fly to Albuquerque tomorrow."

Which was what I *wanted*, I reminded myself—him leaving. Sex with a stranger I'd never see again.

So why did knowing he left in twelve hours or so cause a twinge? *Just bummed you won't see his cock again?* my snarky side suggested. Redirect! "You aren't pulling my leg? About the hotel connection?"

That explained the old SUV, then. A loaner. Family favor and all that.

"Gary's my dad's uncle if you want the nitty-gritty, but they're practically the same age. Weird family dynamic but no matter." Jeff brushed it off as he brushed his fingers over my skin, a casual caress I felt in a most uncasual way.

When he did it again I could only be thankful that I'd shaved earlier and with one of those triple-blade razors. Which brought to mind Jeff's smooth cheeks and how we'd caught him fresh from the shower—me and Rurik. Brought to mind Rurik's bristly jaw and the sensation of his thin, cultured beard gently abrading my skin when we'd kissed. When he'd kissed me—intimately.

How would Jeff's stubble-free face feel between my thighs?

A silent moan passed through me.

Still horny, hotcakes? that annoying, all-knowing voice asked. *That's a record, isn't it? You got off— and off—and yet you still want it? Bravo!*

Okay, so what if before tonight a single orgasm had been enough to tide me over—until the tide once again ebbed and flowed with the moon? If a monthly date with a dildo, after boyfriend one and then two were out of the bedroom picture, had satisfied the urge, put the yen for sex to bed —so to speak?

Weren't women supposed to come into their own, sexually, once they matured? Hit their peak somewhere in their thirties?

I was still a number of years shy of that, so maybe my body was just warming up.

Waaaaay up, my conscience confirmed. *Think he can see the steam rising from your crotch?*

While I'd been debating the evolution of my sex drive—from zero to sixty in one encounter flat thanks to a Tulsa Tornado forward and the team goalie—Jeff was conducting a normal, informative conversation. But as what he was saying registered, I realized maybe it wasn't so normal after all. "Wait a minute. Your uncle owns the hotel *and* the local hockey team?"

"Yep. That's who we battled tonight."

"Then why aren't you playing for him instead?"

"For the simple reason the Tornadoes traded for me my third year in the league and haven't wanted to let go. I'm fine with it. I don't want the other players screaming nepotism, not that they would, but a healthy rivalry works for me. And hey, if Uncle Gary wants to clear out a floor when the Tornadoes are in town and give us a cushy place to crash so we can whoop up on the hometown boys, who are we to argue?"

As we halted in front of yet another light, it occurred to me what a crazy schedule he had: games, practices, plane rides, spending time driving me across town. "Shouldn't you be with him? Your uncle, I mean. Visiting or something?" Not flirting with the girl your roommate picked up in a bar?

"Usually I would be but he's in Hong Kong this week."

"Dang. And here *I* thought hiring a driver for the twenty-mile trek to a swanky downtown nightclub was going to some effort."

"Hope we were worth it."

"You know you were." My voice had softened without my permission.

His cheeks spread wide at the admission and his fingers tightened to the point I flinched.

Regretting that unintentional, telling confession, I blurted, "So how'd you know I hadn't done this before?"

"This? The romp with two guys?"

I jerked a nod, then quickly indicated left when we reached a major intersection. "There's another route we can pick up a couple miles down. Might be less traffic. And forget I asked. About the other." How lame could I be? Bringing that up again when he'd—mostly—already told me. *Just makes you look needy, huh?*

Forget that, it made me *feel* needy.

"Are you kidding? When I walked in, your whole body was shaking so hard I thought you were gonna roll right off the bed."

Dang it. *That*'s why he'd changed his mind? Gone from angry to willing—because I'd looked like a frightened dork? "Well. Thank you for taking my embarrassment to new heights."

The light changed and he spun in the direction I'd suggested, shifting his grip higher on my leg. "I found it endearing."

"Sure you did."

"I did," he insisted. Then he ruined it by adding, "Because I could see in your eyes how bad you wanted it."

I wanted to cry and claw his hand off me. I did neither. "So the sex-starved moron earned herself a pity fuck?"

His arm tensed on the wheel, making the vehicle swerve. "Dammit, that's not what I'm saying."

"Well, that's what I'm hearing!" And why was I yelling? Getting all defensive? *Now?* When I'd gotten what I wanted—a good roll in the hay. A fast, super-fun fuck. Why'd he have to go and tell me about his uncle Gary? About his married teammate who'd just become a father?

Why'd Jeff have to go and start screwing up the illusion of spontaneous sex with a *stranger* by starting to become something more?

I growled out loud.

He snarled back. "I could tell you didn't give a damn about the hockey part, *that's* what sealed it."

"How?"

"How could I tell you weren't just there to bang a player? That any of us would have worked?"

Against the restraining heat of his hand branding my thigh, of his entire body warming my left side, I made myself stay absolutely still. No more wiggling my heated crotch on the seat, no more shifting to press my thighs together.

My body might be aching all over—sexual soreness in core places, newly roused desire in others—but it was my confidence that hurt the most. That needed to know *why* Jeff had slept with me, especially when he hadn't wanted to at first.

If he was going to insist there was something different about me, something that wasn't moronic or worth being embarrassed over, then by God, I wanted to hear the details.

I wanted to salvage my pride. "Yes. *Why?*"

"There were no sycophantic stars in your eyes, no 'I can't wait to brag to my friends who I bagged tonight' looks, simply the honest burn of lust. So that scored one for you, a big one." He tapped his index finger on my leg. "Two"—tapped his middle finger next—"you were turned on, that much was obvious but it was real, raw, not a polished act so you could be fucked by a pro player and claim bragging rights."

"That happens?"

"All the time." His next finger joined in, pressing deeper. "Three. You looked floored by the idea of a threesome, turned to stone when you first saw me, so I knew *I* was a surprise. And I knew that you were interested. You couldn't hide that either. You didn't try. Hell, I don't know. It was flattering." For the first time, his voice turned defensive. "And I wanted you, okay? Can we stop talking about this now?"

I'd heard enough. I was a happy girl. "Hey, you brought it up."

Jeff sliced me a look that said he disagreed, but he'd let it slide.

"And don't forget," I said with a little punch of giddiness, "I *am* wearing your favorite color, after all."

"That's not enough to bring my dick to your door, sweet thing. *You* did that. Why don't you believe me?"

Yeah, I'd done that.

But he knows tonight was a first. A one-off for you. Said it was obvious.

And just like that, my newfound confidence took a nosedive.

When He Realizes He Wants to Impress Her

MY PLEASURE in our exchange plummeted.

Because then, it wasn't Jeff's voice I heard. It was the years-old complaints of another. Of two others. "God, Caro, if I'd known breaking in a virgin would be busting my balls for *this*, I would have skipped the last three months. What a waste. You just lie there and take it. Hell, I can get that from a blow-up doll." And too: "Goddamn, Caro-whine-a, would you keep it down? The way you're going on, you'd think I was stabbing a cow. Just lemme finish, the game's about to start."

Maybe I wouldn't have groaned so much if it hadn't hurt. If it hadn't been all about him and his dick. What he wanted and when.

The first guy, I could forgive. We'd both been young and clueless. Puppy love leading to penis-and-pussy lust that quickly gave way to disenchantment. And him tossing me over for the "stacked" girl in school. But the second?

A real considerate lover he'd been, the jerk I'd lived with for nearly three years, more fool me, until finally realizing that happy alone trumped miserable together. It'd taken distance away from my well-intentioned grandmother in order to finally "see" things clearly. For far too long, even after she was gone, I'd practiced what she'd taught me—the importance of pleasing my man. The only problem was, she'd forgotten to teach me the most important lesson of all—how to know if he was worth it.

So that's who I was yelling at, at least deep down: the selfish shmuck I'd wasted years on. "You like the inexperienced sort, is that it?" I accused Jeff unfairly, old bitterness getting the better of me. "Get to break them in yourself? Can't wait to chat up the 'new girl' with your teammates? Fling my bra around the room and regale them with stories of the one who sucked?"

Heavy, heart-pounding silence met that.

While I stewed in my own juices, he abruptly swerved and pulled into a strip mall parking lot, the stores long since closed. The tires squealed in protest when he turned a tight circle, coming up to some trees lining the road. He punched down on the brake and put it in park, the SUV lurching with the abrupt stop.

Jeff's fingers were gone, off my leg and balled into a fist he slammed into his thigh. "Let's get one thing clear, shall we? I might share with one or t— Shit."

Two I swore he was about to say.

"Might share with one of the guys and yeah, sure. We're gonna talk between us afterward, might comment on something we liked or didn't. It's natural. But I don't go dissecting play-by-plays of my sexual encounters with anyone, whether they participated or not. And I *don't* go telling tales to anyone who's not present and accounted for during the main event. It's none of their damn business what any of us do behind closed doors."

"Oh." Why didn't that make me feel better? Why did I yearn to experience it over again? With him *and* two of his friends? *You are so messed up!* But to ride Jeff again, to see him naked and explore his chest and body as I hadn't had the chance to do earlier…

Just the thought made my desperate need for panties ratchet higher. I squirmed on the seat and tried to pull my short skirt down, past my butt where it'd ridden up, up, *up* during the disjointed drive home.

"Well?" He seemed to expect some sort of response.

So I gave him one. "That's just jolly. But I don't know why you think I care or why it should make a difference. Or why in the heck we're even discussing this!" Or why my heart was tripping over itself, my teeth digging into my lips, my body flushing, blooming under his silent regard.

He was the one who'd been cranky five minutes ago; what had turned the tables? Why did I now feel horribly guilty, not for what we'd done or what I still wanted to do, but for taking my past out on him?

Maybe because his unexpected intensity stole the breath from my lungs, steamed the space in the close confines of the vehicle, and deposited all that hot air right between my thighs?

Who cared if I didn't have much practice in the bedroom and he'd picked up on it? Why should that matter? What had happened to my wonderful, *non-emotional* one-night stand?

You mean two-stud stand, don't you, ducks? And you could be lying between the whole team if your chicken-hearted core hadn't risen up and—

Shut the hell up! I ordered my gloating conscience. Then to Jeff, "Get back on the road, please. I want to go home."

"Ah, darlin'." He killed the engine and brought the back of one finger to my face, just beneath my eye. When he drew his arm away, I was stunned to see a sparkle of moisture on his knuckle. "Quit beating yourself up over whatever refrain you hear in your head. I promise, despite whatever you're thinking, you didn't suck as you so eloquently phrased it." His eyes flicked downward, toward his crotch, then back up, catching my gaze, a half smile curving his lips. "Well, okay. You *did* suck, but I liked it a lot. That was your first time, wasn't it?"

"Of course not! I've had sex—"

"Not sex. First time taking a cock inside your mouth. Your first blow job?"

Crummers! I was that obvious? That bad?

Jeff swore. "Someone did a real number on you, didn't they?"

Though I'd kept myself from voicing my dismay, he'd picked up on it. Drat him! One-night-stand

men weren't supposed to be sensitive! Or…
or…*nice*, darn him! "What makes you think—"

"Shhh." His index finger pressed against my lips.
"Don't answer me if you don't want to but don't
lie or bluff your way out of it."

He held his finger in place, kept my gaze snared
until I jerked a nod. Taking that as agreement I
wouldn't proffer any more empty excuses, he allowed his finger to slide free, the pad snagging
on my bottom lip just before he pulled it away.
"Good girl. Now don't assume 'new' or 'different'
or 'inexperienced' equates with bad, hmmm?"
He brushed several fingertips against the seam
of my lips, back and forth. "As long as your teeth
don't break the skin of his precious anatomy,
most guys are gonna love you going down on
them, no matter how practiced you are at it. I
did."

"Did what?" I asked just because I wanted to
hear him say it.

"Loved having your virgin mouth on me. You
were all true hesitance and fresh eagerness. You
wanted it but didn't have a clue."

Gee thanks. The amateur entertains the pro.

He just stared at me, one eyebrow raised and I heard my own outburst echoing around us. "Shoot. I didn't mean to say that out loud."

"But you did. Which tells me something— starting to have second thoughts about what we did? Is your conscience trying to heap on the guilt?" He assessed accurately, giving me an explanation for the snarky thoughts.

"Yeah." I nodded. "With mine, it's a real love-hate relationship. Guilt for doing both of you. Then a lecture for not taking on the team." My self-effacing smile let him know I wasn't serious about the last one.

"Don't let it. Guilt's a useless emotion to carry 'round. Time only makes it weigh more, I've learned. You need to seize every day, live it to the fullest without regret." I wanted to ask what had happened. What grave event had taught him that lesson. But I didn't have the right—and he wasn't finished. "Tell me, did you have fun tonight?"

That was a *no, duh* question if I'd ever heard one. "Uh, *ye-aahhh.*"

"Are you married? Seeing anyone seriously?"

"No! How could you think I'd do *all this*"—my hand flailed back and forth between us, indicating the entire night and everything we'd done—"if I had someone waiting at home? Someone who might be hurt by it?"

"Exactly," he said with satisfaction. Under his breath, he added, "A lot of people don't feel the same, I'm sad to say." After a deep exhale, his voice firmed. "Don't worry about it, then. Zero reason for guilt."

"Easier heard than done."

"Hey, if you weren't betraying anyone, practiced basic safety, and had a few enjoyable moments, what's the harm? Don't beat yourself up over it."

His practical, easygoing attitude was infectious. "Enjoyable? Try *ecstatic* moments. Long ones. Lots of them," I assured with a relaxed smile. I settled into the seat and closed my eyes, allowing my head to drop sideways against his shoulder. "Think maybe I'm starting to adopt your philosophy."

"Be my guest. But just remember, I still need to hear those promised views on religion and politics, you know." At that, my eyes popped open and my head jerked upright. The lines of his face looked somber, stern almost, but then those green eyes glinted.

Sure, we'd joked about discussing those things before he penetrated me earlier but that'd just been foreplay. Banter, right? "Tell me you're not serious."

"Later. Before we get any more philosophical though, there's something else I need to do." Jeff leaned over and placed both hands on my thighs. "Come here, dollface. I've noticed you've gotten all squirmy, leading me to think you may be as wet as I am hard."

I glanced through the tinted windows at the deserted parking lot. The stores were dim, the patrons long gone. But we were next to the street, busier than normal now because of the freeway closing.

The trees gave good cover, allowed us a semblance of privacy, in theory if not in fact. All this I took in during the few seconds when he undid my seat belt and skimmed his hands under my dress until he met my heated flesh.

"Jeff?" I'm not sure exactly what I was questioning.

"That's me." Releasing his hold on my legs, he placed his hands at my waist and pushed me away, shoving my shoulders toward the passenger door and hauling my legs onto the bench seat, flattening my back and tugging me toward him.

"Here?" It was an excited squeak. "Now?"

"Yep." He hunched toward me, smoothing his fingers over my breasts, palming my nipples through the snug fabric. "Come on, now. Dress up. Panties off." He suited action to words and dragged his hands down to scrunch the velvet sheath up my thighs. "Oops. Forgot you aren't wearing any."

Because he'd torn them off! But I couldn't be upset at the loss of the frilly, expensive thong, not when he said, "I like the thought of knowing those babies are back in my hotel room, dressing up that dark green carpet with a little splash of pretty purple."

"Lavender. Not purple, exactly," the anal part of me just had to clarify.

He took it in stride as he ducked to inspect what he'd just exposed. "Whatever. Lavender, purple, paisley or plaid, they're in my possession now, stiff with your juices. Your spice. Just might need to have a sniff or two later tonight."

My face flamed at the image of him inhaling my panties. My body responded accordingly too. I knew I was wet. Didn't need to see the heat in his eyes or hear the hitch in his breath when he widened my thighs, pressing my outside foot to the floorboard and my opposite leg firmly into the back cushion before angling into the space he'd created to sweep the pads of several fingers up and down my slit.

"*Uhmghm*," I choked, flinching away and then immediately into the caress. My flesh was so sensitized from what we'd done earlier that every glide of his fingers proved to be acute, erotic torture.

The crude, anything-but-suave visual of us humping like teenagers in the backseat of Granddaddy's car rolled through my head. It wasn't enough to stem my growing arousal nor slow how my bent leg tensed against the seat, bringing my core closer to him. The upholstery creaked a protest.

"Really?" I shifted against the vinyl. "We're going to do it in the front seat?" When I was already sweating everywhere? Everywhere the vinyl touched me. Everywhere it didn't.

"No, not what you're thinking. But something else? Definitely yes." His thumb insistently spread each side of my labia outward, revealing the moist crevice it then nudged into. I gasped at the gentle invasion, gaining an inkling of how very swollen I must be by the tremendous fullness his mere thumb provided. Or maybe I gasped at the concentrated expression he wore snugging it into place.

A single streetlamp far across the parking lot arrowed a bluish beam through the windshield, illuminating one side of Jeff's face. I found him easier to concentrate on than the achy desire he brought rolling forth. His mouth was flat and tightly held, eyes glittered behind the glasses. The angle of one sideburn was clear, the other submerged into shadow. "You are so fine."

The stupid observation and old-fashioned-sounding compliment didn't faze him. His thumb delved deep and pressed, stretching inflamed and, prior-to-tonight, little-used muscles.

Scooting his hips back against the door, he leaned in. "I didn't get to taste your cream last time. Rurik's the only one who had the pleasure." He brought his mouth within two inches of where my honey trickled freely. "How can he and I be expected to compare notes," Jeff teased as he took a moment to remove his glasses with his free hand and place them on the dash, "if I don't avail myself of a few drops?"

Practically before he finished talking, his tongue was at my core, following the trail his thumb made as both slid down my weeping center. "Mmm."

After a couple sinuous glides, he lifted his head and changed the angle of his wrist, shoving in deep. Then he applied himself and his tongue to licking me again, his warm mouth savoring and eating its way up the right side of my cleft. "Damn seat," he grumbled, trying and failing to pay equitable attention along the other side. "Can't maneuver."

When his head failed to gain the access he wanted, Jeff brought his chin to my mons and looked at me through hooded eyes. Hovering over the apex, he eased his thumb free to the accompaniment of my hissed groan. Then he deliberately placed it directly atop my clit. "Oh, darn. Guess I'll have to settle for snacking here a bit."

Flexing his knuckle, he raised the tented flesh and latched on to my now screaming clit. Warm, rhythmic motions bathed my flesh as he sucked it inside his mouth and danced his tongue over me. His lips released and repositioned, a bit wider, and he sucked again, all the while lashing his tongue over and around the responsive nerves.

The intimate caress fed my desire for more. It also made me think of the last man who'd generously given me the same pleasure—Rurik, just a scant hour or so before. I could understand now what I couldn't have previously: comparison was natural. Though technique, intensity, and the audible appreciation they each expressed differed, I'm happy to report my body took delight in both, responded to—

As though he sensed my attention wandering—though not far, I could've assured him *if* I'd had the ability to speak—Jeff plunged his thumb back in and sucked a bit harder, flicked his tongue a bit faster.

My pelvis shimmied against his face. Streaks of arousal snaked through me, every one starting and stopping where his hands opened me, his mouth devoured me.

My fingernails creaked against the vinyl near my hips until I dug them in to quiet the sound. Would the next round of hotel personnel or hockey players to occupy the vehicle find little half-moons carved in the seat? Would they smell the lingering scent of my desire? Know what Jeff and I had done?

At the thought, a moan threatened. I clamped my lips but it stubbornly broke free, a near-silent whimper, a testament to how excited I was. My thighs started to shake, miniscule vibrations quivering all through me.

He licked deeper, harder.

My stomach seized in a glorious cramp. I canted my hips and strained in place, careful not to dislodge his attentions.

Jeff lifted his head. "Stop holding back. Yell, participate. *Scratch me.* Do whatever you want. Better yet, *tell* me what you want."

With an offer like that, how could I help myself?

"I want you to fuck me." Once uttered out loud, the obscene word I usually reserved for mental fantasies—or stubbed toes—sounded decadent, not dirty. "Fuck me with your mouth. With your tongue. Make me come and don't give me a choice."

"That's what I wanted to hear." His thumb slipped free leaving me hollow. But not for long, as he slid several fingers inside my passage and pressed deep. With a decisive grin, his mouth returned to laving attention on my delicate flesh.

My toes flexed, drawing my notice. When had I wrapped one leg around his back? The other at his neck?

I reached for his hair, sinking my fingers into the thick, sun-gilded strands for the first time. Nails locked on his scalp, I held him steady as my hips flailed.

Knowing it was his tongue causing this response—such a personal, private part of his body in such intimate contact with mine—ramped the sensations all the way to naughty. Not a word I'd ever thought of in conjunction with my typically tame self.

As though he approved of my fierce grip on his head, Jeff groaned into me. Searing desire coalesced in my abdomen. The rush of arousal slid through my lower body as every individual muscle grew tight. "The seat! I'll get it—"

"Do it!" he lifted his mouth to order. "Don't hold back." His fingers jackhammered into me so fast, his arm was a blur between my upraised legs. "Stuff washes. This can't wait."

At my gasp, he withdrew his fingers and fluttered the flat of his hand over my clit. Fast. Furious.

"Aahh-eeee—" I speared my teeth onto both lips, refusing to shriek like an idiot.

Faster, fiercer, his hand flew. The other snuck between my buttocks where he settled one fingertip at my anus and just held steady. Lightning blasted through me as I rocked between his motionless touch on my ass and the frantic, practiced wave of his fingers on my clit.

"Come on, Care, how does it feel? Let me hear it."

No one had ever shortened my name like that. In his whiskey voice, the adoring sound zoomed from my ears to my toes and everywhere between. A shower of sparks blasted beneath his flying fingers and the one at my anus wedged itself a little deeper.

Every muscle contracted, then released, sucked him in and refused to let go. Just as I refused to yell, biting down on my tongue to still the impulse as minuscule muscle spasms swarmed through my pelvis, over and over and...over...

I sighed, bliss floating me up to some sort of sexual nirvana heaven.

"Oh, baby." The endearment was soft, coaxing. His finger flexed, just barely inside my anus. "You didn't scream like I wanted but you sure did come." He bent and licked up my seam, then leaned back to swipe his tongue over his lips. "How was it? If you won't let go all the way, you have to tell me. Call it a penalty."

With penalties like that, who needed promises?

"Fucking fabulous." The words sounded nicer than they were. Maybe even a bit tame, coming from me. But that was okay. As my trembling hand stroked over his hair, smoothing the pricks my nails had left behind, it was the perfect descriptor. "Your record for immensely impressive acts of fornication just keep on coming tonight, don't they?"

"Impressive, huh?"

Hell, yeah. "Heck, any more and I'd faint on you."

"I can think of worse fates."

FOUR

When He Decides to Shower Her With New Experiences

"SO SPILL."

"Crude oil or my guts?"

"Our postcoital conversation topics," Jeff reminded with a *tsk-tsk*. "How quickly they forget."

There was never supposed to be any postcoital conversing! my conscience fairly screamed. *No emotion, just raw sex.*

After I'd caught my breath and lowered my dress, after he'd pulled me upright and plastered his lips to mine, kissing my mouth with the same talented thoroughness he'd shown my core, I was bemused, baffled, and beyond thought for once. I allowed him to belt me back into place and we resumed the trek toward my apartment.

Now that it was later and farther from the closed freeway, we zipped along, making good time on the sparsely occupied roads, swiftly closing in on the end of this magical evening.

Once he'd started the engine, the first words off my salty-essence-flavored tongue were, "So that's how I taste?"

"What?" He'd seemed surprised, overly so in my opinion. "You've not sampled your...juicy cunt before?" I could tell he'd paused and chosen his words for maximum effect, and what an effect it was. Named "juicy" parts lived up to their reputation and I clenched my entire lower regions, half afraid I was about to turn the bench seat into a Slip 'n Slide before the ride was over.

"I'll take your wiggling silence as a no. Glad I could introduce you." The cocky rat had laughed but I got the impression it was more at the situation than me, so I was mostly okay with it. Knowing I'd again advertised what a rookie I was, I chose not to confirm his assumption and we'd continued on, minus conversation, companionably for several miles.

The question he posed now, discussing what we'd first flirted about in his hotel room, caught me totally off guard.

"I don't know," I hedged, "um, isn't there supposed to be some sort of one-night-stand protocol whereby lengthy discourse on weighty subjects is prohibited?"

"So says the gal who's newly indoctrinated into the art of sex with strangers." His low rumble of a chuckle reached through the sex-drenched interior and tickled my vocal cords, making me want to respond in kind. Want to get to know him better.

That way lies foolishness and heartache.

Can it, I ordered, but couldn't yet relinquish my hesitance to answer.

"Come on," Jeff cajoled, sounding like a third-grader. "I'll tell you mine if you'll tell me yours."

"Remind me of the topics again." As if I didn't already know. Things you're *never* supposed to discuss outside of close family and even closer friends.

"Religion, politics, and sex."

I knew there were others, but those were the three I'd stupidly mentioned first. "What the heck, I'm game." So I told him the truth. "Raised conservative Christian. Raised to vote Republican. Taught not to have it."

"And now?"

"Now?" Boy, I sure could play dense when I wanted.

But he wasn't fooled. "Now that you're on your own. What are *your* views and practices?" His voice lowered. "Your sexual pleasures?"

"I no longer vote straight ticket—for any party. But don't let that get out."

"My lips are sealed," he promised, licking them blatantly and ending the action with an audible *smack*. "Sealed with your flavor."

I ignored that.

Hah! As if my mouth could forget what he'd shared with his. Or my body could stop shuddering, deep inside, where that last tongue-lashed orgasm seemed buried like a fault line, tremoring through me at odd intervals, causing little cracks in the armor I'd trained myself to don around guys I found sexy. "I try to look beyond party lines and make individual choices on issues I care about," I explained, pointing to a group of two-story buildings ahead on the right. "There, that's home. The code to unlock the gate is 0077. As far as religion goes, it's there if you need it. Some people do and I respect that."

"But not you?"

Baring my soul was actually starting to feel a bit liberating. "Nah. Too confining and narrow for where my beliefs have gone. Once I started branching out and visiting various places of worship, I came to recognize I'm a lot more spiritual than I am religious."

"So no church on Sunday?" He braked, lowering his window to punch in the code.

"Rarely. But I do pray, just…informally. Your turn."

The big gate inched open but he didn't drive through. "You forgot about sex."

No, I hadn't. "There's nothing more to share that you need to hear or I want to say."

"So you're pleading the fifth?" It started to close back.

"Something like that. Hey, aren't you going to give it some gas?"

The air left his lungs on a long exhale. I could tell he was contemplating whether to accept that I was done with the topic or argue about it. His next sentence showed that my unspectacular sexual history was off the table—for now. "Okay. My turn. Ah, crap." He'd entered the numbers again and flubbed in his haste. After waiting for the console to reset, he pushed each button decisively. "Where to?"

"Building F. The road is a horseshoe and it's all the way around back. You can probably park right by the stairs." At least this time of night you could. Though it was late for me, on Fridays and Saturdays, it was still considered early according to the party crowd, and enough young singles and not-yet-with-child married couples lived in the complex that date nights still reigned.

"Got it." He raised his window and wound through the complex, his headlights highlighting the stately trees and well-maintained grounds of the place I'd called home the last few years, liking the management, the neighborhood, and my personal space well enough not to move. "All right, I'm a recovering Catholic and no, I don't attend Mass or confession these days. Nor do I feel guilty about skipping either. I toyed with the idea of atheism for a while, but my belief in a higher power shot that to hell."

I couldn't stop my chuckle.

"Laugh at me, will you?" But I could tell he saw the humor in how he'd phrased it. Jeff nodded when I pointed to my building and slowly pulled into a vacant space near the stairway. He killed the engine and shifted to look at me, making no move to get out. "Those were some troubling times, I tell you. Debating the meaning of life and my place in it. Not easy stuff and you dare mock me?"

"What can I say? You're surprisingly easy to talk to, ergo, easy to mock." I intentionally monotoned my voice. "Forgive me, Father, for I have sinned."

"I ain't your daddy, doll, and don't you forget it."

There was never any doubt.

My gaze skimmed over the familiar wrought-iron railing and concrete steps leading up to a small landing with two doors branching off. Mine and that of a married couple who'd just moved in. Part of me wondered what they might think, if they chanced to look out the window. They'd see me—sedate, usually in-bed-by-ten me—sitting in a big vehicle with a sun-streaked blond who could sell suntan lotion on the subway just by holding out the bottle, start a run on Wayfarer frames just by blinking, and cause a condom shortage just by smiling.

Cause me to *want*, a lot more than was safe. Or realistic. But did I skedaddle my butt up to safety? Oh no. "So tell me—what side of the ticket do you pull?"

Did I really want to know? Or was I just pro-longing the end? Delaying the inevitable?

When he answered, I realized I did want to know. Was curious about what made this recovering Catholic, God-believing, non-atheist, sexy-as-hell goalie tick. "I make it a point to only cast a vote in races where I've met the candidate face-to-face. Shaken their hand, taken their measure. I trust my gut and you can't do that wading through online bullshit, a thirty-second commercial, or a televised debate—whether it's a free-for-all yellfest or a stilted affair."

"Sounds to me like you're taking the easy way out. Don't happen to meet them, don't have to care?"

"Just the opposite. If it's a race I'm eligible to vote in and a candidate's going to be in town, I make it a point to go. And I admit, I've gotten suckered into more than one of those Town Meeting phone calls, to hear what they—"

"To *hear*? Isn't that cheating? Discounting your go-with-my-gut theory? You can't exactly shake hands over the phone."

"Ah, but I can learn a candidate's views and see whether it's worth spending any more of my time and the earth's oil investigating them further."

Darn. He got me coming and going. "You must've had one heck of a social studies teacher, to care so much about government and how it's run."

"For the people, *by* the people," he said emphatically, gripping the top of the wheel with his left hand and sliding his right along the seat back, under my hair, and coming into firm contact with my nape. "Too many of these political bigwigs and families have lost sight of that. And yeah, my senior year I had a terrific teacher who made us write every state and local elected official, but more than that, my great-grandmother —or was it great-great?—anyway, she was one of the suffragettes who picketed the White House right after World War I. She died well before I was old enough to hear her talk of it, but my grandfather regaled me with stories of her courage time and again. He was so proud of her and the fight she wouldn't let go of, and he made me promise not to let that be in vain even though I was his rough-and-tumble boy instead of a dainty, pink-frilled granddaughter."

"I'd say you're not." I inhaled and leaned back into his arm, told my lower half to cool its jets. We'd already had round two in the front seat. There was no sense angling for more.

He did say hockey has three periods. Aren't you curious about what might be in store for the last?

"That's...touching," I said about his story, refusing to acknowledge my inner voice. *Inner yearning, you mean?* "I'm ashamed to admit I never thought of women's suffrage. I'm sure I learned something in school but I don't remember any of it. I never knew there was picketing."

"That and a lot more. Easy enough to look up. Check it out if you're interested. She had eight boys and no girls, my great-grandmother, and that's why it was so important to her that her boys teach their kids to make an effort and do what's right for the country. Even when it involves personal sacrifice."

Dang. I'd known him, what? Two hours? Maybe three? And this was probably the "deepest" conversation I'd ever had with any of the—now four—men I'd slept with. Weird.

Phenomenal, really.

He drummed his fingertips on the wheel. The ones on my nape flexed.

"You probably need to get back. I'm sure the freeway's open from this direction. All you—"

"No." His fingers stilled, tightened. "There's no one clocking me tonight. As long as I report to the boarding gate on time, I'm good."

And that was my cue. Did I ask him in? Or save myself the humiliation? Wasn't two cocks, two tongues, and countless climaxes in one night enough?

Not for me!

Hand on my seat belt, I stalled. Once I unclicked it, there would be nothing keeping me here. No reason not to leave.

I stared at Jeff in the inky darkness, stunned when he quietly asked, "Can I come up?"

"I..." Wanted him to, with everything in me.

I was also afraid.

Because at some point since being taken in his hotel room by both him and Rurik and during the ride over here, I'd come to care, damn him. About what, I couldn't exactly identify, wasn't even sure if I knew. Him? My performance? Crushing on the wrong guy? I didn't know.

But still, some elusive emotion was starting to creep over me, causing me to hesitate and second-guess the whole night. To ponder where we went from here—upstairs together, for more adventure? Or me alone, to boring safety?

"I want you again," he breathed into the strained silence. "Want to fuck your tight pussy, feel you shatter around me with no one else watching. I want your nails scoring my back. But if it's *no*, just say the word. I'll go back to the hotel to sleep. That's it."

That's it? "Meaning you won't... What?"

"Meaning I won't go out. Won't snare another cunt in your place. Not tonight."

"Why?" Why did his crude phrasing turn me on? Excite me to a whole new level? *Fuck your tight pussy...with no one else watching.* "Why even tell me that last part?"

"Hell if I know. I guess I don't want you thinking that you're interchangeable. I've enjoyed talking with you. Tasting you," he said bluntly. "I like the innocence in your eyes. Even now, after all we've done to corrupt you, Rurik and I, it's still there, shining bright." He gave a tight laugh. "Blinding my common sense perhaps, for telling you this. But I've been hard for you since I went down— Hell, since we left the hotel. Talking about church and doing our civic duty hasn't changed a thing. Or dulled the edge."

That confession surprised me. Surprised me because not once had Jeff hinted that he was horny or pulled my hand toward his groin, forcing me to stroke him. Not once had he indicated since he'd gotten me off, it was my duty to return the favor. Not once had he acted entitled. And that only made me want him back with a desperate yearning that was so foreign to my typically sub-dued sex drive I hardly recognized myself.

"Oh. I figured since you came earlier, you were done. Not interested in more." At least that'd been my prior experience—one good fuck, roll over and start snoring. That's what I'd gotten used to. What I thought was the norm.

"Hardly. I know I let the subject drop earlier, but I'm starting to think you haven't had the best of luck with men. So put what ever preconceived notions you may have in the incinerator, hmmm? Start fresh," he posed, stroking my neck, "starting now?"

I didn't need any more prompting, other than his sincere tone, to give him a single, silent nod.

"Good." Jeff's fingers trailed across my shoulders when he pulled his arm down. He scooted my listless hand away and unlocked my seat belt. "Your expression was so skittish at the hotel, so arresting," he commented idly as he tossed the belt to the empty passenger side, then undid his own. "I can't get it out of my mind. When I came out of that bathroom and you registered what you were seeing, I thought for sure you were about to bolt. Go running for cover. But you didn't."

He exhaled a measured, contemplative sigh. Then he shifted and faced me in the shadowed interior. "You didn't bolt then. Are you going to now?"

"No." It squeaked out of me, timid and unsure. So I said it again, more decisively. "No. Come upstairs with me."

"Are you positive?"

No. "Yes."

"You sore?"

Yes. "No."

"You lying?"

"Through my teeth. But come up anyway. You've got a plane to catch and time's a-wasting."

"NICE JUNGLE," Jeff commented after I'd un-locked the door to my apartment and gestured for him to precede me. He gingerly brushed aside several leafy falls of Herbert, a beautiful pothos hanging from the ceiling, so he could walk inside.

"Herbert, release our houseguest." My breath was coming fast and furious, and I knew it wasn't from climbing the stairs. "I sort of have a thing for plants."

Two steps in, he spun in place, narrowly getting sideswiped by Rupert, a solid green spider plant whose baby offshoots never seemed to stop growing. I hadn't trimmed them back in months and they were only inches off the floor.

"So I see." His eyes raked my not-quite-hyper-ventilating form from my toes upward. Plum-tipped toes that did a little wiggle under his re-gard. My breasts responded too, nipples knotting tighter at being subject to his admiring gaze. He flicked his eyes to the side and did a quick inven-tory of the entryway. "Plants and purple."

I'd installed motion sensors on most of my lights, along with sliding dimmers. So the instant we'd pierced the darkness, my overhead foyer light had flashed on, bathing the area in a warm golden glow. Well, sort of golden. Due to our surroundings, it was almost pinkish because above the ornate chair-rail molding that ran horizontally throughout most of the apartment, I'd painted the textured sheet rock a rich shade of lavender.

Jeff craned his neck to look past the hanging plants. I guessed he was taking in the living room and what he could see of the kitchen beyond, as well as my office, a small square room that branched off the entry. Finished with his perusal, he turned back and grinned, snaring my gaze with something I could almost take to be appreciation if it weren't for the choked way he voiced, "A *lot* of purple."

"Um-mmm." Without looking, I reached behind me and turned the deadbolt, locking us in. My recently reclaimed purse slid to the tiled floor with a soft thump. My keys weren't so considerate, clattering loudly from my nervous fingers.

His eyes had remained on mine, holding me captive, observing my every move peripherally; only the slight tilt of one eyebrow acknowledged the crash of my keychain, but his hands had been busy—digging in both of his back pockets for a moment, then foraging one in the front. "Ta da!" Like a kid excited about show-and-tell, Jeff whipped out my bra with a proud, beaming smile. "Told you I'd return it."

But it was no longer the gorgeous purple tiger stripe push-up I'd worn mere hours ago. Now it was crumpled. And in pieces. Tattered pieces. "So that's what you did with it? D-dissected it like...like a *dead frog*?"

"Guilty as charged." But he didn't look guilty, not a bit.

He'd divested the cups of their precious padding, had apparently stuffed the now shapeless, forlorn satin in his front pocket and crammed the beautifully crafted push-up foam in his back pockets.

And he'd sat on it the whole way here?! My Mentionables marvel? The one that made near mountains out of my molehills?

"Jeff! You ruined it!" Then why wasn't I mad at him? Raging at him for destroying my favorite bosom enhancer? Why was I just standing there, staring at this tanned, Wayfarer-wearing, surfing-styled god holding out the one item—now useless—that had given me the confidence to go through with tonight?

Maybe it was because he didn't give me a chance, dropping the mangled pieces and covering the tiny bumps on my chest with his palms to push me back, flat against the door.

"I did but I didn't mean to," he whispered hotly against my mouth. "And sweet Care, if I can get you to cry my name like that again, I might just massacre every one you own."

He took tiny nibbles of my lips as though coaxing another cry from me. What I gave him instead was a sigh as my hands found anchor against his shirt collar, my fingers gripping the doubled fabric as if that could strengthen my knees and keep me upright.

Which was unnecessary, given how solidly he supported me. How the strong length of his hard body kept mine firmly in place. His willing prisoner.

But so very necessary when his mouth paid homage to mine, going from playful to passionate in a blink, when his hands cupped the slight swells on my chest, massaging them through my dress and bringing a fiery heat to my nipples that made me flash on earlier tonight, when he'd folded back the edge of my bra and first licked me there.

My bra! I whimpered.

But not because it was gone. No, because he'd wedged one thigh between my legs and leaned into me, using the door at my back for leverage as he lifted me, angling his leg so that I was nearly riding him. My dress hiking up of its own accord, my pussy sliding, rubbing over the denim. My breath catching, evaporating.

My mind reeling.

Little voice yelling, *Hoorah!*

Lips and tongue now engaged in a battle I hoped to lose. Needed to lose. To the victor went the spoils and I was spoiling for his cock. Oh wait, wouldn't that make me the winner?

My fingers climbed from his collar, up his neck, and into his hair. I tugged his head back to look at him.

His breath came as hard as mine and just as fast.

I watched his nostrils flare, saw the pulse flickering rapidly at the base of his jaw, tempting my tongue to return, to taste him there.

You are so dang fine.

As if he heard what I'd only thought, he pinched my nipples and pushed his leg higher. My feet hung suspended a few inches off the floor. I depended upon him to support me, to keep me safe.

A tiny moan worked free. "You killed it," I said forlornly, surprising myself because I'd honestly thought I didn't care anymore. "It was a gift."

"A gift?" A shadow passed over his eyes. "The bra?"

He lunged backward and forward again, causing my crotch to slide over his thigh.

"From...from a friend." I kept staring at his mouth, feeling his fingers fluttering over my nipples.

His fingers pinched my nipples as his gaze darkened. "What kind of friend?"

"Girlfriend. C-coworker," I stammered out as the pressure loosened, turned playful. "Kathi says I'm not adventurous enough."

"I'd say you're proving her wrong tonight. And if it helps, it wasn't intentional. Not at first." My body started to slip downward. He swiftly traded stimulating my breasts to holding my waist in order to halt the unintentional retreat. "When I snatched it from Rurik, I saw some loose threads."

"Loose threads, hmmm?" It was impossible to mind, not when he was pulling me forward, abrading my intimate flesh on his thigh, then pushing me back. My toes curled against my sandals, wishing they were free to curl against him, to scrape over his legs. "That doesn't explain how it ended up in pieces and *in your pockets.*"

"One side was really loose and I started picking at it." Now he did look guilty. I took perverse pleasure in that. And decided not to admit that I'd been lazy and had started washing it in the machine. Who said I had to reveal all my secrets?

His fingers firmed at my waist and my thigh-ride stopped. "Hell, you were in the bathroom for an hour—"

"An hour?" I started fiddling with his glasses, tracing his ear where the black frames rested. "That's a crock!"

"A slight exaggeration. *Maybe.*"

"A fifty-minute exaggeration but go on." How many other opportunities would I have to make out—half naked—with a sexy guy in my foyer? I slid the Wayfarers off and wiggled my pelvis. By now, I was sure my juices had soaked through the denim of his jeans. I really should have been bothered by the thought. Tough cookies, I wasn't. Guess I'd be glued in place. Hung up on a hung hottie. Oh darn.

"Forty minutes, then. Anyway, and this is going to sound really dumb"—nothing he ever said could sound dumb, not in that rich, bedroom voice of his—"but I didn't *want* to give it back. You seemed more vulnerable, more real, once it was off. Besides, how can I look at your nipples when they're covered up with three feet of stuffing?"

Really? He wanted to see my nipples? Holy happiness, Batman, I almost came on the spot. His spot. God, just the thought of coming on his jeans made me wetter. I hooked his glasses behind my ears and blinked at him through the distorted glass. "How do I look?"

"Adorable. But like you're hiding again." He pulled them off and slid one earpiece into a link on Herbert's overhead chain. His leg flexed once beneath me, then tilted to provide a short ride down.

My feet landed on the floor easily enough. It was my pride that stung. "What do you mean, hiding?"

"Like you do behind fancy bras and silence."

"Silence? We've been talking all night." My sex felt so hollow. *Not your sex, your psyche. He's pegged you! And after only one poke!*

Dang. How in the heck could this man I'd just met sense my secrets so soon? Recognize my vulnerabilities and strip me of my armor so easily?

Does it really matter? He likes your nipples! Run with that!

"So, Miss Carolina." As though backing away from the touchy subject, his voice changed, grew almost as perky as my just-played-with breasts. "I've got a question for you."

"Ask away."

"Ever shower with a guy?"

FIVE

When He Realizes the Importance of Stocking Condoms—On His Person

SHOWER WITH A GUY? "*YOU MEAN NAKED?*"

"No, Care. I mean in a tux. Oops." My jungle had caught him again. After getting his arm untangled, Jeff draped one of Rupert's long-hanging offshoots behind him and leaned closer to me. "*Of course* I mean naked. Silly girl."

Not waiting for my reply, which was so obviously a negative, he twirled until his back was at the door. Legs spread wide, he drew me into the vee and with one hand on my butt, pressed me into his groin.

His erection was a solid presence between us.

Sticky residue from earlier mixed with fresh arousal, slicking my inner thighs. I couldn't believe I had any cream left. Considering how much I'd given up to his mouth and jeans, I should be all out.

"A shower would feel nice," I admitted, deciding to brave my way through this. *This* being *bonus-one-night-stand* sex. I'd be a fool not to grab on to anything and everything Jeff might want to show me. Do with me. *To* me.

I leaned back at my waist, keeping my lower half nestled firmly against his, and brought my fingers—the darn things were trembling, I saw with dismay—to his shirt. Under his watchful gaze, I slipped the top button free, followed by the next, exposing the skin beneath his collarbones.

His hands flexed on each of my butt cheeks. Flexed, then dug in, lifting the velvet sheath higher over my ass. I couldn't hold back my moan of appreciation.

My fingers echoed the sentiment, getting the hang of it and tearing through his remaining buttons with the speed of a lightning strike. Eagerly, I pushed the edges apart and gazed, once again but up close this time, at his magnificent chest. "You've got a surfer's body, did you know?"

He rocked me back and forth and side to side, over and against his erection. "You get a lot of surfers here in Cinci?"

I brought my hands to his pecs and mapped across, bringing the sensitive hollow of my palms into contact with his nipples...where they lingered. I leaned forward and drew my tongue down the center of his chest, in the open space between my splayed fingers and inhaled him as deeply as I could.

He grunted and stopped the methodical rocking. "Carolina? The shower? Can I take that to mean ye— *Wuhm!*"

I'd moved one hand lower to make room for my lips and nipped the muscle just above his left nipple. Something told me Jeff wouldn't complain.

I opened my mouth and scraped my teeth over more of his flesh, not biting exactly but definitely not kissing either.

"'S that, uhm, a yes?"

Yes? What was he talking about? Impossible to remember when I was licking his torso for the first time. His skin didn't taste the least bit salty. Wasn't flavored with sweat the way you might expect after a vigorous sex session or vehicle seduction. No, all my tongue encountered was the fresh, clean fragrance of good-quality hotel soap, probably some triple-milled French stuff. That seemed like The Riviera. The soap scent, the hint of citrusy aftershave and Jeff, a faint residual of something masculine and yummy. Sandalwood maybe?

His fingers continued their flex and retreat, working my dress all the way up until they completely met the bare skin of my bottom. He inched them closer to my center and another wave of I-want-your-body passion flooded through me, threatening to coat his delving fingers—and my floor if we didn't get horizontal quick.

The wave of wetness reminded me—surfing. That's what he'd asked about, so in between insistent nibbles over his chest—my mouth didn't seem in any hurry to leave—I told him, "I've seen *Baywatch*, saw *Point Break*. I know a lean and sexy surfer when I see…" I licked over a nipple, started flailing the tiny tip with my tongue. "One."

When his fingertips met in the crevice and slid along my slit, wedging ever deeper, all the way from my anus to my passion-drenched curls, my tongue slowed and I started sucking on his chest. My nails dug in, just a bit, and my toes curled again, lifting me higher, giving his searching fingers better access.

A low, growling noise erupted from him and his intimate advance halted as his hands tensed in place.

Another sound emerged from his throat. I couldn't tell if it was a laugh or a snort. Maybe a snarl. "You're a fan of *Baywatch*? And I look like a surfer? God, you're priceless. And apparently don't have a problem with water..." Without warning he bent low, interrupting my exploratory chest kisses, my feasting on his body, and curved his hands around my knees. In one easy motion, he stood, flipping me over his shoulder. "So it's to the shower we go."

Dangling there, I watched my living room pass by in an upside-down haze as he plowed through the apartment.

"Watch out for Beauregard!" I tried to holler when a few stray ivy leaves drifted to the floor, but with his hard shoulder bisecting my stomach, the words came out garbled.

Carolina! My uncharacteristically quiet—for the past few minutes at least—inner voice piped up, sounding surprisingly panicked. *It's Friday! You haven't done Saturday's list!*

Who cared about lists when—

You do! I do! Because when everything around you is falling to pieces, if your corner is neat and tidy, then you're all right with the world.

"Wait!" The protest was instinctive. I clawed at his denim-clad legs, seeing my hallway come into reverse as Jeff paused before open doors until finding the one he sought, various lights flicking on in our wake. *Stop him!* "Jeff!"

That voice wasn't mine, the one preaching about corners and lists. It was my grandmother's. The woman who raised me after my deadbeat dad, whoever he was, didn't stick around for my birth. After my mom, misguided but well intentioned, got herself killed in a robbery gone bad while working three jobs to make things right. To help out her mom who'd taken us in.

Twelve years old when my world fell apart, and my one remaining relative kept me sane by teaching me structure and order. By preaching a neat home not only made a good impression, it gave one a measure of peaceful contentment.

So when Jeff put me on my feet and the blood rushed away from my head, leaving me grasping at his forearm for balance, it wasn't the achy edge of desire speaking, it was long-held teachings and often-practiced habits. "I haven't cleaned since last weekend." I spun toward the cabinet where I kept the cleaners and scrub brushes. "It'll only take a sec. Just let me—*Ompf!*"

Whirling me around and bracketing both hands on either side of my face, he commandeered my full attention "Care." His eyebrows shot skyward, floating a good foot above those emerald beauties I could see so clearly now, then they slammed down in a fierce frown. "Really? *Clean the shower?* That's what occurs to you when I have my hands in your slit? When all I want to do is fuck your heavenly body and make it sing? Make you scream? Have you clawing at mine because you're about to pass out? To hell with the shower, baby, you need a lesson in *need*." His fingers tensed against my cheeks, thumbs edged toward my mouth. "Maybe punished, for such an asinine thought."

Punished? For wanting to clean? "But it will only take—"

"Shut up." To make sure I did, he thrust one thumb in my mouth.

Now this tasted slightly salty. Completely different than his cock but still...him. His flesh, his body. Pliable, supple. Inviting.

Inviting me to hollow my cheeks and suck it deep. Dance my tongue over the tip and close my eyes as I imagined doing this again to his thick shaft.

"Vixen," he swore.

When he started to pull it out, I used my teeth to keep him there. "Uh-uh," I mouthed around his thumb, just before I sucked on it as hard as I could. His eyes flared red hot, going from emeralds to rubies, promising retribution if I didn't stop right quick.

So I distracted him with one hand, sliding it down his chest to his stomach while I gentled the pressure concaving my cheeks, allowed my tongue to turn soft and persuasive, curving it around his thumb as I licked.

And caressed the hard plains of his stomach.

And reached behind me with my other arm, blindly searching for the cabinet where I housed the cleaners.

He caught sight of the action in the mirror. "Goddammit!"

Wrenching me away from temptation, he did something totally unexpected, thrusting three fingers inside my mouth, filling me, consuming me.

That need he wanted me to learn crashed through me like a tidal wave, obliterating old habits and stray thoughts. Grazing my teeth over the cock-sized intrusion, I turned to him, to his waistband specifically, and busied myself with getting the button open.

His jaw came down to my cheek when he leaned in. "Ah, much better." He eased his fingers from the depths of my mouth and once again possessed himself of my head. Tilting it to lick a line straight up my neck and totally interfering with my zipper-unzipping efforts, he coaxed, "There now. Isn't this"—another swipe of his tongue, a half inch over—"so much better than cleaning?"

"But you're a guest." I groaned as he started to suck on the sensitive skin of my neck. "You—"

"I'm a guy, not an effin' houseguest!" He sucked hard, punctuating his claim with a hickey mark I knew would be visible come morning. "A guy who's hard for you, hard and ready to fuck! Trust me, we don't notice if the place hasn't been cleaned for a month. Month*sss*." He made it clear the state of my home meant less than diddly squat. "Dammit, Carolina, as long as there's nothing growing in there, I'm good."

Dang it! Just when I'd decided to say *screw the scrub brush* without looking back, he had to go and say that? "Uh…" My gaze veered behind him. Toward the shower.

"Hell, woman. Mold doesn't take root in a week." He released me and hauled back the shower curtain, muttering as he did so, "Purple, by damn." Then he started to laugh, giant stomach-wrenching hoots that told me more than anything he was having a grand old time. At my expense.

Funny how I didn't mind, could actually feel myself relaxing as I stopped caring about the cleanliness of my shower in favor of caring about *who* had just stepped into it, clothes and all.

Still chuckling, he asked, "And who have we here?"

Jeff fingered the Davallia I'd hung up just yesterday, a wilted, crisp-looking specimen that a fellow real estate agent had found abandoned in a recently vacated property. He'd brought it to the office hollering *mayday*. In addition to standard-fare fern fronds, this guy had furry little offshoots poking out of the basket.

Wanting to join the man occupying my shower —hey, I might have some issues but I was no fool—I bent to scrape my sandal straps down and off. Having no patience for unbuckling, I willed my ankles to shrink and allow the coil of straps to slide over my heels. My left shoe cooperated, coming off without too much balking. The right? Stubborn as a hungry mule waiting for hotcakes.

"Carolina?" Jeff's voice was tempered now, soft as a kitten's purr. "Your tenant here?"

As determined as that mule, I stubbornly kept working the remaining strap but looked up to answer. "That's Carlton. A rabbit's foot fern I'm nursing. Hopefully back to health." I kept fighting with the strap. "He's a recent arrival and I thought the steam—" There! The sandal finally whisked away, I stood and climbed into the tub beside Jeff, turning the hanging basket to inspect Carlton from all angles. A crunching conflagration of yellowed, dried leaves wafting downward protested the movement. "I thought the steam might help revive him, that and the shade. But I don't know…" More leaves drifted forlornly past my face, landing on the porcelain floor of the tub, textured with old-fashioned stick-ons. "It might be too late."

The falling leaves had drawn Jeff's attention to our feet. "We're standing on frogs?"

"I thought they were cute, went good with the purple." Lime green frogs decorated the shiny surface, hopping about merrily in place. "And they make for good traction." I defended my frogs.

He dragged the toe of one shoe over one of the goofy-smiling critters. "Have you named them too?"

"No, just my plant buddies like Carlton here." I fingered one sad, not-quite-furry foot. "Herbert you met. And that was Rupert behind him. And Beauregard you almost creamed in the living room."

"Ah, so you live with a whole horde of men?"

Huh. I guess they were all manly names. "Looks that way." Giving Carlton one last pet, I started to exit the tub.

"Hold up." Jeff braced one hand at my waist and, in a blink, both of his leather slip-ons went sailing toward the hallway, his cell phone skidded onto the counter and he was leaning around me. "We'll just help the old fella out."

Before I knew his plan, he'd pulled up on the handle, sending a frigid spray of water gushing from the showerhead and straight onto my shoulders.

I shrieked.

"Oops." He laughed harder, straightening to grasp my shoulders and ease me around him, toward the back of the tub. "Oh shit! It's cold!"

"And drenching your clothes." Mine too, but I lived here.

"Sorry 'bout that. In my family, we always aim the showerhead into the wall when we're done. I didn't think it would get you. Come here." He pulled me to him, still protectively keeping the waterfall away. "Mmm. It's warming up."

He thrust one arm behind him to adjust the lever and, with his free hand, snugged me flush against his body. "Not bad, eh? Giving Carlton a little steam."

"In my family, we don't hop in fully clothed."

"Who says you're fully dressed?" Jeff's hands made quick work peeling my soggy dress up and over my head. "See? I remedied that. Now you're not dressed at all."

Once freed, my hands settled around his neck. I fingered the soaked plaid, made a mental note to toss the crazy man's clothes in the dryer. Then directed my glance downward, between us. My naked form standing just an inch or two from his. Blue denim quickly turning almost black from the water, his red shirt open, revealing a sexy slice of chest and stomach. Ah…his stomach. His waistband. Where a tempting piece of his anatomy was, just barely, making an appearance.

I didn't pre-think it, just lowered my arms until my hands hovered over the tip of his erection, peeking out from his jeans.

"You want it?" he encouraged, an extra husk in his whiskey-smooth voice. "Take it, baby. I'm all yours."

The second I fingered the smooth, smooth pyramid of flushed skin emerging past the denim prison, his breath hissed free and his head fell back under the spray. "God, yes," he said into the water, his hands pushing mine aside to undo his fly. He dipped his head forward to look at me while he worked the fastenings and shoved his sodden jeans and briefs past his hips. It took some effort, the fabric clinging persistently. After a near fall, he bit out a couple of swear words, cursing the jeans to some violent, unholy death. That was followed by "Sorry" and then more cussing.

Smiling at his jean-strangling antics, I stepped back, ducking to avoid Carlton's basket, to give Jeff more room.

"Now isn't this better than *cleaning*?" Given how he'd taken advantage of his bent position to swipe his tongue over one nipple, I'd have to answer *Yes*.

I steadied him, hands on his shoulders, as he fought to get his legs free. "Hey, can I help it if I was taught that cleaning took top priority?"

"There!" He slogged the dripping denim over the side and stood, wearing nothing but his open shirt, to grasp my hips and bring us into contact. "Ummm. Yeah"—he was breathing hard —"and I bet the walls always had to be white and plants were considered taboo."

Da-hamn. I didn't know whether to be impressed or insulted. "What? Is your mother a shrink?"

His chuckle vibrated through me. "A hair-dresser, but it amounts to the same thing." Drops flew when he tossed his head. "At least to her."

With every syllable, every motion he made, my water-slicked body felt the arousing slide of his. My hands scooted beneath his shirt, then down. The skin of his hips was like molten marble. "This feels decadent, rubbing up against you like this."

My face was level with his pectorals. Again, his leanly muscled mass reminded me of a California surfer and not an ice-skating hunk who regularly slammed into others. Digging my toes over a couple of frogs, I leaned up and nudged the red plaid aside to kiss the colorful bruise on his shoulder, just to the side of the stitches. I wanted to ask more about how he'd gotten it. About what Rurik had done that caused the accident. But my lips didn't want to move, not off his skin.

The stitches felt slightly bumpy, a little prickly where they were tied off on one side.

I had a man in my shower! Standing on top of my frogs! I was so delighted I could have hopped to the moon.

"You just wait. I know something that'll feel even better." Leaning back, taking his shoulder out of reach, he held out one hand, palm up. "Soap, please."

"It's behind you, hanging off the showerhead. It's a gel, an all-in-one soap and shampoo combo."

He worked the dispenser, gaining a dollop of foam. Then he went back for two more. "Peaches. Smells nice."

Overhead, he slapped his hands together, generating bubbles, loads of them. The next thing I knew, both of his hands were on my butt, sliding over my flesh and hauling me firmly into his.

Where his mouth took mine.

No further preliminaries, no more banter, he kissed me hard while his bubble-slick hands slowly roved everywhere—up my spine, over my shoulders, massaging the tight muscles of my neck...down my back, over my bottom...between my thighs...

During this wonderful, soapy seduction, his mouth enticed and enchanted mine all over again, lips and tongue feasting from me as though I were a banquet, feeding me as though I were starving.

"Time to rinse," he murmured against my mouth as droplets rained down, sliding past my lips to mix with our saliva.

He held tight to my hips, shuffling us around until the warm spray hit the back of my head, then my shoulders when he adjusted the angle, and coasted downward, taking soap and suds with it. Kissing me all the while, first my lips, then jaw, shoulders, and nape, he twirled—okay, gingerly spun—me in place, allowing the pummeling water to caress and cleanse everywhere he wasn't.

After a minute or so of shower-spray torture, I blinked open misty eyelids to see him nodding with satisfaction.

"Now you do me." He stepped back until he bumped into Carlton, then stretched out his arms.

"You're still dressed," I accused, getting my own squirt of soap, my breath coming faster now that I could see him. *All* of him.

When I hesitated, he brought my soapy hands to his chest and started moving them up and down. "Don't you see? I'm multitasking here. My shirt's getting washed the same time we are."

"Ah." I thumbed his nipples, then lifted my fingers to his neck, soaping both sides above his wilted collar. "You are so smart. How did you get to be so smart?"

"You're just now figuring that out?" he asked with a wink, but I could tell he was preening under the praise.

"Turkey."

He closed his eyes once I reached his face. "*Smart* turkey, don't forget," he mumbled, barely moving his lips as I approached his mouth.

"Smart *ass*."

"That too." His lips spread in a smile when I scrubbed my fingers over his chin. He dipped his head, giving me easy access.

I washed his squared-off jaw, paused a second, then skimmed over the sides of his neck, the tops of his ears...thinking again of the retro eyeglasses he wore with such flair, the look that just made him seem more approachable and, conversely, so far out of my league, it was a wonder we spoke the same language.

Shower now, dictionary later.

I went back for more soap, ready to concentrate my efforts lower.

My courage faded once I reached his groin. I skirted his cock, running my fingers around the base while avoiding the shaft. Spreading soap over the tops of his thighs and his abdomen, I watched his stomach suck in on an inward groan, feeling my own.

"No guilt, remember?" he coaxed when I stalled.

My eyelids fluttering against the mist, I looked up. "Not guilt," I confessed. "Nerves."

"You touched me earlier. Took me into your mouth." His thumb pressed into the grooves in front of my shoulders. He gave me a tiny shake. "Why nervous now?"

Yeah, but that had been with Rurik. Before I knew Jeff as a person. *Before you knew him at all.* "This feels more intimate."

I thought the noise of the rushing water washed my whisper down the drain. Until he whispered back, "It is."

Not waiting for me to grasp him—which I was just about to do. Really!—Jeff slid forward and meshed our fronts. He wiggled against me, spreading soap and silliness and a yearning so deep this was all I could ever fathom wanting.

Then he spun me around into the splash of water. "Playtime's over," he said at my ear, dragging his hands over my body and rinsing the residual suds. His fingers lingered at my core, delving past my inflamed opening to sweep inside. "Dadgum, darlin'"—he sucked on my earlobe —"you are wet in here, silky wet. And hot."

His teeth bit down and his fingernails scraped a path across my inner thighs, hurting good. He did it twice more, each time digging in a little deeper, going a little farther, until his hands ended up on either side of my ass. He gripped me, grabbed at the flesh and massaged it and another answering wave of arousal churned through me. "Go get on the bed." One last squeeze and his hands were gone. "I'll be right there."

With a whimper, I nodded, scooting the shower curtain aside with a shaking arm. Acutely noticing the lack of his touch, I wrung my hair, streaming water from the length, then I stepped onto the plush rug beside his discarded, soaked jeans and my dress.

Part of me wanted to grab a towel and dry off; the other part just wanted to please him, to jump in my bed and be there waiting. Despite the water droplets falling from the ends of my hair, it was that second part that prompted me to by-pass the towel rack.

At the door, I turned back. I couldn't help myself. But my reluctance to leave him, my eagerness to be touching him once more, was rewarded.

Jeff had left the shower curtain open and ducked under the spray. His eyes were closed, jaw clenched tight.

He'd braced his hands on the wall, on either side of the showerhead, and the muscles in his forearms stood out in stark relief. He inhaled and his shoulders lifted, his thighs flexed. But his cock hardly moved beyond the sopping edge of his shirt. His flesh stood straight out now. Heavy in readiness. Impatient.

My mouth watered and I instinctively took a step toward him.

His eyes blinked open. Water rebounding off his face, he turned his head and gave me a hard look. "The bed, Carolina. Now. Don't make me tell you again."

When had he turned all abrupt? Dominating and assertive? And why didn't I mind?

Beads of water chilled on my skin as I gazed at those cascading over his hard muscles. Several rolled languidly down my back. The spray from the showerhead pummeled his front. But the bite in the air was nothing compared to the heat he'd created in my center.

I froze in place, thinking of licking him. Of sliding once again against all that hot, slick skin and over those flexing, whipcord muscles.

"Carolina! Dammit, I told you to *move*."

Just when I was about to tease him about being so bossy, he started tearing at his shirt, clawing it off without any attempt at finesse. "Please." The single word was guttural and he jerked his eyes from mine, staring up at the ceiling. "I don't want to embarrass myself."

He turned the tap all the way to the right and dropped his shirt where he stood. To his whispered chorus of "Shit, fuck, *shit* it's cold," I scurried toward my bedroom not bothering with a towel.

All I wore was a giant smile.

JEFF JOINED me two minutes later. Erection still impressive, frown still in place.

So was my smile.

On my elbows, snug beneath mounds of covers, I remained happily horny and torridly wet, but at least the sheets and blankets had served to dry off my skin, if not my hair.

Once in the bedroom, I'd adjusted the dimmer, keeping it bright enough we could see but not so bright we'd be hollering for sunglasses. Watching him now, advancing like a predator coming in for the kill, I was glad I hadn't turned craven and turned the lights down more, as had been my first inclination. I could clearly see how tiny crystals dotted his skin, shimmered and blinked atop muscle and sinew as he prowled forward.

So he hadn't dried off either. Too impatient for me?

That was a nice thought.

I wondered what he might think of my bedroom. Discounting Mac (which realistically, one couldn't as Macmillion was the granddaddy of all plants, a gorgeous heartleaf philodendron who'd exploded beyond my wildest dreams) this room was different than the rest of my apartment, softer, more representative of the real me

—usually quiet and serene, not always purpled out.

"Pretty bed." Jeff nearly snarled the compliment as his gaze tracked the tentacles trailing down all four posts of my big bed, the pine green fronds cocooning me in my own little forest. "Not what I expected."

He finished on a growl but his words only widened my smile.

"I'm glad to hear you like it." A king-size wrought iron canopy in a beautiful sky blue, it was unlike anything I'd ever owned before. I'd treated myself after choosing happy solitude over crummy couplehood.

You're the first man to be in it.

I started to tell him but that little voice chided me not to. *Smacks of desperation, ducks.*

I agreed, so instead I asked, "Why didn't you jack off? I thought that's why you wanted me to leave, so you could—"

"Uh-uh." At the foot of my bed, he stretched out those muscles I had so recently admired and grabbed handfuls of my puffy, blue-and-white comforter and started pulling. "I'm not as young as I used to be," he explained with a scowl. "I already came once tonight and I wasn't going to risk it."

He kept tugging, ridding my big bed of first the comforter, then the blanket, and then the eyelet-trimmed top sheet. Pillows toppled but stayed, more or less, near my headboard.

"AARP, here you come," I quipped, feeling oddly vulnerable and alone, more so with every layer he discarded until I reclined on top of a nearly stripped mattress, with nothing but a few pillows for company. That and the fire in his eyes.

Evidently the bed was how he wanted it, because Jeff joined me, climbing right up between my legs, forcing me to my back. Amazing how quickly I wasn't lonely anymore.

He kissed my jaw. "You makin' fun of my age? Saying the retirement home is just around the corner?"

I thrilled at the heavy pressure of his weight on me, his body pushing mine into the mattress.

My arms slid around his back. "Hey, bud, you started it."

"And it's time I finished." His jaw nuzzled mine but before my lips could meet the invitation, he started skating back down. "Want me to lick you again?"

Again? Was he for real? I thought guys only did that when they *had* to. You know, the carrot before the cart. Actual sex being the cart.

In answer, I made a noncommittal moan. Just a soft one.

Pausing to lick a circle around my breast, he snaked one hand between us.

"God, you're wet. You ready to do a little screaming?"

I was tempted. Sorely tempted. I didn't believe Jeff would call me names or accuse me of being a mood killer. But even if I *could* let go around him, what might the neighbors think if they heard me? Would they know what I was—

"Yes!" His fingers wrung the cry from me when they danced over my hooded clit.

"You sure?" Rising up on one arm, he angled halfway off me and looked down, bending my free leg at the knee and placing my foot on the bed. Opening me up. Way up.

His moistened fingers scratched a teasing trail through my freshly washed curls. "'Cause I plan on making you holler real loud. That's how I know you like it." He spread my folds open, one at a time, arranging the plumped lips on either side so he could swipe several fingers down my cleft.

Oh, I'm liking it.

But would he? If I truly let go? "Really? You like it when a girl—"

"*You.*"

"When I...yell?"

"Hell yeah. That's how I know you've lost control." He circled his fingers over and around, toying with my entrance, spreading my cream. "Then I can lose mine."

But I'd been taught to keep my lusty screams to myself. A total turnoff, or so I'd been told. *You sound like a pig on a spit*, my second lover had claimed, the swine. But with Jeff's encouragement, no longer was I starting to *think* maybe I'd been duped, I was beginning to *know* it. I'd fallen victim to the complaints of a jackass—or someone with overly sensitive ears. And underly developed sexual prowess.

Or maybe someone who didn't know the meaning of control. And *how to lose it.*

For once, my inner voice sounded rather mature. "Okay. I might."

He swept his fingertips over the perimeter, causing my breath to hitch, my pelvis to tilt. "Might what?"

"Scream." Maybe. If I could forget about the neighbors.

"You will."

He separated one finger from the pack, deliberately drawing that single digit over my swollen flesh, sliding up and down my opening in a languid journey, coming closer and closer to where I needed him most. After a shallow nudge, then retreat, he returned full force to glide it deep. My inner muscles clamped down on the welcome intrusion.

"Oh yeah," he complimented, twisting his hand and brushing his thumb over my clit. "What do you want? Another finger? My tongue or my dick?"

"Yes."

Smiling like a fiend, he scooted downward, his tongue taking over for his thumb while he pushed a second finger in, squeezing it alongside the first. He sawed them in and out of me.

My body ate at him, clit rejoiced at the feel of his lips and tongue, thighs opened wider and hips lifted higher. Then promptly crashed back to the bed. Over and over, my lower body surged and grasped at his, melted and flooded around his fingers, under his mouth, as his duel attentions brought another pending release ever closer.

When he raked one hand up my chest and fondled the tight knots of my nipples with all the attention any woman could ask for, I nearly came apart.

Instead, I scrambled backward. "Stop. Stop." My breath rasped as I ordered my body to hit the pause button. "Cock and mouth. Ready now."

Easing his fingers out and wiping them on the inside of my thighs, Jeff gave his tongue a final little twirl around my clit and firmed the gentle touch on one breast, giving it a pinch. Humming an appreciative sound the entire way, he started sliding back up, his body giving mine one huge, core-shattering caress. "My cock? My mouth? Since you asked so sweetly and they can't both go in the same place at the same time, I'm thinking you want another kiss." His torso undulated against my stomach, rubbing the already fluttery-feeling area and causing another kind of acute agony. Everything he did made me burn for him, fired the flame hotter. "Lucky for us both, what you want is what I need. Come here, Care."

My leg flopped inward, landing against his hip as he slid by my breast, tongue out for a fast nipple swipe, then his glorious lips were on mine, his mouth kissing me with more hunger than he'd shown yet. Voracious, violent almost. Sweet as all get-out.

Just to be wanted so fiercely, it was heady. Flattering. And it made me crave him more. My nails flexed on his biceps as they came up to support his weight near my head. And still the dynamite, can't-get-enough-of-you kisses continued. So much for the soft, flirty ones he'd given me before, these kisses dominated. Took without asking. Drugged me like an addiction. "Mmm."

"Umm," he responded, never breaking stride.

Our tongues dove and rolled against each other, hands held on tight and bodies surged, automatically aiming for the fit that would feel so right. Would satisfy the ache and douse the blaze.

The long column of his erection brushed my thigh, his hips arched and it landed on top of my abdomen. Granting my tongue a sensuous bit of sucking action, Jeff pulled back. "Where do you keep the condoms?"

Huh?

My head slanted upward, finding his mouth open and ready. His kiss transported me away from my bright and feminine bedroom, back to the hotel where we'd met, when I'd first realized *need* had a name.

Carolina.

I no longer had to be afraid of fucking up a good fuck. Didn't have to always wonder or worry or question what a sex partner might think of me: Was I too loud? Too demanding? Too flat-chested?

Because Jeff had shown I wasn't. Not for him.

Which meant there were likely others who shared his tastes. And thanks to that bit of confidence-inspiring wisdom, I realized I no longer had to obsess over what I might think of myself: Did I listen to my little voice too much? Was I afraid to take chances? To risk? To—

He pulled back from the kiss. "Carolina!" For once, his voice shredded my name like a blade. "Condoms. Where are they?"

I whimpered, my lower body seeking his, needing that satisfaction he promised. The end to the ache he'd created, roused into a beast with nothing more than a flick of his tongue, a quirk of his lip.

"Hmm? Condoms?" My breath hissed inward. *Condoms?* "Don't you have one?"

"Fuck." A shudder went through him. Then another.

He rolled to his back, taking me with him. Grabbing hold beneath my armpits, he hauled me higher until our eyes met. "Are you saying you don't have any?"

My hands flailed, then gripped his head, fingers tunneling through the sun-streaked strands. "*Are you saying you didn't bring one?*"

SIX

When He Notices She Says A Cock, Not HIS Cock

JEFF'S LOOK OF WOE, of regret, of I'm-pissed-at-*myself* told the tale. "Shit! I don't believe this."

I pinched the short hair at his nape and twisted. "And here I thought you were smart! Don't you keep any in your wallet?"

"Yeah. The ones we used back at the hotel. Dammit!" Then he started to laugh, holding me to his chest, his arms twin vises when I would have lunged downward and impaled myself anyway.

No you wouldn't. You're not that *stupid.*

But my level of smartness—or stupidness—didn't have to come into play because Jeff was there. Taking responsibility, taking care of me.

And still laughing like a horn-crazed hyena. "Of course you don't have any. You don't do this kind of thing!" he howled. His arms moved lower, hugged me tighter. "And I didn't think to bring any because I *stopped* doing this sort of thing. I swear." His vibrant laughter jolted his torso against mine. "I only had those two because Coach hands them out at the start of every season. At the start of every game in fact, but I never used these so here they are. Or there they *were*." Which seemed to tickle his funny bone more than anything that came before.

Just hump his leg, you need to get off!

What the naughty, nasty little voice suggested was tempting. Tempting but too crude. *What happened to mature?* I inquired. *Put a sock in it!*

Put a cock in it!

Desire clawed through me like a heat wave, every particle of my being on fire for his, burning hotter now. Now that I knew I couldn't have him.

I slugged one shoulder. "And you—you just had to hop in the shower. With your clothes all wet, you can't even go get any!"

Which only made him laugh harder.

"Damn. Damn. Double-dick damn!" He took a deep breath and his hands lowered and molded to my butt cheeks. "Okay." Another long inhalation shuddered through him. "Okay. Sixty-nine?"

I might not have done it before but I knew what it was. "Works for me."

Me too!

Not needing any further encouragement, I scrambled around, rotating over his body until I was hugging his legs, my face on level with his shins. Sexy shins. With just a light covering of hair.

"You're way too far," he grumbled, tugging on my hips and helping me crawl backward until his cock bumped into my chin.

I was acutely aware I had my crotch *in his face*. The gloves were off—I almost giggled, realizing we both wished one was on him—but metaphorically speaking, the heart of me was now exposed in a way it had never been before and the somersaults in my stomach told me I wasn't exactly nonchalant about the matter.

Yeah, he and Rurik had both licked my passion-drenched privates earlier but I'd been on the bottom; they'd been in control of angle and pressure. Now I was on top and it made me vulnerable in a wholly different way.

I tried not to think about how my thighs were splayed wide on either side of his head or how he could no doubt see my most intimate muscles contracting with nerves and excitement. See the unmistakable evidence of how much I wanted this, wanted him. Tried but failed. It was all I could think about. Well, that and the impressive erection just waiting for *my* attention.

I stuck my tongue out, eager to fulfill my half of our mathematical equation, and tried to lick his cock but it bobbed away. I chased after it, but when I felt Jeff opening me, his fingers pulling apart my labia to make way for his mouth… When I felt that first, sure glide of his wet tongue on my already wetter anatomy, I just about lost it.

My hips jerked, smashing my flesh to his face. Embarrassed, I tried to climb away, but he only dragged me closer and did some twirly thing with his tongue I thought would set me on fire.

"Oh God," I eked out. *Oh God, oh God!*

He firmed it and dove his tongue inside my passage, then retreated to fly it over my clit. His head tilted between my straining legs as he brought that gorgeous, squared-off chin into play. His hands roved up and around my thighs and each gripped an ass cheek, pulling them apart while pulling me closer, ever closer.

"I... God..."

I sought out his cock again, needing it in me. My pelvis flailed within his grasp, against his face, and I thought again of the neighbors. The young couple seemed so dang chipper, so happy every time we crossed paths. Did they do this? Have sex like this? Did normal couples go down on each other in such an earthy, raunchy way and then still behave so properly afterward?

Could they be on the other side of the wall, even now, climbing over each other's naked bodies, licking, touching, *tasting...*

One of my arms gave out as a spike of lust tore through my lower half. I tumbled forward into his legs and held on for dear life, trying to scoot over and secure his shaft in my hand.

Did other couples experience this reckless, restless craving for debauchery and decadence?

"Come on, Care"—he eased my loins forward, breathing hotly over my core—"let me hear you, baby. Tell me what you like."

Then his mouth was back, fused to my pussy, dancing over my flesh like a maestro. A genius.

Like a real smart guy—who'd forgotten condoms.

I snickered.

He heard me and slapped one side of my ass.

"Uhm." A protest? Appreciation? I wasn't sure what I uttered, but I wanted him to do it again. Do everything again. Maybe never stop.

"Louder, Carolina." He spoke against my cleft, his words bringing a maelstrom of quivers strumming forth. "I can't hear you."

My left arm was trapped between us. Who cared? I only needed one. I dragged my right hand to his groin and grasped his thick shaft.

He slapped me again, the other side this time.

Smiling at the slight sting, I brought him to my lips and tried to kiss but got distracted when he licked faster, harder, when he slid his fingers inward and nudged my anus, rimmed it, teased it... Just as Rurik had earlier. *Holy hotness, Batman, I slept with two men tonight!*

And one of them was in *my* bed!

It was that thought, combined with the tongue in my twat, that sent me hurtling straight into orgasmic bliss.

Teeth tightly compressed, I held his shaft to my mouth but didn't do more than let my convulsing lower limbs vibrate it there as "mmnnn" emerged from behind my closed lips and stars exploded beneath his tongue and in front of my eyes.

The twitchy, tingly, overwhelming buzz of release pounded from my clit outward, encompassed my entire abdomen, racing to my anus, blasting tendrils of satisfied desire everywhere. Absolutely everywhere.

I was practically humping the poor guy's face, over and around and up and down, up and up and *up,* then *d-o-w-n,* grinding my core on any body part he had available—and the riotous sensations just kept coming. So did I, when he slid one arm along my crack and must have done some contortionist thing with his wrist so he could push his thumb into my depths.

At the thick sensation sliding through my swollen tissues, I gasped and grasped, hugging the intrusion when another orgasmic wave trembled through me.

His words of praise, his soft petting of my hiked-in-the-air butt helped gentle me back to earth.

As the firestorm eased, I no longer feared smothering him. Or biting that which is *not* meant for teeth. His cock, patiently contained within the circle of my fist, hovered against my lips where I'd locked it, but now my mouth opened and I snaked my tongue out, ready to lick him, eager for another taste.

"Forget it." Jeff groaned the words the second I curved my tongue around his crown. His body jackknifed beneath mine and he was on his knees, staring at me and breathing hard.

Forget it? Forget giving me another taste? Forget the whole *I need to fuck you, but you don't have condoms so let's sixty-nine* thing? Forget what? Tonight? It was fun but now I'm gone? Or… forget licking me again because you suck at it?

"Forget *it*?" I tried not to sound disappointed. I tried not to sound hurt. I tried not to whine. *"Forget what?"*

"I've changed my mind. If I get in your mouth, I'm gonna blow deep and blow hard and you aren't ready for that."

I'm not? "Why not?"

"Trust me. Last thing I need is your drowning on my conscience."

"Then what—"

Before I could finish, he flipped me over, facing the mattress, and crawled on top, lowering his torso directly over my spine with an appreciative *mmm.* "This is what." His voice had a hard edge that thrilled me. "I'm gonna come..." He worked his fingers between me and the mattress, criss-crossing his arms over my chest and anchoring each palm atop a breast, fingers stretched wide, gripping as much of my flesh as he could. "Holding you...like this."

His legs wedged themselves on the inside of mine, opening me up. His cock, his hard, hot cock, pushed down, making a place for itself at the very top of my butt and onto the small of my back.

I felt surrounded. Consumed by his heat and hunger.

"You okay?" After he asked, he scraped his top teeth over the side of my neck.

With his entire weight supported by my body, I could hardly breathe. *That's okay—he's worth it! This is so very worth it!* For once my conscience and I were in accord. "Better than." I grunted the whisper.

He moved against me and the solid column of his erection pressed deeper, spreading the cheeks of my ass to make way for its length. The angle of his pelvis ground my clit into the mattress. A tiny flare of that just-satisfied need awoke in me.

His hands tensed over my chest. Fingers flexed and fondled. "I won't take long."

"Take all..." *Breathe*, dang it. "The time...you need."

He rocked his hips slowly, sliding against me once, twice, another two times and then he groaned and froze. Was that it? I'm not sure exactly what I waited for, but somehow I expected more. My teeth clamped over my bottom lip, stilling my instinctive protest.

Since he'd rolled me over and climbed aboard, he'd been controlled, methodical. And I didn't feel the warm ooze of his semen either.

I made some sort of questioning hum in my throat. When all he did was hug me tighter, my teeth released its prisoner so I could ask, "Jeff?" *Are you finished?*

He licked up the side of my neck where he'd lightly grazed his teeth. "Just hitting the pause button. Making it last."

"What happened to drowning me?" From the way he'd acted, I'd thought an erectile explosion had been imminent.

"This isn't your mouth."

"So? What difference does that make?"

He twisted his hips, making me very aware of our intimate connection. Our loins might not be melded together in the truest sense but their proximity was pretty darn close. The action also served to remind me that *I had a naked man on top of me!* How cool was that?

"You're so damn innocent."

I couldn't tell if that was a compliment or a criticism. "So?"

He slid his hands an inch or two lower and rubbed his thumbs over the hard knots of my nipples. "The difference is that one takes me to the moon, the other just feels real good."

"*Good?*" I managed to imbue a wealth of disgust in that single syllable.

"Great, darlin'. Fuck-*in'* great."

Though that was a balm to my ears, I still couldn't help but wonder. I mean, he'd withdrawn after barely giving me a split second to taste. And here I'd been looking forward to improving upon my previous performance. After all, I had at least two hours' maturity since the last time I'd given him a blow job. Although he hadn't blown that time either, I recalled with a frown, staring down at the mattress. "Are you sure it's not because you hated how I did it at the hotel and—"

"God, perish the thought." Before I could doubt further, he thumbed my nipple again and chided, "You came apart under my mouth but you didn't scream for me, sweet Care."

"You didn't come in mine." Wow. Weird. I sounded grumpy about it.

He laughed and his chest quaked against my back, sending quivers straight through me. Sending that tiny flare of need a notch higher. He nuzzled my neck just beneath my ear and I turned my head to accommodate him. "Sounds like that's something we need to remedy."

What? My screaming or his coming in my mouth?

"Another time." I thought that's what he murmured. I wasn't sure because he started kissing me like a man gone mad, whirling his tongue over my neck and it drove me bonkers. "Right now, be still. I need to concentrate." When he spoke, I felt his words more than heard them, the timbre of his voice vibrating through me from his chest to my crotch.

Be still? Was he nuts? When I kept thinking of where his mouth had been moments ago? My pelvis flexed, ready for more of that direct stimulation.

As though responding to my restless need, his teasing tongue forays changed to more of a lip-involved neck seduction. The side of my head not receiving his attention melted into the mattress as I arched into his kiss.

My hands were clenched into painful fists. I'd tried to grip the sheet but being freshly made, just that morning, there was nothing to give. Nothing to grab. So while Jeff made love to my neck, I ordered my fingers to stop strangling each other and bent my left arm back to touch his head, rubbing my nails through his hair, over his scalp. My right arm I snuck downward. After a harsh exhale, he started rocking his hips again, sending his shaft over my flesh in longer, even more controlled thrusts if that were possible. "You smell nice."

He nearly grunted the words.

Considering we both smelled the same, I was able to kick it back. "You too. Good, ah—" Timing my advance with his pumping motions, I slipped my right hand under my body, palm up, and crept several fingertips over my hooded clit. "Ode to peach cobbler."

He chuckled but didn't break rhythm. "Your skin feels so smooth." His warm hands massaged in place, rousing my nipples to tighter peaks. "And pointy."

Every time he lunged against me, I was forced deeper into my fingers. My eyelids fluttered, then slammed shut and I started imagining he was in me again, forging his cock through my passage, all of him invading me, his mouth possessing mine.

I licked my lips, swirled my tongue over their perimeter, thirsting...

And then I pressed my face into the sheet to muffle my squeal because I was on the verge of coming again. On the verge, but something was missing, something—

"Care...o...lina?" He paused mid-thrust. "You—"

"Don't stop." I sounded haggard. But he was too heavy. I couldn't buck him off, couldn't ease the ache without his help. "Keep going, *please*."

He did. And I did, heading closer and closer to another orgasm. Closer to identifying what it was I missed. What I craved.

"Carolina?" He still sounded concerned, guarded almost.

My mouth worked against the mattress but nothing came out. I tried to move my hand, to get more direct stimulation, more pressure on my clit, but he pinned me in place, his groin keeping mine stationary now that he'd stopped again.

"Jeff—move!" Renewed desire turned me cranky.

"Care. What is it?"

You know what you want! You can almost taste it. My conscience was right. It was there—on the tip of my tongue. My lonely, abandoned, yearning tongue. "Jeff. I..."

Fuck it, tell him already!

With such lovely, supportive encouragement, how could I do anything else? "I—I want a cock in my mouth."

"Now? While I'm on you?"

A short nod was all I could manage.

He immediately loosened his arms and dragged one free. His hand came up to my face. He opened my lips and pushed his middle finger in along with the command to "Suck!"

Whether it was the way he said it or the way he filled me, having part of him inside, and tasting of what I craved, set me off.

Blind, intense need driving me, I pulled him in and sucked hard. My abdomen spasmed over my fingers, my clit and mouth working together to spark off another orgasm that had me bucking beneath him and squealing in earnest.

Like a match to a powder keg, that triggered an end to his control. He jammed his finger deep and rammed his cock along my back. A hoarse shout marked the moment he spilled his seed harmlessly on my spine.

My ears rang with the sound. My heart tripped over itself. My vagina clamped inward over nothing as wave after wave of satisfaction powered through me. But my mouth was full and I heard a tiny but audible *pop* when I finally released the suction and my jaw relaxed.

Our joint breathing was harsh. Neither of us seemed inclined to move.

Jeff was the first to remember how, slowly pulling his finger past my lips and drying it on my hair as he tucked it out of the way so he could kiss my cheek.

From far, far away, I heard him say something out of a dream.

"Do you want…" His arm constricted beneath my chest. "Do you want me to bring Rurik with me next time?"

With me next time! The refrain sounded sweeter than any Hallelujah Chorus.

I had to lick my lips three times before I could speak. "Will he mind, do you think?"

"Hell no. He'll be thrilled."

Will you mind? I wanted to ask, *if he joins us?* But I didn't voice the question.

Because what if he didn't?

SEVEN

When His Actions Prove He's Still Thinking of Her

A STRANGE SORT of groggy awareness came over me. I was sleeping but barely; I was awake but not quite. I drifted and dozed and had never felt more content in my life.

A warm leg brushing against mine brought me from the fringes in one second flat. I was wide awake now. But I didn't move, choosing instead to remain motionless and savor the wealth of sensations and memories that poured through me.

When the leg nudged mine again, this time accompanied by a soft groan whispering past my temple, I languidly turned toward its source. My eyelids fluttered open.

Looking as replete as I felt, Jeff's green gaze warmed when he smiled. "Hi there."

I liked the sight of him sharing my pillow. "Hi yourself."

"Looks like we dozed for a bit."

"Mmm. And forgot to turn off the light." It was still dark outside. I didn't think I'd slept deeply, figured maybe we'd been out for an hour or less.

What a night. Satisfaction oozed through me. What an amazing, miraculous night. Even once my pretty magic bra bit the dust.

Thinking a quick trip to the bathroom was in order, I rolled toward the edge. But I didn't get far. The clock read 5:33 a.m. "Jeff!" My throat closed up on itself. "Di-didn't you say your plane leaves in the morning?"

"Yeah," he yawned the word, coming up on his elbows. "At seven. Why—" He caught sight of the clock. "Oh, hell no!"

He blasted out of bed like a rocket. "My clothes!" He spun in place. "Shit! Where are my clothes?"

Shit was right. "They're in the shower! Ah, dang it, I'm sorry! I didn't mean to fall asleep. I—"

"Hey, don't blame yourself." He looked incredibly ticked. Horribly mad. At me or himself, I wasn't sure. But when he spoke, it was almost gentle. "It takes two to tango and all that. I slept too."

Dadgum! This was all my fault, us falling asleep, his obvious panic—at being caught with his pants down. Which somehow struck me as funny and I started to laugh, bending to tug the discarded sheet around me like a toga as I tried to sober up and think straight.

He'd already retreated into the bathroom to fight with his wet jeans and shirt, if his battle cries were anything to go by. The image of him taking them off still made me smile but my laughter dried up. I'd totally forgotten to put them in the dryer. Not to mention that he could get into real trouble if he missed his flight and that wasn't funny, not in the least.

I heard him talking. "What's that?" I called, rushing toward the bathroom only to find him on his cell phone. I started to back away but he waved me in.

His jeans were in place, unfastened, and he was struggling to button his shirt one-handed while searching the bank of drawers for something.

"What do you need?" I whispered.

He looked exhausted but sexy as all get-out. Day-old whiskers shaded his jaw. My inner thighs did this pseudo-tingly thing, as if they were imagining him between them and I stomped my feet in protest. None of that now! Hadn't I had enough?

You'll never get enough. He's spoiled you.

"Hold up," he told the person on the other end. "And quit griping at me. I know I screwed up." To me, he said swiftly, "A pen. For the flight info."

"He should text it," I suggested. Less to keep up with that way.

"Battery's on fumes. Forgot to charge it."

"Gotcha." While I ran for a notepad, I overheard him arranging for Rurik to pack his stuff and see that it got checked in.

"Have him bring you a change of clothes," I whispered, coming back to hand him a sticky pad and pen.

Jeff nodded and I left to find a robe.

Holy sleepovers, Batman.

Traveling with the team or not, wasn't he supposed to check in ninety minutes *before* his flight?

Kaboom, a jagged thunderbolt crashed down on my head, raining loads of guilt over me. What if he did miss his flight? Got penalized by the team or something?

Shoving down that unpalatable thought, I raced into the kitchen, whirling from the sink to the pantry to the fridge. What did you feed a guy after hours and hours of sex? Or non-intercourse sex play? Something that you could fix in two minutes and he could eat on the run?

As fast as I could, I pulled out stuff he could take with him, arranged it on the counter and hoped for the best.

The best being that he wouldn't hate me.

Wouldn't lose his job.

Might—if I was really lucky—think fondly of me, his purple-wearing, one-night-stand gal in Cincinnati.

The toilet flushed and I heard him cussing at his jeans and apologize to Beauregard when he passed him in the hall. I almost smiled at that. But I couldn't. I felt more wretched by the moment.

Here it was, all the awkwardness and unease I'd expected. The Morning-After Awfuls, compounded by the number of orgasms I'd been served.

As though the universe was paying me back for being amazingly generous last night, this morning sucked.

And it was all my fault.

He came walking in as though he had a scorpion tucked away in his jeans and one wrong move would spell disaster.

"Those wet jeans have got to feel terrible." *And isn't that nice of you to rub it in?* Ugh!

"They do. And I hope you don't mind—I left my briefs in the bathtub." When he gestured, I saw he'd retrieved his glasses from Herbert's basket. "Too damp to hassle with."

"No problem. I'll have them bronzed, put them on the mantle."

He gave a bark of laughter. "I like your wit."

I like your cock. Heck, so far I liked everything about him. "I like you—ah, yours too."

The lack of time seemed to press in on us both. Twice he started to say something, then stopped.

Knowing that leaving was his top priority, I pointed toward the counter but he noticed the fridge instead. "Whoa." His eyes went wide. "I'm being stared at by a zoo. A whiskered, pointy-eared zoo."

Water! I'd forgotten to get him something to drink. As I hauled booty to the pantry, he crossed over to my refrigerator, inspecting the multitude of adoption certificates papering the doors.

"Just my wildcats," I said over my shoulder while reaching for a bottle of water and another of apple juice. "I give to a sanctuary in the Northeast, sponsor their beautiful rescues and—

"Oh!" When I turned with juice and water in hand, I came into contact with his chest. He'd come up silently behind me and was *close*. His shirt fairly radiated soggy humidity. "I..." My gaze flicked to his and I saw he'd put on his black-frame Wayfarers. They didn't do anything to shield the emerald glint flaring behind the glass.

Owlishly, I blinked up at him. *You are so darn fine.*

And he's standing in your kitchen—commando!

"I'll take these." He whisked the bottles from my grasp and secured them in one hand. He wound his free hand behind my neck and tilted my head with his secure grip. "It was a wonderful night. Thank you." Half his mouth quirked upward. "I'd hug you but I don't want to get you wet."

Oh baby, get me wet!

He angled my head a bit more and leaned down for a hungry, swift salute of his lips on mine. No tongue action, just a thorough swamping of my senses, a crumbling of my defenses, as his mouth practically wooed me into a simpering puddle. My pulse kicked into high gear and my arms zoomed around his waist, his damp shirt be damned.

I rose to my toes and kissed him harder. His fingers tensed on my nape and I knew he was about to end it, so I did it first.

Dropping to my heels, retracting my arms, trying not to lick my lips or drool like a dog, I bounded away, pasting a giant, bright, *fake* smile on my face. "Thanks yourself. What a way to wake up." *And say goodbye.*

He looked rueful, his attention darting between me and the food on the counter. "For me?"

"Take whatever you want. And here…" I handed him scribbled directions to the airport I'd dashed off. "It's messy, but will get you there if your phone conks out." I glanced at the clock on the stove. "You've really got to go. It'll ruin everything if you miss your flight and get in trouble. Thank you for a great time. Really. You and Rurik both. I… It was—I…"

I was a babbling idiot but he didn't seem to mind. Or be paying attention to my rambling nonsense.

"Hey now." He shrugged one shoulder and I saw how his shirt had stuck clammily to his form, thanks to my ill-timed hug. "It's all good."

He grabbed up two protein bars and three containers of applesauce. Unzipping the plastic bag I'd laid out, he flashed me a grin that quickly turned to a grimace when he dropped two tubs of applesauce in his haste.

"I'll get it later," I assured him when one of them rolled under the table. We were both talking and moving at fast speed, adrenaline supercharging the exchange. "Here, take another. Oh man, I'm so sorry—"

"Carolina." He went for a box of raisins instead. "Stop worrying. If the stars are aligned in my favor, I can make it to the gate before the plane takes off and they'll let me board."

"I hope that's the case. If not—if not—"

"Then I'll just catch a different plane and catch hell from the coach." Finished with bagging the snacks and a plastic spoon I shoved his way, he slapped the sticky with his flight number on the outside, then held out the pad and pen. "Here. Write down your phone number for me."

As though the yellow pad was a viper, I backed up a step, yanking my hands aloft. "Why? We both know you won't call." If I give you my number, I'll only get my hopes up. And for what? Another mind-blowing orgasm?

Are you crazy? That's worth getting your hopes up over!

"We play here again next month. I'll call."

No you won't. "What do you need my number for? You know where I live."

YOU WON'T CALL. Stated with such conviction Jeff knew she was right. What moronic minion in his mind had made him ask?

"Shit!" Preoccupied with the woman sending him on his merry way from her second-story, plant-shrouded balcony, Jeff nearly slammed his left foot with the vehicle door. He gritted his teeth against another oath and returned her jaunty wave with an abrupt nod.

She was that eager to see him off? He tore his gaze from his sudden unhealthy obsession and fired up the engine.

"Talk about unexpected distractions." He skewered his penis with a glare that withered. "Letting you do all the thinking? I ought to be shot."

Nah. No need to waste the bullet. Coach was gonna be beyond pissed. Would take care of it for him. Hanging at High Noon, he could see the headline now.

Cringing inside, Jeff fished his phone from a dank pocket. His uncle would be thrilled to learn management had to send a couple employees all the way out to the airport to retrieve his vehicle.

You won't call.

Of course he wouldn't.

Two fucks and a shower—one that still made him suffer—weren't worth the aggravation.

"Shit." *One* fuck, that's what it'd been. The first one, last night—*with Rurik*. That and an enthusiastic but ill-performed blow job, and one aborted fuck. Not a single condom in her apartment? What century was she living in? Miss Carolina—Jeff noted the name of the apartments as he paused before exiting onto the street—of Heartridge Oaks?

His fingers tightened against the wheel. He'd never make it. But, God, she had cute toes. And that nail polish? The prettiest, richest shade of shimmering purple—

"Ah, hell." Punching the gas when somebody behind him honked, Jeff scrubbed one weary hand over his face and pulled out of the complex. "If I wanted to obsess over feet, I'd do better to think about the big, booted one I'll be getting up the ass if I miss this plane."

BRIGHT AND EARLY MONDAY MORNING, Kathi was at my desk, tapping out an impatient *t-t-t-t-t-t* with her tongue stud against her top teeth. "That's *it*?" Her voice rose to glass-shattering heights. "*All* you're going to share?"

I guiltily looked through the glass wall separating my office from the common area. As though I knew a neon sign flashed over my head, loudly proclaiming *I just had my first one-night stand. With TWO men!!!*, I'd practically slunk in at the crack of dawn, hunkered down behind contrived mounds of paperwork, and hid out. Both despairing and conversely looking forward to the moment when I would no longer be the only one in the office and prey to my whirling thoughts.

As I'd expected, my crazy girlfriend had been the first through the doors. Fortunately for me, given the topic and her record-breaking, mega-decibel screech, we were still the only ones here.

"Honestly, that's really about it. We all had sex and then…" I kind of glossed over how the night ended. "I went home."

"But still! You got it on with *two!*" Her eyeballs did cartwheels at the prospect. "I am so proud," she gushed, starting to pace in front of my desk, her indigo hair extra bright, extra rich. But still the same shade it'd been last week. Hmm. Something was up. Kathi changed her hair color as often as I did my sheets. "I mean, I thought you might, *might* get some *cojones*, man up and go out. Get in a good grope or two, maybe… maybe…go home with a hung hunk. But two? Girl, you take the cake!"

Heck, it wasn't as though I'd done something really impressive. I hadn't run a marathon or jumped out of a plane. I hadn't passed the bar or won an Oscar.

I'd screwed a couple of guys. Big whoop.

Gorgeous guys, my conscience reminded me, *ones you hadn't known from Adam.*

True.

A little of Kathi's obvious pride in my accomplishment transferred itself, and I felt it bubbling up within me—giddiness over what I'd done. "Beefcake," I concurred, grinning inside. "Beefcakes, plural, don't forget. Two of them."

While making that important proclamation, I stood. It was dang difficult to be taken seriously behind a mountain of manila folders—and the wall of guilt surrounding me.

A strange sort of perplexing guilt. Because some time between saying goodbye in the wee hours of Saturday morning and waking up in the dead of night today, too restless to sleep, too energized to try, I'd *stopped* feeling guilty and started feeling awed—of myself, for having the courage to do something so intimidating and foreign, so ballsy and brave.

And that's what the guilt was about. How could I be proud of myself for no-strings sex? For indulging my inner vixen, solely because it felt good?

Was it just because of Kathi's influence? Had our at-work friendship evolved into something more? That's when I realized I hadn't called a single other girlfriend over the weekend, had kept the juicy details all to myself, savoring the encounter while envisioning Kathi's reaction. I knew then she'd become a lot more than just my daily chat buddy.

I not only admired her bold approach to life and love, I depended on her. Because for all of her over-the-top antics and attention-getting ways, Kathi was as efficient as they came. Top-notch at keeping the office organized and running, and fabulous on the phone. It was only in person she gave clients pause and by then, they already adored her.

We all did, except…

"Fun time's over." I nodded toward the entrance where two other agents had just arrived, one of them aiming a malevolent glare our direction. "I don't ruffle his normally sedate feathers, so why are Trevor's eyes hurtling poison-tipped daggers at you?"

Without glancing his direction, Kathi stiffened. "That prig? No idea. But back to you—" Her sincere smile beamed like a spotlight. "Beefcake, pound cake, sock-it-to-me cake, *whatever*." She raced around the desk to give me a gleeful hug. "Cupcake, I'm so happy for you!"

"Golly gee whillakers," I said when she released me, afraid I might be blushing. "If I'd known how much it would mean to you, I would have gotten laid sooner."

"Don't ridicule. Good sex is…well, better than good. It's great for everything that ails you." She eyed me speculatively. *Tap. Tap.* "You turned a corner this weekend."

"If you say so." Thinking the conversation was over, I retreated to my chair, automatically smoothing my navy skirt down the sides of my legs. So much longer than the micromini I'd worn Friday night, I needn't have bothered.

As it should be at work, everything about me was buttoned up tight. Except my mind. It continued a free-for-all, reliving every kiss, every caress, every hard thrust.

To stop the moan that was working its way up from my panty region, I assumed Professional Mode. "Now then, seeing as how I emptied the bottom two drawers of my filing cabinet and given how I have clients coming in after lunch, I probably should do something with this mess."

Audience or not, Kathi wasn't finished. "Later." She shoved aside one pile, narrowly avoiding sending another flying off the desk, and perched on one corner. "Okay. So, to review, Friday was great." Her voice lowered—something to be thankful for. Especially given what she said next. "Two guys. I'm so damned envious. Did you do them both DP or one in front, the other in back?"

"DP?" Granted it was my favorite soft drink but... "Dr Pepper? What's that got to do with sex?"

She trilled a laugh, one which caused heads to turn. In the past few minutes, the office had filled to regular 8:00 a.m. capacity, people in motion, ready to list and sell properties and bring home a hefty commission. "Sometimes I forget what you don't know. Double pen-ne-tra-*shun.* Capeesh?"

She said it just like that. As though English was my third language.

Double pen— Double *penetration?* "You mean...?" My face grew hot. "N-no! We... They..."

Kathi leaned forward and her abundant breasts, a beautiful pair I couldn't help but notice as she wasn't shy about showing them off, threatened to pop buttons off her straining, low-cut blouse. Hmm. New blouse, same-color dye job...something was definitely up.

"Try to stop blushing, sweetcakes—you'll catch your eyebrows on fire," she said patiently, for once in her life whispering. "And to spell it out, I'm talking two cocks. In your pussy. *At the same time.*"

As though her job was done, she straightened and smiled, a little cat-ate-the-cream-dipped-canary barracuda smile. "Okay, so I can tell by your expression things didn't go in *that* kinky direction. Bummer, I wanted to hear what it felt like."

"You h-haven't...?" The question hyperventilated out of me. "People do that? Women *can* do that? It's possible?" Holy porn flicks, Batman!

"Only in my dreams. Besides, big ol' baby heads come out of there, of course it's possible." Airily, she brushed the concept aside. "But we aren't talking about my fantasies, we're talking about you and reality. When—"

"Kathi," I interrupted, pointing toward her desk where Trevor stood. Immaculate, powerfully built Trevor, the newest addition to our office, he'd transferred here from another branch three months ago. Trevor, the late-thirtysomething who dressed like a bank president but with his beard and build looked more like a wilderness guide. The man who usually didn't have a grumpy bone in his body, glowering at Kathi as though his sole ambition was to get his hands on her neck and *squeeze*. "Don't you think you should go see what he wants?"

After a quick glance his direction, she turned back to me. "Pah. Want in one hand, piss in the other." She discounted him with a snort. "So...*you*. When do you see them again? Got your next night of sin lined up? Need any company? Because I am so game. With the guys or w—*owmth*..."

Without, I thought she almost said even though she strangled the word off.

"Uh...company?" As in a foursome? Share Rurik and Jeff? With another woman? One endowed with more confidence, more bravado and definitely more bosom than I?

That didn't seem palatable, not at all.

And was she saying something *other* than what was on the surface? Or was that implausible thought niggling my brain just my overactive libido and confused mind playing tricks?

Did Kathi go for...girls? *Kathi?* The gal who banged so regularly, if her stories were all true, it was a wonder she could walk? Banged guys. That's all she'd ever talked about, all I knew of.

My fingers fluttered on my desk. By design or simple klutz factor, they sent the tallest stack of files toppling to the floor. And thanks to the domino effect, a barrage of others followed, crashing down all around me just like my chaotic thoughts. Now I had an ocean of typed, white pages, legal contracts, pink phone messages, and manila folders to contend with. I was tempted to shred the whole lot.

Maybe throw in Kathi's outrageous tongue. Double penetration? *Join in with a friend?*

The mind reeled; the body reacted slowly.

Before I slid from my chair, Kathi had jumped to assist and was on her knees, systematically corralling the massive mess.

Behind the cover of my desk, she paused and flashed me a consoling smile. "Relax, chickadee. Yeah, I swing both ways. I just never said anything before now because I didn't want it to mess up our friendship. I guess maybe I should've kept—"

"No! No. You're fine. It won't," I rushed to assure her, holding out one hand as though I was swearing on a stack of brownie mix. "You just caught me off guard. That's all."

"Are you sure?" She sat back on her haunches. "Maybe I shouldn't have said anything. If it helps, given one over the other, I'd go with men. There's something about a real cock no vibrator or strap-on can replace." She ignored the gurgling sound coming from my throat. "But sometimes I get a hankering for pussy juice. And nothing else will satisfy, you know?"

I didn't, but I could feel my body responding to the carnal images.

Though the idea of going down on a female didn't tempt me, I could tell just opening up and thinking and talking about sex in a whole new way was making me more receptive...to more. More talk, more possibilities, more naughty nights on the town. And even though exploring with *men* was all I wanted to pursue, I suddenly needed to tell Kathi, to confide what I'd done. More accurately, *who* I'd done it with.

"They were hockey players." It came out hushed and she leaned toward me, silent for once, her expression rapt. "They were only in town for the night and that's why I won't see them again."

I ignored the pang saying it out loud brought on.

"Hockey players?" She tasted the idea, tested it on her tongue. "As in *professional* hockey players? As in they skate on ice and crash into other buff men for a living?" I thought she might swoon. But Kathi definitely wasn't the fainting type.

I nodded. "They both had bruises. One had stitches."

"Hot fuckin' damn! Who?"

"You mean their names?"

She nodded so exuberantly, it was a wonder that silver tongue stud didn't go flying out of her mouth and into the glass wall.

For all of her flashy ways, Kathi was trustworthy. I knew that based on the conversations we'd had about our pasts. We'd both suffered deadbeat dads, but more than that, we'd each had to deal with the loss of our moms early on. While I'd shut down and turned inward, anal to hear her tell it, she'd gone all-out in the opposite direction, turning wild child overnight and not looking back.

So why did I hesitate now? Would the magic of my special night fade if I spread it around? She'd only asked for their names, not their social security numbers and penis sizes. "I—I'm not ready to say."

"You're not? Well, crap." She tipped her head as though evaluating a new species of insect and made a contemplative humming sound. "That's fair enough I suppose." Abandoning her entomological study, Kathi started piling folders again. Shooting me a quick glance from beneath indigo bangs I'd just noticed—those were new too—she added, "Still too fresh, huh? Want to savor it a bit first?"

A muffled noise had her peeking over my desk quick as a flash. "Dickhead."

I knew that meant Trevor. A jackrabbit started hopping around my stomach. "Did he overhear?"

Frowning at the few remaining scattered files, she climbed to her knees. "Nah, he was walking the other way. But I better get out there. The natives are getting restless. Can't have them cannibalizing each other."

"No problem. I made the mess, I'll clean it. And I like the bangs, by the way."

Self-consciously, she reached up and feathered her fingers through the short, gelled spikes covering half her forehead. "They aren't too soft? Don't make me look like a dipshit?"

I laughed at her word choice. "Not a bit."

"Thank God. I started regretting them the minute I cut." Flicking her fingers as though her hair didn't warrant another thought, she rose to her feet, looking almost motherly for once. Totally implausible because I was slightly older. Totally absurd, given how she dressed. "Hey." She placed two fingers on my shoulder and tapped lightly. "I'm here if and when you want to talk. Dish the dirt. Shower me with all the raunchy details. And I'll probably keep asking their names, you know. Is that all right?"

"And I'll probably tell you. Eventually."

She took one step toward the doorway, then halted. "Have you looked them up online yet? Gotten their stats? Made sure they weren't married?"

That last was almost comical because what would it matter now? "They weren't but no, and I'm not sure I will. I think I'll let a great thing be just that—a one-time, wonderful deal and move on from here." I nodded toward her desk where Trevor had once again taken up his scowling position. "What happened with you two? I know you yank his chain every chance you get but he's not the type to yank back. What'd you do to get him to go all draconian on you? He looks ready to breathe fire."

"I..." Her gaze skittered from mine to his and then her back went poker straight, the action thrusting out her breasts. Still staring at him, she said, "Part of me is still puzzling that out. But I'm starting to think I'm ready to get burned."

IN THE END, I held out for two weeks before sharing their names.

I never did look them up online.

Kathi did it for me, giving me winks and high-fives when our paths crossed in the office and keeping me apprised of Tornado games and league rankings. Information I secretly craved but outwardly shrugged off as unimportant. Unnecessary.

Just when I'd finally begun to *not* think of that monumental night every single time I went to bed or woke up or took a shower or watered a plant or ate applesauce or…

It arrived. A package from Jeff.

He sent me a card. A greeting card.

With a simple drawing of a dog wagging its tail on the front and the pre-printed message "I get excited thinking of you" inside.

Below that he'd written:

Since I couldn't call, I decided to tell you the old-fashioned way. Jeff

Below his name, he'd even penciled in his phone number. An afterthought. Because his words were in ink.

That's partly what kept me from dialing. That and what else he'd done.

Yessiree, my one-night stud had sent me a card. *Along* with a box of condoms.

A big multi-pack, not just some skinny box with eight or ten. No, he'd sent the stock-up special.

I didn't know whether to be offended or honored. To laugh or cry.

I went with honored. After all, he'd taken the time to find and buy the thing. To mail it with a cute card I couldn't forget. He'd taken the time to wrap it all up and to write down my address—abbreviated though it was, the package coming to:

Carolina, Upstairs Left-side Unit, Building F, Heartridge Oaks Apartments plus the city and zip, et cetera.

But still. Tacky or not, presumptive or sweet, it was my very own present from my very own one-night stand.

What girl wouldn't be flattered?

At the least, it was worth a laugh. And a sigh. And a place in my bathroom cabinet.

The condoms, that was. The card and envelope, I tucked into my underwear drawer.

EIGHT

When She Learns Not Everyone is as Confident as She Thought

"HERE. I MADE A LIST." Kathi came marching in to my office midmorning a few weeks later.

"A list of what?" I didn't remember requesting anything.

Her sassy walk should have warned me. It grew saucier as she approached. "Of the cute Tornadoes."

She plopped a crooked stack on my desk. I scanned the topmost page, a summary sheet of sorts, soaking in what she'd done. On a surprised laugh, I said, "Kath, that's the whole team."

"No, it's not. I skipped the three who were married, anyone under five-eleven, and the two who've been out all season with injuries." One blunt nail tapped the page. "There's a lot of Europeans in the league. I was surprised by how many. Well, that and Canadians."

"The league? You've checked out other teams?" The more I studied her "list"—and caught how she'd starred two names—the more I felt my cheeks and forehead heating.

Oh boy. There it was, marked with incriminating yellow highlighter, all but written in blood—the two men I'd slept with.

"Should you really be spending your time on this?" is what came out of my mouth when I really wanted to holler, *What if anyone else sees this?*

"What do you think lunch hour is for?" She scooted the summary page out of the way and pointed to a four-inch square beneath. "He's a cutie, wouldn't you say?"

Printed in color on the cardstock square, a baby-faced sweetheart with a full smile and devilish sparkle in his amber eyes stared at me. "A charmer," I agreed, thinking he was. Thinking more about Jeff and Rurik and wondering if they really would come over this weekend. The date I'd tried very hard and completely unsuccessfully *not* to keep track of.

D-Day, as I'd started calling it in my mind. D as in *desire.* The last time this season the Tornadoes played in Cincinnati. When he said he'd be back.

But I'd never dialed Jeff's penciled-in phone number and he hadn't sent anything else. My sensible side doubted I'd hear from him again. Why would I? Why would he go to the trouble for me when any number of willing women likely presented themselves at the end of every game?

Why are you being so down on yourself? Darn voice, always having to pipe in with something. *What does your sultry side think?*

Why don't you get a muzzle?

Unaware of my turbulent mental meanderings, Kathi flipped the card over. "See here? I wrote in their stats."

Relieved to be doing something other than arguing with my conscience, I skimmed the column of numbers: Lance Howell, 43, 6'2", 200#, Left, March 19th, 28, Goodland, Kansas.

"Hey, an American. But what's this?" I indicated the first number. "There's no way he's forty-three." Not with that bright smile and those fresh, unsullied looks.

"That's his jersey number. Followed by his height, weight, what direction he shoots, his birthday and then how old he is. Got it?"

And she'd looked this stuff up—charted it—for every one of the Tornadoes? "Kathi, *Kathi*! Did you even think to look at our hometown team? Consider familiarizing yourself with the Sidewinders instead of guys residing several states away? Maybe *countries* away, during off-season?" The Cincinnati Sidewinders. At least I'd taken the time to look that up.

I'd also managed, by the skin of my teeth, to restrain myself from doing anything more.

"Yep, it's already done. Left that chart at home. I needed something to memorize in case I crossed paths with one of them at the grocery store. But forget about them. Look at *this* one." She shuffled the cardstock squares again, placing another front and center.

Chet Holloway, 14, 6'3", 217#, Left, May 24th, 25, Windsor, Ontario. Canada.

"He's hiding secrets," she said with conviction, "that or hatching nefarious plans—look at those eyes!" She'd come around behind me to peer over my shoulder. She almost sounded dreamy. "Isn't he the cat's meow? *Rrreowww!*"

What made Kathi so impassioned over this particular player? I looked at Chet again. Something about him seemed vaguely familiar. "That's a coincidence. His last name." It was Holloway, just like our agency.

"Who cares about a silly co-inkydink? Would you *look* at him?" She was still hovering, waiting for me to say more.

I picked up the card and stared at the picture, studying him critically.

"Come on, tell me you see it too," she said eagerly. "Scrumptious, isn't he?"

While her enthusiasm didn't necessarily transfer my way, I still thought I'd seen him before. Giving up on figuring it out, I flipped the card back to my desk. I'd probably just seen him at the hotel, in the hallway or something, the night of my…

Well now. I didn't know quite *what* to call it. The night of my sexual breakthrough? Multiple orgasms? Fantasy fuck? None of those totally worked.

"Why, Kath," I teased, trying to get my mind off the past, off the coming weekend and firmly in the present. "You're not crushing on hockey players now, are you?" I couldn't fathom it, not with all the in-person, real-time action she saw.

"Hell, I'll crush on and crash *in* to anything with legs. You know that. When I'm horny enough."

I stretched in my seat, raising both arms overhead to get the kinks out. Swiveling toward Kathi, I gave her an evaluating once-over. "And are you? Is that what's prompting this new fascination?"

"What, horny? God, yes!" She gave her hips a little twist and seemed to wince when she did it. "Damn clit ring," she whispered. "It might have been a mistake. I've had it a while now and no one's seen it yet!"

"No one?" Talk about implausible!

She colored, then backtracked mighty fast. "Well, almost no one. No one who counts anyway."

Releasing the stretch, I relaxed back into my chair, my gaze seeking out Trevor's desk, a corner office on the far side of the building. It was empty. That's right—I'd seen him head into the conference room with clients a little while earlier.

Following my gaze, Kathi whipped her arm around to retrieve her precious Chet card. "I see what you're thinking." Her voice was flat. As flat as my chest. Which wasn't like her at all. "You're wrong. Completely wrong. Way, *way* off base."

"You and Trevor? He's seen your latest piercing?" I said out loud, incredulity giving way to conviction when I realized what it was about Chet that had struck a chord—he looked like a younger version of Trevor. "'Hatching nefarious plans'?" I echoed what she'd said about him. No wonder he was the player she fixated on. "That's what you see in him! He reminds you of Trevor."

She was standing at the side of my desk, a little belligerently it seemed to me, shaking her head for all she was worth. So I scooted my chair back and opened my middle drawer, fishing around for a nail file. Giving her some space. "It doesn't take a genius to see the obvious," I said lightly. "But really, you and Trevor? I know you two give off more sparks than the Fourth of July, but I thought you claimed he had as much person-ality as a trash bag."

Her exact words had been *trashed toilet paper* with *crap bag* thrown in there somewhere. I didn't think she'd mind the paraphrase. I made sure to pretend filing my fingernail was utterly absorbing as I offered, "When you asked him out and he said no, I thought you decided the idea of dating him wasn't worth another breath. Seems to me that you're giving him plenty."

"There's a lot more to him than meets the eye," Kathi defended hotly. When I hadn't even gone on attack!

I slowly lifted my head. Kathi had made me face the reality of my empty sex life and do some-thing about it. Maybe it was my turn. "I'm sure there is. Ah-ah…" I stopped her from inter-rupting with a wave of my nail file. "The ques-tion is, Ms. Hot 'n' Horny and Cruising for Hockey Players—online, where it's safe, I might add. The question is, what are you going to do about him?"

Releasing her gaze and dropping the file back in my drawer, I turned to gather the Hockey Stud

Cards she'd made, realizing as my hands shuffled over what she'd dumped on my desk, that there was a veritable bounty of them. Almost like baseball cards, each square had a hunk's face printed on the front and his stats handwritten on the back. I couldn't resist one more jibe. "Now I know you're efficient, but this"—I held up one of the cards—"*this* is beyond ridiculous. A grown woman, one with your personality and interests, would only spend the amount of time this took on something this dang *tweeny* if she was avoiding something. Or someone."

By now, I had all the cards piled in a deck. Tapping the edge on my desk, I challenged, "Since when have you been afraid of anything or any guy? Never, not since I've known you. Trevor's a decent guy, he's got a good job, everyone here likes him."

Although, come to think on it, he had kept to himself since transferring here from one of our out-of-town locations. He was polite but not overly chatty. Came in later than most of us, but stayed later too. I'd never seen him outside of work, which said as much about me as it might him. Still... "What's he hiding under that pinstripe suit you so abhor, I wonder?" The suit she complained about, saying it was something only a pompous prick would wear on casual Fridays. I held out the homemade cards. "Aren't you itching to find out?"

Kathi looked oddly uncertain as she slowly reached for the deck. I started to think she wasn't going to answer, was simply going to ignore the elephant who'd just emerged from the conference room and was heading toward his desk, his sharp glance skewering my office and zeroing in on Kathi as though it was a tracking device. Staring at the cards in her hands, unaware of Trevor's attention, she whispered, "More than I'll admit."

"Well? What else?"

"Okay. Fine." She raised her narrowed gaze to mine. "I'm starting to think the guy's a rash I can't get rid of. Yeah, he makes me itch."

When she stopped there, I snapped my fingers next to her head. "*Hel-lo!* Then why the heck aren't you doing something about it? Telling him? Showing off that fancy piercing and getting that"—I lowered my voice to stealth status

—"particular cock you crave? Instead of developing a manufactured crush on someone you don't know and will likely never meet? *Why*, Kathi?" When she didn't answer, just stood there wavering on her feet, I challenged, "Man up and spit it out."

She smiled at my attempt to sound like her but it didn't reach her eyes. "Because I'm afraid he might be more than I can handle. And if I'm honest with you and myself, I think I might be too afraid to find out."

KATHI–AFRAID? Not something I'd ever thought to hear.

With her stunning confession still ringing in my ears two days later, I remained on alert, ready to welcome my studs. Not that I *expected* them to show up.

Or was even hoping for it, not really.

Liar!

I ignored the taunting voice.

Being a pragmatic realist, I knew better than to think sexual lightning might strike the same spot twice. *My* spot. But still…

I couldn't stop hoping. *Wanting.* Worrying.

Solace came, as it always had, in the regular routines instilled in me since childhood. Saturday's list? Check. Sunday's list? Double check.

The apartment was tidy, the shower spotless. Plants watered and even trimmed. Sheets changed, legs shaved and lotioned.

Even my toenails were freshly painted, and it wasn't superstition that made me put on the plum color Jeff had so admired. It was…a desire to please. Yeah, that was it. A desire to please myself, please him maybe.

Maybe? Liar!

The homemade spaghetti sauce was hot, the wine was chilled. Not that I expected them to show for dinner. They did have a hockey game to play first. Who knew if they would even be hungry? For food or for me?

But being prepared never hurt.

It was the waiting that got to you.

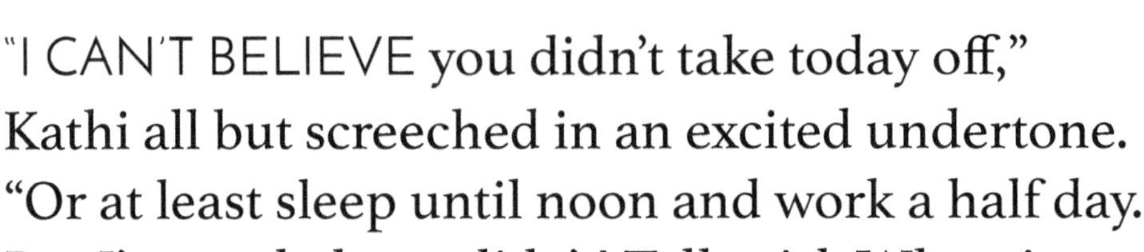

"I CAN'T BELIEVE you didn't take today off," Kathi all but screeched in an excited undertone. "Or at least sleep until noon and work a half day. But I'm so glad you didn't! Talk, girl. What time did they arrive? How'd it go? Details this time, *please*."

For once, *she'd* been late to work, some appointment or other, but the moment I saw her push through the large double doors, she'd beelined for my office, not even stopping to drop off her backpack or stick her lunch in the fridge.

She'd just zoomed in here and shut the glass door. Giving us total privacy. Audible privacy, that was. Because thanks to her zealous arrival, all eyes were on us. "Well?" She was giddily impatient, practically skipping in place. "I wanted to call you over the weekend, give you a pep talk. But after last time, I figured you had this one in the bag. Plus, the fun run was this weekend and I was swamped." She mentioned the annual fundraiser event she volunteered to organize, rubbing her palms together as though anticipating something delightful. "Come on, girl. Dish the dirty dirt already!"

I went back to filling in the contract. It was my third attempt to spell the buyer's name correctly. The act of doing it by hand and foregoing the computer was supposed to have grounded me, helped take my mind off what-ifs and silly regrets and put it where it belonged—on work.

It hadn't. Worked, that is. My mind was still a muddle, full of memories of what *hadn't* happened.

"Well?" Eager, excited fingertips tapped on the top of my desk, nudged the contract aside. "Spill, Carolina."

"Nothing to serve up. He didn't show."

She pounced. "He?"

"*They.*"

Her palm slapped across the page. "What do you mean *they didn't show*?" Bafflement colored the question. Then dismay. "They didn't show? But the Tornadoes won! The game was over by ten!" Realizing she was practically screeching, she toned it down. "I was positive they'd swing by to celebrate, do a little swinging with you in the middle."

Nudging her stiff pinky with my pen, I tried to write around her hand. "You thought wrong."

Her fingers wilted along with the enthusiasm that had carried her through the door, coiling into a listless fist to hammer on top of my desk. "But I was certain they'd be back. I mean, you're a sure thing. He sent you a box of rubbers!"

Every word she spoke was a spike shredding into my already shaky confidence. Hadn't I stayed up, for hours and hours, telling myself the very same thing? Doing what I'd sworn I wouldn't, despite my mental assurances the last weeks that I knew better? My promises to myself to not get excited, not *expect* anything?

In the end, disappointment had hit me hard. Making it clear, if I hadn't expected them, then by God, I'd *anticipated*. Looked forward to. And, for all my schoolgirl hopes, had wound up with *nada.* Nothing but a punch to the gut. And an empty bed.

Kathi's fist flailed again, punishing my desk, pounding so hard my butt felt the vibrations all the way in my chair. "He mailed you a gift, fuckin' dammit! Guys don't go to the trouble of taping something up and hassling with the post office unless there's a reason!"

With both hands, I caught her flying fist midair and halted its ferocious descent. "Hey there." I finally looked up, sure by now that while my eyes might be swimming in tears, I wasn't naïve enough to let one fall. "Fun sex, a great night. Fabulous memories. That's *all* it was. All it was ever supposed to be, remember?"

I reminded us both, repeating the litany I'd been preaching to myself since 2 a.m. when I'd finally faced the truth. I slowly released her clenched fist. "I love how you're coming to my defense. If I haven't told you lately, you've been the best friend ever about all this but ease up, okay? Everyone is staring—" And I did mean *everyone.* "They probably think we're about to come to blows."

"What?" she snarled. "They want a show?" She looked over her shoulder and I could only imagine the killer glare she was giving as gazes dropped and feet shuffled, attention slowly turning away. At least for most of them.

"Did Trevor just wink at you?" Seeing that surprising, flirty action brought about my first real smile of the day.

Kathi jabbed her fist at him once, then gave our audience her back. "Fuck him. I'd give him the finger if I wasn't such a professional."

I snorted at that, one of those really good ones where you get tickled unexpectedly and your nose starts to run. Grabbing a tissue, I wiped. Then smiled some more. "Think they were hoping for a catfight? The way you were attacking my desk, they probably thought we were about to go after each other."

"Nah." She retrieved her backpack and lunch. They'd fallen to the floor sometime during her tirade. "I only fight with girls when we're all greased up. And in a ring."

And that picture kept me snorting and smiling the rest of the day. Or at least for the next ten minutes.

CAROLINA.

Jeff couldn't stop thinking about her. No matter how much he tried.

For a woman whose name he'd had trouble remembering initially, flashes of their first night together played a little too frequently in his mind's matinee.

Carolina.

The curve of her waist drove him nuts. The gentle slope of her breasts with those puckered, dusky nipples? They drove him to distraction.

Especially now, as he drove the sedan he'd just rented to her place on this hot and sunny early evening.

"Hey, man, I'm honored," his passenger, Lance Howell, was saying while scooting the seat back to make more room for his long legs. "Glad to be invited to this little shindig. Wait—" The seat adjustment stalled and he looked up. "Or was I last choice?"

"Nah, you were the first," Jeff told him, checking mirrors as they merged onto the highway from the rental place. "Don't let it go to your head, though."

"Oh! I feel so used!" Lance gave a mock protest and slapped the back of one hand to his forehead in a feigned swoon. "You only want me for my dick."

The guy could be a ham. "Don't be such a drag queen."

Lance's magnified protests halted on a screech. "Don't you mean *drama* queen?"

Gotcha. "I did, but you responded better to 'drag'."

"Har-har." Lance started fiddling with the radio. "Does she know this is your last year? That you're retiring when the season's over?"

"No."

"Why?" Lance paused to slide Jeff a Groucho Marx raised-eyebrow leer. "Afraid she's a groupie who only likes you for your stick?"

"She's not, you goof. And I'm not saying any-thing because I haven't made up my mind." Which was true. Granted, it was something he thought about with increasing frequency.

Sort of like Carolina?

He growled under his breath. "So consider the subject closed and yourself on thin ice. I'm starting to regret I asked you."

"No, you're not," Lance said accurately, finally settling on a Top 40 station. "But I am curious why you did."

"Hell if I know." Because though they'd been teammates for several years, Jeff had never shared with Lance before. And though he'd never admit it out loud, he'd seen a considerate side to the guy more than once. A quality he thought Care might respond to. Be comfortable with.

Even if something about the idea didn't sit quite right in his gut. Made him feel, just a bit, as though the shrimp tacos he'd had for lunch had been off. Or maybe it was just the sunlight streaming through the car windows, steaming his patience. Frying his nerves.

"It's because the ladies love me," Lance gloated, changing over to a country station. When that failed to get a rise, he added, "And because I'm so well-hung."

"It's because you know how to *listen*. When you're not flapping your jaw with penile praise, that is," Jeff told him. Mainly it was because he liked the younger man. He knew the ladies liked him too. Good-natured and always up for making people laugh.

He'd also noticed Lance didn't plug it in every available hole every time one was offered. The man showed *some* restraint (unlike some of their teammates) and that earned Jeff's respect.

But Lance wasn't finished extolling his own virtues. "Let's not forget I'm the top goal maker three games running."

Jeff stifled a chuckle. "Let's not forget I'm the one behind the wheel."

"So?"

"So if I decide to strand you on the other side of Cincinnati, it'll be a long walk back to the hotel."

"Fuck, man. You're really serious about this girl."

Muscles tensed. Hackles rose. "Whoa. Where in the hell do you come up with that?"

Ugh. Stupid after-work traffic was making the drive take longer than he'd expected.

"You never act like such a prick. You've talked about her enough, it's easy to see."

He had? Sure, he might've mentioned her *once*.

Maybe twice.

But more than that? Nah.

"Usually if I yank your chain," Lance continued, "you just yank back, don't get angry. Go-oll-ly, I'm glad you're getting some tonight. You need to unwind."

"Unwind my fist against your face," Jeff muttered, flexing stiff fingers on the wheel, unwilling to admit Lance was right. That he *was* acting like an impatient dick. Certainly unwilling to announce the reason behind it—because he was anxious about their reception. Hell, *his* reception. Would she be happy to see him? Regardless of who he'd brought along to ride shotgun?

Damn, it was hot. He cranked up the air-conditioning.

"Methinks your agitated cells need a soothing symphony." Lance backtracked to a classical station he'd bypassed earlier. "Here. Have some Haydn."

Huh? The guy knew composers? And his cells were just fine, agitated or otherwise. Dammit.

"Just tell me what you want and where you want me," Lance said. "That'll take the pressure off junior here."

"You *like* to be told what to do?" No wonder the kid listened so well on the ice, his skating and shooting automated to such a degree he'd earned the nickname The Cyborg Slicer from the other players.

Jeff was the opposite. He needed to be in charge, more so with every year that passed. Maybe that was why Uncle Gary's latest offer tempted him more than any of the others. He and Coach had been batting heads frequently too. Especially since that last Cincinnati trip.

Maybe it really was time to consider hanging up his skates and finish his degree. The one he'd abandoned when professional hockey called and he was so excited to answer.

"What about kink?" Lance interrupted his musings. "Has she got any toys or costumes?"

"Costumes? You missed your calling, buddy. You belong on the stage. No, no costumes. No toys that I'm aware of. Nothing too kinky. Not tonight." Jeff didn't want to scare her off, assuming she'd let him back on. Back in. Her apartment. Her life. Over a month was a long time without contact. Why hadn't she called?

Even if it was to say "Stop harassing me, buddy. Keep your card and your box of condoms to yourself"?

Face it, she might not have given you a single thought since.

True. But ouch.

He hadn't imagined the chemistry between them. The conversations. Or her mesmerizing looks of sexual awakening. Of wonder.

But what if he had…?

Maybe he was getting delusional in his middle age.

Too many knocks to his noggin on the ice.

"No problemo," Lance said. "Vanilla sex is still s-e-x. Works for me." He brushed his fingers over the dash in time with some stringed instrument, going to town. "Besides, I kind of like the idea of being your get-out-of-jail-free card."

"Don't think sex is a given," Jeff cautioned. "It's not. *She's* not. Hang back, would you? While I talk with her first." If she was even home. *If* she'd even speak to him. Had she been there last night? Waiting for him? Thinking he'd forgotten her completely? Wondering. Worrying…

"She's not a dog, right?" Lance asked, his musical recital stalling out as he angled in his seat. A quick glance showed he was grinning. "Even if it does mean getting you out of the doghouse, I'm not fucking a two-bagger."

"Snipe found her."

"Ah."

Yeah. *Ah.* That said it all. Rurik had a knack for picking up lovelies anytime he went out, and the entire team knew it. Most of the women he brought back knew it too, their confidence often laced with a brittle edge that Jeff found more and more abrasive as time went on.

Carolina now? He didn't remember a single hard thing about her. "She's innocent. If that makes sense."

Innocent? Hell, Lance would never buy that. Not after knowing that she'd "partied" with him and Rurik both. "I mean," Jeff backpedaled, "she comes across pretty wholesome. Yeah, wholesome." That sounded right. In his head, at least. But when he heard it echo in the car? Not so much. "Know what I mean?"

"Not a bit." Lance laughed as though Jeff was a one-man comedy show. "Wholesome? You've known her what—a month? Oh wait, that's too generous. You knew her a single night!"

"Shut up."

"I'm starting to think that you're toast, man, the way you're acting. Cooked and buttered." Lance stretched his tall frame and leaned back in the passenger seat of the rental, opening his legs as though the continued discussion was riling certain anatomy. "To have you so smitten, she must be gorgeous and stacked and—"

"I said *shut up*." Jeff forced his tone back to neutral, his strangling grip on the wheel to loosen. "And don't say anything about her boobs. She's—"

Hell. He was *not* about to tell Lance he'd sensed her self-consciousness over their size. "Just follow my lead, okay? She's not like other—"

"I get it." Lance turned the music up a notch. "Chillax, dude. I'll be fucking Prince Charming bowing to *your* every whim, King Jeff. But you owe me for this."

The sign indicating his exit *finally* loomed into sight. "I owe you—for getting you laid?"

"That's gravy. No, you owe me for all the grief that's come before. Hell, you're liable to give me performance anxiety, the way you're obsessing about—"

"Fuck off."

"Hoping to, dear Jeffrey."

"And don't call me that." The words were gritted out with a career's worth of exasperation. While other guys on the ice picked up cool nicknames, either from each other or the press—Tazor, Snipe, The Toledo Torpedo—somehow he'd gotten saddled with "Jeffrey". And that wasn't even his real name.

"So..." Lance's long pause nearly gave him heartburn. What was the guy going to badger him about next? "You ever have any trouble in the erectile-function arena?"

"Where the hell did that come from?" God, he hadn't extended an invitation to ride double with a lame horse had he? Feeling the heat more than ever, he turned the a/c to full blast and shot his passenger a narrowed glance. "Is there something you need to tell me?"

"Just curious." Lance shrugged. "Planning for the future and all that. It's got to happen sometime, right?"

"Hopefully not tonight." Why'd she have to live so far from the hotel? The way this was going downhill, they'd be buried in quicksand before they arrived.

"No problem there," Lance assured. "I'm more than half hard already. As long as she wants it, the other half will jump in line."

"She might need a tad of coaxing but if I wasn't sure, we wouldn't be wasting our time." At least he sounded confident.

"What are you going to tell her?" Lance questioned. "About last night?"

"What happened." What else would he tell her?

He slowed to exit the freeway. Next stop—Heartridge Oaks Apartments.

"You think she'll buy it?"

"It's the truth. I don't see why not."

"If she was my girl, I'd make up something that sounded better. Extra practice, team meeting, earthquake, food pois—"

"Earthquake? Because the Midwest is just riddled with them." His girl? Why'd that sound right? It shouldn't. He was just having fun. Playing the field with a fun filly.

Who intrigues you. Who occupies far more of your thoughts than she should.

Dammit. "And she's not my girl."

"When's the last time you waited five weeks and drove across town in a car you rented just to nail some chick?"

Jeff pointed to a panhandler on the side of the road. The guy held up the requisite "Will Work For Food, God Bless" cardboard square below his grimy face. "That's you in ten seconds if you don't find something else to harp on."

"So...that latest spate of superhero movies..."

"What about 'em?"

"Nothing. Just changing the subject."

"You couldn't have thought of something better?" Jeff wanted to toss Lance out the window as the guy's observations settled uncomfortably in his gut.

His girl?

When the thought of that made his pulse stampede, Jeff knew he was in deep shit.

MONDAYS WEREN'T EVER anyone's favorite workday. But today had been especially brutal. It was unusually hot and—despite what I'd bluffed to Kathi—I'd been distracted and somewhat down, despite my efforts to put the weekend disappointment behind me.

During the drive between the office and my apartment, I shook off any lingering doldrums, deciding to plan my next big night out. It didn't necessarily have to be sexually focused but it did have to be something fun. Something sociable that took me beyond my apartment and into the public arena. Putting myself out there, where it was at least *possible* to mingle and meet datable men.

A concert, a play—heck, maybe I'd take salsa lessons. What I refused to do was sit around and let life, and lust, pass me by, not anymore.

I'd been home half an hour, just long enough for a quick shower and to put the chocolate syrup ingredients on to melt. Homemade bliss, my grandmother's recipe—just sugar, cocoa, and water.

Kathi had offered to drop by bearing ice cream and a chick flick if I needed the distraction. I thanked her for the offer but told her she didn't need to, that I was fine.

I meant it too, but I wouldn't put it past her to come over anyway, hence the chocolate syrup. If she didn't show in the next hour, I could always drizzle it over last night's spaghetti, toss back the bottle of wine and have a grand ol' time for one.

Yippee.

Not!

Thinking it'd heated long enough, I dipped a finger in the saucepan for a taste.

"Mmm." It was good, hot on my tongue and very sweet, extra rich too because I'd used a new gourmet cocoa.

"Drat." And dotting my shirt, I saw when I leaned forward and turned off the burner to let it cool. "Just great."

My sleeveless white knit top, which I wore over a tied-at-the-side-of-my-waist skirt fashioned from a colorful sarong, now sported chocolate splatters smack between my breasts.

Shoot. I didn't know whether dried chocolate would stain as bad as grape juice or tomato sauce and I didn't want to find out. Better to put it in water to soak than ignore and regret it later. Frowning down at the chocolate splotches, I reached for the bottom edge of my shirt.

That's when she knocked.

Good, dependable Kathi.

"You came!" I hollered, releasing my shirt and feeling my face spread in a smile as I headed to-ward the door. "I told you that you didn't have to!" I flipped the lock and swung the door open, still preoccupied with the stain. "But I'm so darn glad you did." I glanced up and— *Gulp*. My smile fizzled. "J-Jeff."

Remarkable how I didn't swallow my tongue, given the way I nearly choked on it. "Jeff. You're *here*."

Okay, so the observation was inane but this time I truly hadn't expected him. Not *tonight*.

A noise beyond my porch drew my gaze to the base of the stairs twelve feet below where a handsome hottie, arms crossed in front of his chest, one hip resting against the rail, grinned confidently, cockily up at me. A dark-haired charmer, dressed in faded jeans and a snug-fitting black T-shirt. A hunk, with pale, golden eyes I could see all the way from up here, silently waiting.

My gaze zipped back to Jeff. Standing there, two feet away. Two feet that felt like miles. I was barefoot and without those extra three inches, Jeff seemed bigger, more impressive, more male. *Face it, ducks, he's more everything.*

"Jeff." That's all I could manage: his name. Without bowing at his feet or tripping over one of mine. I couldn't stop my eyes from drinking him in. He had on dark jeans with casual boots, and another short-sleeve, untucked shirt, this time in a green plaid.

"Hi there." He was wearing his contacts not his glasses. He stared at me with a hopeful, expectant expression.

What? Did he expect me to invite him in? Just like that?

Invite him in!

"Hi yourself." *I got the card and rubbers you mailed, thanks*, I could imagine myself saying, adding a sultry grin worthy of Kathi—yeah, right. *Want to come inside and use them up?*

But nothing else came out other than that not-quite-garbled greeting. My mouth was too dry to say more, my throat too painfully tight.

He appeared just on the edge of solemn. Just shy of uncertain.

And that's what kept me from kicking him to the curb.

I didn't like the idea of being taken for granted as a "sure thing". A near-sure thing, *maybe.*

When I just stood there, one hand on the door, the other balled into a fist behind my back, he nodded once, decisively, and stepped forward, halving the distance between us.

"Carolina." He breathed my name as though it were a caress, but he made no move to touch me.

I waited, unmoving, curious what else he might say, my attention divided between him and the man silently evaluating our interaction below.

"We wanted to come by after last night's game, would have but one of the guys got a concussion and I ended up at the hospital for several hours."

His explanation sounded dubious to me. *Just be grateful he's making one!* "Don't they have medics for that sort of thing?"

"Sure, when it happens during a game. The dumb-ass slipped in the shower at the hotel afterward, hit his head, said he was fine, then promptly passed out. The coaches were watching a replay of the game somewhere and most of the guys had already gone out. It fell to me and Lance to get him to the ER."

There was just enough sincerity in his eyes that some of the starch went out of me. "Is he okay? Your friend?"

Jeff nodded. "Right as rain this morning, but he was grounded from today's game."

"Today's?" It was then I noticed how his booted foot was swiftly sliding over the concrete, his toes traveling back and forth while his heel stayed in place. A nervous gesture?

"Yeah. We played an exhibition game earlier today with the Sidewinders. Doesn't affect the standings, just something to help raise funds for the family of a coach who's worked on both teams. His home was destroyed by a tornado last—"

"His family? Are *they* all right?"

Jeff's toes tapped on the concrete in quick succession. The muffled noise halted when he nodded. "Waited it out in an underground cellar, but their house got churned into matchsticks. Anyway, that's why we're still in town, heading out first thing tomorrow."

Jeff pointed over his shoulder. "That's Lance," he introduced unnecessarily. I'd already recognized the stair-leaning hunk from Kathi's timely Stud Cards—the cute charmer, #43. But there was no way I'd admit I knew that.

"Rurik wanted to be here, was looking forward to seeing you again but he had a family emergency back home." Jeff paused and I thought he was going to stop there. Then a shadow crossed over his face, shading his eyes and carving a line between his brows, and he added, "His grandfather died and Rurik flew back for the funeral."

Before I could comment, Jeff leaned in, so close I caught a subtle, inviting whiff of his cologne beneath the lemony scent of his aftershave. Definitely sandalwood. "I would've called last night and told you about Serg and about Rurik and asked about Lance, checked if the substitution was okay—"

"But you don't have my number," I finished for him. *And whose fault is that?*

NINE

When He Thoughtfully Orders Her a Lap Dance

"IT'S ALL RIGHT," I told him, feeling a strange, peaceful calm come over me. One that told me I didn't think he was feeding me a line or stringing me along. "Serg, is it?" I repeated the name, hitting the hard G as Jeff had.

"Sergei Dolohov," he confirmed. "One of the best D-men around."

"Best what?"

"Defenseman," Jeff explained, as I heard his foot start shuffling again. "That's his position. Lance back there is a center."

Seeing Jeff gesture toward him, Lance raised one hand in a casual wave. Without doing more than giving him a brief nod, I told Jeff, "I miss the glasses."

His eyebrows shot up. "Wha—? Oh. Mine?"

I nodded once, drinking him in. He looked wonderful, gorgeous to me, breath-stealingly *here*. The reality of it made me lightheaded.

"I'll wear them next time," he promised easily.

Next time, huh? Did I want to be his Cinci fuck buddy?

Hell yes you do!

Little voices could be so astute. "I'll look forward to seeing them."

Jeff's posture eased, his foot finally stilled and he gave me a half grin, one that *asked* rather than said, *is everything okay? Can we stay?*

"Guess I need to get Serg some frogs." When his forehead creased in confusion, I added, "For his tub."

I heard the breath go out of him then. A sigh of relief?

His cheeks lifted when his smile grew. He stepped close enough to lean down and brush my cheek with his. My stomach did a triple flip off the high board. "And Lance?" Jeff whispered near my ear. "If he meets muster and you aren't too pissed at me, can he come up?"

"He knows the score?" That—out of my mouth? Heck fire, I sounded as though I did this sort of thing all the time now.

Jeff slid his hand along my arm, freeing my fingers from the doorframe where they'd gone numb, thanks to my death grip. He tugged me to him, practically hugging my groin to his while undressing me with his eyes—outside my apartment where all the world could see. Outside, where he couldn't miss the chocolate splotches front and center between my non-enhanced, braless breasts.

Funny how neither bothered me—that we might have an audience or that I wasn't armored in a magic bra.

"Is Lance here to fuck you, you mean?" Jeff practically purred the words and they sounded like a seduction, especially when he nuzzled my forehead with his lips. "Yeah, that'd entered his mind." His mouth moved a little lower, over my cheek. "But only if you approve and only if I'm part of the picture."

I thought he motioned for Lance to come on up but I wasn't positive because then Jeff was framing my face and kissing me for all he was worth, walking me backward, through the doorway and into my apartment.

I'M NOT sure what I figured might happen next. That maybe we'd sit down after I nuked the spaghetti, flirt and exchange hot glances while eating and sharing a bottle of wine. Maybe that

Lance would shoot me sultry glances over the rim of his glass, lick his lips as though he was tasting *me* while Jeff led a round table on finances and immigration, two of the topics we'd failed to cover during our previous night together. And of course, during this weighty conversation, he'd slip his hand under the table, skim it beneath my skirt and over my thighs. Then explore between…

That maybe we'd relocate to the living room, stream some music and dance, me with one of the guys and then, after a song or two, the other. Then maybe both. Standing on either side of me, their sheer size and intimidatingly good looks dwarfing my insecurities while rousing my desire. Certainly, that would have been lovely, perhaps even a touch romantic but that's not what happened.

Not at all.

Stopping barely inside, once Herbert streamed over our shoulders, Jeff halted and tightened his fingers on either side of my face, kissing me harder, if that was possible. Humming his appreciation, he curved one strong hand over my head to release my hair from its messy knot. He stroked strong fingers through the strands, easing the tension from my scalp, from my day.

A second later he groaned and stole his hands away. To steal them under my shirt.

"God, Care." He spoke into my mouth, his lips and tongue too busy engaging mine to move far. "I've been dying to get my hands on you, my lips on you." He shoved my top up with the backs of his wrists, his fingers speeding over my torso until he cupped my breasts with the flat of his palms. "These dark nipples have been driving me insane since you opened—" *The door* never made it past his lips.

But I heard it as clearly as I felt his hands, demanding more. The driving need Jeff couldn't seem to tame driving mine higher. With every plunge of his tongue, every flex of his fingers. Every beat of my heart.

Though hazed with passion, I registered Lance following and locking the door.

Jeff kissed me as though he couldn't stop, his mouth moving over mine by turns tenderly and torridly, teaching me what kissing was really about—communicating need, communicating urgency, or so it seemed. His palms teased my nipples below the constriction of my bunched-up shirt, sliding lightly over the hard points, then grasping at my chest, pulling my flesh outward and upward.

I moaned deep in my throat, taking little, choppy breaths whenever Jeff slanted his head for a different angle. I realized two could play this game and started tugging his shirt from his jeans.

"Hell, Jeff," said a new voice, "she doesn't need a lick of coaxing after all." Lance came up behind me, reminding me three were playing this particular game. Three of us on the ice and ready to shoot for the goal.

I could've taken offense at his gloating statement. But why bother? He was right. The moment I'd seen Jeff, seen how happy he was to see me, sensed his sincerity, any reserve or resolve to resist had melted like milk chocolate in a hot car.

"I guess introductions can wait," Lance chuckled as he put his hands on my shoulders and drew them together, lifting my hair to place a kiss on my nape.

Jeff eased back to scrape my shirt over my head. "Lance, Carolina. Care, Lance."

My chocolate-dotted top was gone and now both men kissed me with delirious, suffocating intensity. But who needed to breathe? Not I, not when Lance nibbled on one side of my neck where it met the curve of my shoulder while Jeff ducked his head to suck on my breasts, lashing his tongue against my nipple as his hands worked at the knot of the sarong.

"Hi—ah—*mmm*, Lance," I attempted, finally succeeding at getting Jeff's shirt unbuttoned. "Nice to—ah—meet you*ooee*!" I ended on a squeal when one of his hands slid from my shoulder to pinch the nipple that wasn't in Jeff's mouth.

"What a coincidence," Lance murmured as he gentled the pressure and smiled against my neck. "I was just about to tell you the same thing."

"Undress now, talk later," Jeff said, kissing down my stomach, his hands grappling feverishly at my waist. "Can't get the damn thing untied."

This close to his head, this close to his *mouth*, as though they too remembered everything he'd done between them, my inner thighs pressed together and clung. I felt so swollen, so impossibly horny, and it had happened so quickly. As though just the sight of him, of them, had triggered the response, ratcheting my body up to the saturation point in seconds.

This is what I'd craved the past few weeks. Another taste of the mindless passion that supersedes all else, where I'm transported to a plane where satisfying the swirling ache is all that matters. Where I'm left *alone* inside my head, without a taunting little voice or bouts of niggling doubt.

My restless hands went in opposite directions, one coming up to grip Lance's wrist as he continued to play with and pinch my nipple, the other going down to thread through Jeff's short hair. "Stop trying," I told him, referring to the knot. "Just lift up my skirt. I'm..." When Lance changed his nipple torture to soft plucking motions and redirected more of his mouth's attention on my nape, I sighed, "I'm ready." *So very ready.*

Jeff immediately abandoned the knot and stood, his eyes a little wild. He shrugged off the shirt I'd unbuttoned and threw it to the side. His hands went to his jeans. "I'm not fool enough to pass up an invitation like that." His gaze flicked over my shoulder. "Lance, keep her hot while I get... this...off..." With no finesse whatsoever, Jeff scraped the denim past his hips and shoved it downward, doing this half-hopping thing on alternating feet. "*Without* falling on my ass."

Lance dropped to the floor behind me, skimming his warm palms over my torso and sarong-covered hips on the journey down. Nestling his face against my lower back, his fingers circled my legs and stroked down to my ankles and then higher until they halted above my knees and tightened.

Heeding his unspoken instruction, I widened my stance. When he slid the back of one hand between my legs to nudge my center with several knuckles, I wavered but didn't try to stop the eager moan that escaped.

"Steady now." Lance leaned solidly into the back of my legs. He wedged his knuckles higher, forcing my panties just inside my labia. His breath whistled out. "She's wet and ready, my friend," he said to Jeff, making no move to investigate further.

I stared at Jeff's nude body when he straightened from dispatching his jeans and socks. His fist clenched a condom packet he'd procured from a pocket. It was bunched next to that pale strip on his sexy lean hip, the one that looked as though he wore a form-fitting swimsuit several days a week. The one that swam through my dreams.

I saw him crunch the tiny square. While the rest of him was stone still, his fist worried the packet as though it was burning a hole in his palm. I prodded, "Didn't trust me to have any this time?"

Without alluding to the gift he'd sent, he gave his head a single negative shake. "Didn't trust myself to wait."

Lightning bugs powwowed over every inch of my skin. I glittered and tingled in place, even more when I ripped my attention from the dynamite view he'd exposed to the barely banked fire in those emerald eyes and saw what they conveyed—pure, raw heat. For *me*. As though Jeff depended on my body to put out the blaze, I felt myself start to melt inside, soaking through my panties.

A mew of near-embarrassment emerged and I shifted in place but Jeff wouldn't let me back away—from myself or what they did to me.

He stepped close but didn't make physical contact. His eyes narrowed as he looked at me, and though his stare somehow turned glacial for some reason I couldn't fathom, all I felt was his heat. "Are you sure?" he said to Lance while keeping his gaze on my face. "I need you to be certain."

"Ah…" Lance breathed over the small of my back and I felt his hand between my legs slide away. *Not yet!* I wanted to scream at him, but then it was back, flipped over with nimble fingers active and mobile, this time edging past the elastic on one side of my panties to test my wetness, my readiness, directly.

"Let's see… I'm just now discovering this beautiful new paradise." His touch firmed as he slid it up and down to the accompaniment of my moan. "Well, blow me over, it appears to be raining in paradise." Lance's finger roved past my puffy outer lip to graze over my hollow. After a single inward flick, it traveled upward, seeking out my clit. "Yep, definitely raining." He started kissing my back and running his opposite hand up and down my leg, fingernails engaged in a stimulating way. "Think maybe I'll go skinny-dipping."

With that, his finger dove inside. Right where I needed it most.

My eyes closed against the vision of Jeff, rigid and aroused, every inch of him waiting in pained, silent agony—or so it appeared to me—while his friend explored my depths. My head fell back. The sight was too much.

The finger in my body not enough.

My knees bent as I tried to take more of that probing, pleasuring finger inside me. *Jeff*, I mouthed toward the ceiling, not looking at him, *take me*.

"Fuck it," he swore and I heard crinkling and rustling. "She's ready. Lance?"

"You got it." His finger retreated from my core and both men were gripping me, Lance by my hips, Jeff at my waist, lifting me off the floor and into Jeff's embrace, against his chest, above his erection.

My legs instinctively widened to coil around him. Lance knelt again and gathered the sarong, both hands and head—or so the hot breath on my newly exposed parts told me—beneath my skirt now, tugging on my panties to make room for Jeff's cock.

"Forget this." Jeff swore again, practically throwing me off him as he went after the sarong tie with a vengeance. I whimpered, clutching at his head and shoulders for balance. Four seconds more and the pesky knot slid free, and he was attacking my innocent panties with the same ferocity until they too were down my shaky legs and cast aside. "Come here." Hand at my nape, he hauled me to him, stealing my breath and commanding my surrender with his hard kiss.

Three strong arms put me back into position, my legs around Jeff's waist, his cock probing for entry with Lance below us, spreading my ass cheeks and guiding it home.

Home? Enjoy this while you can, ducks. Don't expect him to become a regular tenant.

I knew that, I did. But right now, I felt too good, *what they did* felt too good, for me to heed any warnings. However well intentioned.

"Ah, God." To the accompaniment of his heart-felt groan, Jeff forged his erection deep. Swollen tissues stretched to accommodate this latest taste of heaven and I strangled off my irritating voice when the Hallelujah Chorus zinged through my brain.

My pussy muscles did their own bit of rejoicing and hugged the thick column of his shaft. I abandoned any semblance of sultry and held on tight. Exposed but not embarrassed; filled but not nearly finished.

Not with tonight. Or with him.

With my fashioned skirt out of the way, all my normally shielded regions were wide open. So every speck of skin sensed Lance closing in, experienced the strong glide of his large hands petting from my knees to my butt, over and again, both restful and arousing. His warm breath came hotly over my flesh, agonizing when he spoke near where Jeff and I were joined. "Lookin' good, Jeffrey." Fingertips fondled one side of my ass. "Looking real good."

He reached my crack and a single finger made the journey downward, skating past my anus to nudge my inner workings, right where Jeff had lodged deep and stalled, his breath harsh against my ear.

Jeff shuddered beneath me. Around me, inside of me.

That was when I realized I'd latched on to his shoulder with my mouth, was sucking on him without thought, my lower body clenched as tight as my teeth.

"Do you think..." Lance mused, and after circling the area where Jeff and I comingled, touching us both—to my surprised inhale and Jeff's grunt—his finger retreated. Then advanced—back toward my anus. "Think this little filly might like having her ass played with?"

Little filly? Huh. He compared me to a horse?

Filly. Fuckwhore. Fruitcake! Does any of it matter? my voice screamed at me. *Go with it! Feels way too good to balk at the bridle now!*

Jeff, his legs and cock like granite, tunneled one hand through my hair to grasp my scalp. He tugged, releasing my hold on his neck and tilting my head until he could look at me. I blinked when tangled strands streamed in front of my face. Through the mangled mess, I saw tiny beads of sweat dotting his temples and the space above his lip. "I don't know but I'm thinking yes," he told the other man while his eyes probed mine. "Why don't you try it?"

Lance wasted no time, rimming my ass with that slick finger in ever-narrowing circles until it was stationary, perched atop the puckered opening.

Under Jeff's gaze, my tongue slipped out. I tasted him on my bottom lip and my anus flared against the pressure, giving way for Lance to push inside.

I caught my breath the same instant my pussy clamped down on Jeff's cock.

"Yeah, she likes it." Jeff smiled with his eyes though the hand on my scalp and the line of his mouth remained unyielding.

"Good, then." Lance withdrew his finger partway only to push it deep once again, starting a rhythmic pumping motion in my anus. "I'll just have some fun down here while I wait for my turn."

As though that set something off in Jeff, he stumbled backward, Lance scurrying to keep up, and began thrusting in earnest, bumping into Rupert and knocking my panties off—so that's where they'd landed?!—but not stopping until his back was at the wall and he could heave into me with everything in him.

Lance must've added a second finger because suddenly I was so full, so close to coming, so—

With a pained shout, Jeff lunged deep and hard. It hurt. But I didn't flinch away, just kept arching toward him, taking him in. Watching the intense look that betrayed what was going on below.

He stood there, cussing through an orgasm while his shaft jerked within me, diving upward in tiny, stabbing jolts as he ejaculated.

"Fuck! Fuckin' dammit!" he all but roared, his customary cool gone under the power of passion, the weight of release. Smoothing my hair away from my eyes with abrupt, shaky motions, he rested his forehead against mine and apologized on choppy exhales. "I didn't mean...to do that. Not...*dammit*...yet."

"That's okay." I hadn't come. In fact, at his unexpected roughness, my pending climax had paused, hovering just before peaking. It scaled down now, maybe in response to his self-directed anger. "Really, it's okay." My legs shuffled against each other, squashed between his back and the wall. The action seated me lower, the short hairs above his cock tickling my clit as our groins came into utter and complete contact. "Due to condom defection the last time, you were overdue."

Lance had stilled in me when Jeff came. Now he laughed as he eased his fingers slowly out and climbed to his feet. "He told me about that. I take it we're set tonight?"

"We're set," Jeff and I told him in unison.

Lance rubbed his chin on the top of my head and gripped my waist. "Good, because this fucker may have blasted off before seeing to you but I won't be so selfish."

He lifted me up and Jeff's cock eased out. Lance braced me while I caught my balance and shuffled to face him. Herbert had swung between us. I brushed one long-hanging, leafy tendril aside and focused on Lance.

I looked up, way up. Then way across. "Dang. You're bigger than you looked downstairs."

The Stud Card might have said six foot two but he towered over me, more muscular than his headshot had indicated. Neither had the fading black eye been apparent either. Goodness, these guys really beat each other up, didn't they?

Adds to the caveman factor, don't it, ducks? I wasn't sure about that but I couldn't deny how it amped up the manly, hotness quotient, especially for someone used to refined, desk-sitting businessmen.

"Yeah, standing at the bottom of a stairway tends to do that."

Good. He could go on thinking that's where I'd seen him first.

While I'd been otherwise occupied, Lance had stripped to reveal a body of divine proportions. Where Jeff had well-defined, lean muscles, Lance sported the build of a fighter. He was broad all over, solid, like a heavyweight boxer. Tan too, or maybe that was his natural skin tone because even his groin and cock were the color of pale coffee. Well maybe not his cock, flushed and reddened I couldn't help but notice, likely aided by the fist he pumped along its pussy-watering length.

"Not scaring you off, am I?" Lance asked, halting his fist when he saw where my gaze had landed. And stayed.

Though I hadn't climaxed, my body felt a strange sort of lethargy from just having Jeff inside. From being the one who had given him release. But now, watching Lance's cock stir under my regard, sweeping my gaze over his sculpture-worthy physique, and feeling Jeff come up behind me, the ache that'd been muted thundered into full bloom.

"She's not scared." Jeff surprised me by answering, settling his hands on my shoulders. "She's just taking it all in."

He repeated what I'd told him that very first night, stunning me with the recollection.

"I'm hoping she can take it all in." Lance released his hold on his shaft and grabbed my hand. "Don't want my business getting cold and shriveling. That's no way to make an impression. Where's your bedroom? And what's that sweet smell? It's been eating at me since we got here."

"Last door on your left." Jeff provided the intel and nudged me forward, whisking his hands from my shoulders down my spine to flutter his fingers over my bottom as I followed his friend.

"Chocolate sauce. I made some earlier."

"Chocolate sauce?" Lance braked at the edge of the living room and spun toward me. His grin was infectious. "No fooling?"

"It's syrup really," I explained with a one-shoulder shrug as my other was immobile due to his warm-fingered grip. "I hope you're not disappointed. After it's been in the fridge a while it thickens up, for now it's pretty thin."

His eyes closed and he dramatically fell back onto the corner wall, releasing me to brace both arms over his chest. "Be still my beating heart." He peeked at me through slitted lids. "You've got milk?"

"Watch it, junior!" Jeff jostled Lance where he'd landed so he could free a bank of ivy leaves. "You trapped Beauregard here."

Lance straightened, his eyes following the leafy triangles up to the hanging basket. "Beauregard?"

"Don't ask." I said it the exact moment Jeff laughed it.

Pointing to Lance, he added, "Nimrod here thinks he's four. He has a chocolate-milk addiction that won't quit."

Hands on my waist, Lance steered me down the hallway. "Me? A kid? Oh yeah?" he tossed over his shoulder. "And who's the doof who came prematurely?"

"Watch it!" Jeff growled. "Unless you want me analyzing *your* performance."

"Oh, wow." Lance froze at the door to my bedroom. He pulled me against his chest and peered in over my head as though afraid something dangerous might be gunning for him. "It's an effing forest."

"Not quite but close." Making himself at home, Jeff scooted around us and strolled in. He immediately went to the bed and started dragging off the covers.

"Why does he do that?" I asked Lance, who'd followed Jeff, bringing me with him.

"What? Strip the bed?" Lance's tone indicated he didn't have a clue or really care. He was too busy inspecting Mac's many offshoots.

"'Cause I don't like having anything in my way," Jeff answered. He finished whipping the flat sheet off with a flourish, leaving the mattress decorated in the baby blue knit fitted sheet I'd put on yesterday morning. "Speaking of strip, did you know Lance used to be a dancer?"

"Now how in the hell would she know that?" Lance sounded embarrassed.

"You mean *stripper*?" Reaching the bed, I tugged on Lance's arm to make him face me. "No way. You look too wholesome." If one discounted the yellowed shiner rimming his left eye.

"Wholesome, huh?" Lance gave Jeff a look I couldn't decipher.

"Wholesome? Him?" Jeff snorted. "That's a crock."

A deep flush painted the latté hue of Lance's cheeks. He glared at Jeff. "I told you I'm trying to live down those ignoble three months. Why'd you go and bring it up?"

Jeff gloated as he stretched out on the bed, bare-assed and totally comfortable. He hooked his legs at the ankles and propped his head on his interlaced fingers. "Payback, buddy, for that pre-mature-ejaculation crack."

Lance, red-faced and stiff-cocked, rubbed one hand over the back of his neck. "And now that you blabbed, I'm guessing you want a demo."

Jeff barked a protest. "Not me, dickweed. Carolina." He unhooked his ankles and used one long leg to draw me to his side. "Am I right? Have you ever been to a nudie bar, sweet Care? Seen a man parade down to his birthday suit to musical accompaniment?"

Having fun at Lance's expense, which he didn't seem to mind overly much, I allowed Jeff to guide me onto the mattress beside him. He drew me down, along his length, and I settled in, as though reclining naked on my bed—with a partner—was an everyday occurrence. "Can't say that I have, dear Jeffrey."

Jeff chuckled.

Lance groaned. The look he shot me was two parts embarrassment and one part pride. "I know when I'm beat." He gave me some unmistakable hip action which made a certain part of his anatomy do its own little jig. "How about it, Carolina? Want your very own personal lap dance?"

I did! But...

Feeling Jeff's hard body luring me closer, I burrowed into his side and used his chest as a pillow. "Only if I don't have to move."

"Nah. I'll do all the work." Lance no longer appeared resigned to his fanny-baring fate. He seemed delighted. That charming, boyish grin grew naughty, excited even, and I got the impression having an audience was turning him on. "If I'm going to do this thing, I might as well do it right. Be right back."

Lance disappeared down the hallway.

"Here." Jeff abandoned his sprawled pose and shoved the remaining pillows behind him, toward the head of the bed. Once everything was arranged to his satisfaction, he again extended his legs, spreading them wide and tugging me between, his arm looping around my middle until my spine was snug against his chest. "How's this? You don't have to move *and* you have front row viewing privileges."

Naked. In my bed with a hot guy—a *naked* hot guy—cradling me against his chest, his long, muscular legs bracketing mine, his hands resting on my hips, fingertips lightly trailing over my abdomen, his chin on my shoulder...

Watching another guy, a formerly naked, now struggling-into-his-jeans-and-shirt other guy —"So you can get the full effect," Lance said with a wink—about to get naked again and dance. For me?

"How's this?" I sighed and relaxed into Jeff's steely heat, my fingers grazing over his hair-roughened thighs and slowing to a stop when his quads flexed. "*This* is perfection. Pure, absolute perfection."

TEN

When His Friend Declares: Chocolate Sauce to the Rescue!

"FRONT ROW IS RIGHT." Who wouldn't be delighted with their own strip show for one? Dadgum, I was a lucky girl.

And about to get luckier!

It was true, so true, and I didn't have it in me to wish my little voice to perdition, not when there were so many other things—gorgeous things— to focus on.

Properly stuffed and zipped, Lance unthreaded his belt and tossed it aside. He palmed his cell and scrolled through several screens. "Just let me dial up some tunes, set it on speaker, and we'll be set."

After placing his phone on my nightstand, Lance staked out his dancing spot in the space between my bed and the door. The first notes of *I'm Too Sexy* rang out, the song fitting perfectly with how he started taunting me by lifting and lowering his shirt.

"Come on!" Jeff blustered with exaggerated impatience, causing me to giggle. "Get to the good stuff already!"

Lance wagged his finger our direction. "Nuh-uh. I'm too sexy to hurry."

Even as he laughed, Jeff hugged me tighter and my body responded, settling deeper into the vee of his thighs.

While Lance turned his back to us and performed some creative, limber gyrations with his hips and ass, my fingers slid downward on the solid rock of Jeff's legs. After a few seconds of the back-and-forth motions of my nails over his skin, I felt the subtle prod of Jeff's cock as it stirred behind me.

Thinking television cop show titty-bar dances didn't count, and the ones in the movies shouldn't either, I wanted to watch my first live strip show. I wanted to admire the flex and play of intriguing muscles dancing enthusiastically before me. Muscles usually not bared to my gaze as a tight T-shirt being toyed with made my eyes play hide-and-seek with sheer perfection.

I wanted to appreciate controlled hip action, abs that should be illegal, and the teasing glint of sexy groin hair when jeans were playfully folded back. I wanted to see more.

The problem was, while my gaze remained riveted on Lance and his amazing body and sultry moves, my attention was split.

Divided between the men.

I couldn't help but bask in what was going on before me, but neither could I stop fixating about what was going on *behind* me, what I couldn't see but could feel. Could sense and even smell.

Jeff's inviting scent. The faint hint of sandalwood captured me. Hiding beneath the citrus of his aftershave, so light it almost eluded detection, the rich fragrance nevertheless caused my lungs to expand as I inhaled ever deeper, hoping for more. The light strokes he delivered first on my outer thighs, down toward my knees, then higher and on top of my legs, his strong fingers moving mine out of the way while his tormented me, rubbing everywhere they could reach and back again, stroking closer and closer to my core. Where I wept for him.

Or maybe my body cried *thanks* for the gift I was being given. Lightning, remarkably, had struck twice. Here I was—naked, by gum!—in front of two men, fine-ass, well-hung men, one of them freakin' *stripping* for me and I wasn't, amazingly, obsessing over my chest, or lack thereof. I wasn't worrying a speck about my performance or doing or saying—or squealing—the wrong thing. All I could think was how I was having the time of my life.

That and how I wished Lance would, "Take it off. Take it all off, baby!"

I hollered the encouragement as Jeff lowered his head and licked a hot path to my ear. "You're really getting into this, aren't you?"

Heck, yeah. All of it.

Restless inside, I shifted, felt his growing erection hardening, lengthening between us. My nails sank into the muscles cording his leg.

My toes clenched together, then stretched. My breath hitched. Cream flowed.

And still Lance danced, now to Rod Stewart's *Da Ya Think I'm Sexy?*, the rounded cheeks of his firm butt coming closer when he spun and shimmied backward toward us, kicking off his jeans to the beat of the music.

When Lance reached the side of the bed, the upper muscles in the back of his thighs flexing with every rhythmic thrust and jerk of his hips,

Jeff tensed behind me. His lips had never left my neck and now he coaxed, "Slap his ass."

At the command, his warm breath blasted into my ear and settled deep.

"What?"

His fingers halted their maddening forays once they reached the border of my pubic hair. "Slap him, Care, right on his ass. He'll like it and I think you'll like doing it."

My sex clenched. *Feel me up already!* "You're not allowed to make physical contact with strippers." I shared my limited knowledge on the subject. "You get kicked out or something."

Jeff laughed. "We're in *your* home!"

"It's a private showing, sweet pea," Lance chimed in, spinning round to snare my gaze. "No need to worry about cops or cuffs—unless you want to." He grinned like the devil and waved his equipment tantalizingly near. "Grab me anywhere you want. For now, it's your show. Pretty soon"—his voice switched from indulgent to inviting, the seductive, raw edge he employed quickening my pulse—"it'll be closing time and *your* turn to shine."

Did he expect me to strip? Not in this century. Not— "Ow-*umm!*"

Oh God.

Jeff had plunged both hands between my legs and taken hold of the short curls residing there. He gave another yank, not excessively sharp but definitely enough to command my attention, hiking my skin and hair up an inch and *hurting so dang goooooood.*

"Do it," Jeff instructed again with a third wonderful-agonizing tug.

The stinging sensation that resulted made me bold. I held out my hand. "Stud dancer, bring that tempting body within reach."

While Lance sashayed his posterior right up to the head of the bed, Jeff gentled his touch but kept my hairs seized in his grip. Keeping me on the edge, expecting. My internal muscles contracted against the pressure he exuded. *Touch me!*

Lance bent forward, facing away.

Interesting.

I guess I'd always thought having an ass shoved in my face, not that I'd ever given it any *conscious* thought, might be off-putting. A little...crass maybe.

Crass? Not this ass.

Muscular and attractively curved, twin dimples topping it off, two honey-brown legs beneath. Oh, yeah. This ass just made me go, "Yum!"

And without being fully aware I intended to go through with it, the next thing I registered was my palm whipping directly across the shadowed crack in the center of those sexy, flexing buttocks. *Thwack!*

"Do it again," Jeff encouraged, pulling upon my pussy hairs in time with my spanking arm. Lance stayed bent over, dancing in place, his feet lifting, knees bending to the music, the tan halves displayed so very clearly and within reach and just begging for more.

Thwack! Pop, pop!

Lance groaned and wiggled a bit closer.

THWACK! "Ohmphth!"

On the last swat, Jeff released my curls to drive his fingers straight down my slit. "That's cheating!" I accused, smacking Lance again, because I could. And because he seemed to dance faster and with more abandon the redder I turned his butt. "Get me all distracted and go in for the grope. Darn player."

Jeff's fingertips fluttered and edged inside. He swept his tongue across my ear. "Complaining?"

"Watch it now!" Lance hollered and flinched.

"Oops! Sorry!" Unintentionally, I'd pricked my nails into his posterior. My thighs clamped around Jeff's wandering hand. "I can't concentrate when you do that. *That's* my only complaint."

Jeff turned my chin with his free hand, the one my thighs weren't strangling and mashing toward my depths, and brought my mouth to his. "You ready for more?"

His eyes tracked over my face, weighing my response.

Lance eased away from my clawing action and I heard him by the nightstand, changing the song selection. As a slow, romantic ballad filtered out, the mattress dipped with his weight. "Yeah. Ready for me to join the party?" he asked, smoothing one hand up my leg.

Was I ready for more? I stared into Jeff's eyes. *I don't know but...* "Show me what you've got."

"Me too?" Lance climbed completely onto the bed as he took hold of my crossed ankles, one in either hand. "Just to be clear—unless I hear otherwise in the next two seconds, I'm assuming that means a party for three."

I loosed my chokehold on Jeff's wrist, allowed my legs to unclench at the gentle insistence from Lance, and both guys went straight for my center, parting hair, separating folds, their fingers becoming slick...my cream running thick...

"Oh yeah. You both." Bending knees and working my hips, I slunk down till my head was on one of Jeff's thighs, his torso coiled above me, both he and Lance doing turn-me-on things to my core. "Do with me what you will. Just give me a cock to suck."

Jeff didn't know it yet, but I had a surprise in store.

He gently scooted my head onto the mattress and moved above me. Kneeling on his knees and stroking his length, he rubbed the tip over my chin. "Thought you couldn't concentrate with too much going on."

"What can I say?" *No guilt, remember?* I heard his refrain from weeks ago and decided to truly live it. "You've given me an appetite and I'm hungry for more." I stuck my tongue out for a teasing lick. "Who wants to concentrate when they could be orgas-*mmmm*."

He slid the head past my lips and I got to taste him again. Finally.

And possibly even better, I had a chance to redeem myself for my first-time-at-bat performance that long-ago night, the one that had branded me a rookie in his eyes.

So, while I might not have *expected* him to show back up in my life, I'd hoped. God, how I'd hoped. I could deny it to Kathi, deny it to my little voice even, but deep down, in my heart of hearts, I'd done all but get on my knees and pray for his return.

Because something about him made me sexually braver than I'd ever been before, made me yearn to walk the line *and* skip beyond it. And though you can't learn everything from books, you can certainly try.

Maybe it was just my way of saying—or sucking—*thank you* to the man who'd taught me about myself and brought me out of my afraid-to-play sexual stupor. Maybe it was part of my personal evolution in the erotic arts.

Regardless of why, I wanted to impress him. To knock his socks off and send him to the moon.

And I wanted to do it with my mouth.

Slanting my head back until he slipped free, I made the request. "Can you change directions? I think I can reach you better that way." *And I know I can get my hands on you easier.*

"You got it."

"Keep yo hairy butt outta my face!" Lance gave Jeff a playful shove as he swung his legs over me and rotated, snugging his knees alongside my torso toward my armpits until, with no more than a slight tilt, I could reach him with my mouth.

"How's this?" he asked.

I nodded. This was perfect. Exactly one of the positions the book had recommended for easy access to a certain little-toyed-with region on the male body.

As I was mentally thinking through how to maneuver—written instructions could only do so much; they couldn't prepare you for the heat, the musk, the *power* emanating inches above you, when faced with such a bounty—Jeff jabbed a thumb over his shoulder to indicate Lance. "Pay him no mind. Jackwipe here's just jealous."

"So you think!" Lance cradled my ankle in his palm and traced the pads of his fingers over and between my painted toenails. What was it about hockey players and my feet?

I pulled back from that direction fast. If I started thinking about how famously Jeff sucked on my toes, I would never move from selfish enjoyment to selfless execution.

"Jealous of what?" Lance asked, massaging each toe.

"Hmmm?" I made a sound to indicate I was interested when really, I was analyzing strategy. Planning my next move.

"That I come by this naturally," Jeff said, sliding his palms over his chest, drawing my gaze up the beautiful planes of his body, covered with just the lightest sheen of pale, golden hair, "and don't waste time like you do waxing or running a razor over—*ahh*—Carolina!"

While the men had postured and preened, which I secretly found adorable, and fluffed peacock feathers over who had the best physique, I'd decided it was time to apply my talents to one "peacock" in particular.

Busying myself on two fronts, I'd grasped the underside of Jeff's cock with my left hand and flipped it up, exposing his scrotum for my first trick. For my second, I simultaneously whipped my right hand in between his thighs and behind his balls to stroke his perineum.

"Car—*Oh! Oh! Oh!*—lina!"

Yes indeed, the book had been right about getting a reaction from *this*. Although, given the way Jeff was starting to turn purple and hyperventilate all at once, maybe I wasn't supposed to be doing both things at the same time.

So I backed off, stopped lip-nibbling one of his balls and concentrated on the stroking motion I'd learned. Simply rubbing a couple fingertips from his anus toward his testicles, petting that tiny, tender slice of masculine anatomy that was supposed to be super receptive to any stimulation I delivered.

Varying the timing of my fingers and occasionally throwing in a little nudge toward "no man's land", just to keep him wondering, I took his floundering cock back into my mouth.

While Lance's touch on my ticklish foot dwindled to light forays over my ankle and shins, I explored Jeff's cock, focusing on his glans and the coronal ridge that flared out just before his shaft. Using first my lips, then tongue, I applied pressure and suction from different angles, taking my cue from the gurgling sounds he made as when to move on and where to linger.

From this direction, I was able to search out his "sweet spot" on the underside of his cock, just beneath the ridge. Known as the *frenulum*—a totally new word to my vocabulary—this little area was considered the closest equivalent on a man's body to a woman's clit.

Who knew?

And it was there I focused an inordinate amount of tongue action. While keeping my fumbling fingers in motion as well.

He must've liked it, a lot, because in between grunts and shouts of my name, Jeff did a little whimpering of his own and his cock firmed perceptibly in my mouth.

"Enough." His trembling thighs surrounding me, he growled the command to stop.

I obeyed.

Partially.

Transferring my efforts from his perineum and sliding my hand away j-u-s-t enough to grab one side of his ass and make him *think* I might go back for more, I tilted my head, allowing his cock a bit of false freedom. My left hand had remained at the base. Staring up at Jeff, I aimed his beautiful, angry-looking erection upward, then downward, made a tight ring of my fingers and pulled on him until he was back at my lips. Until he was hyperventilating once again.

The dormant siren in me had finally come to life and drawing it out as long as I could, I swirled my tongue around his crown. Then once again, slower. Thinking I'd put him through enough torture for a single session, not to mention how the muscles in my lips and throat, muscles I'd honed thanks to exercises in my trusty little book, were starting to fatigue, I sucked him back into my mouth. And hummed.

"Lance! What in the *hell* are you doing back there?" Jeff stared down at me as though he was contemplating taking out a hit on my life.

Having mercy on the poor fellow, I stopped humming and let my tongue turn pliant. Let it become a gentle, rewarding tribute of sorts.

"Lance? Fuckin' dammit, answer me! Where the hell are you?" Jeff didn't look away when he asked. No, he stared down at me, the scowl creasing his forehead slowly fading as I so prettily, so softly licked him.

But he had started to sweat. "Lance?"

Jeff's erstwhile teammate leaned forward so he could see us both. "Good lord, man, I was getting an education from this direction. Did you see where she had her hand—"

Jeff shoved Lance's head away. "I didn't need to fuckin' see it, I was *living* it but thank you for that haunting image of you staring at my nut sac. Now get between her legs and distract the hell out of her. That's an order!"

"Aye, aye, Captain." Chuckling, Lance disappeared. I easily tracked his progress when he shackled one of my ankles and propped my foot on the bed. He nudged my knee until my leg opened wide, spreading my thighs. Spreading my center.

And making me wholly aware of how wet I'd become from licking Jeff. The unmistakable trickle of desire gliding down my sex brought home how wanton I'd become. How wonderfully wicked. Made me stop tenderly tonguing Jeff's precious package and instead hollow my cheeks to pull his crown and the upper part of his shaft firmly into my mouth.

Made my fingers tighten on his butt, and his balls.

Made him groan out another command. "Lance, if your mouth isn't driving her mind to distraction and her pussy to orgasm in two seconds, I'm going to yank off your cock and feed it to the piranhas!"

"The Portland Piranhas?" Lance named another team Kathi had told me about. He laughed against my core, then gently blew over the drenched channel. Without further preliminaries, he braced my thighs and went to town, going down on me and making good, every bit as distracting as Jeff wanted.

The moment my efforts slacked off, just the tiniest bit, Jeff pulled free and came down on both arms, a trickle of sweat rolling from his face to land in my hair. "Holy hell, Carolina. You've been practicing!"

Was that a frown or just shock? Maybe stunned pleasure?

"Have you?" The edge to his voice sliced through me. Was he jealous? Nah, too implausible. "Have you been practicing?"

I borrowed a page from Kathi's book to set him at ease. "Only..." After what I'd just done with my mouth, talking felt foreign. "Only in my dreams."

Jeff leaned closer and brought his face within inches of mine. Another bead of sweat rolled free, this one finding home near my collarbone.

"Are you pleased with yourself?" His voice had gentled. It was almost as though by coming closer and talking softer, he had granted us a private moment.

Was I pleased with myself? I thought of what all I'd done and how he'd responded.

Heck yeah, I was pleased. Taking my time with the gesture, I released his scrotum and dug the nails of my left hand into his flank and scraped toward me, nothing too deep but certainly not a pansy-ass motion either, until I ultimately brought my fingers to my mouth where I proceeded to suck two of them in, mimicking how I'd sucked him. I blinked my eyes once in a sign of assent.

He could make what he wanted to of that.

"Guess what?" At his low words, my right hand tightened on his butt cheek. I expected him to rail at me, to threaten payback, turnabout, to tell me *his* inner workings were off-limits from here on out. What I didn't expect, when I widened my eyes in a show of curiosity, was for him to kiss one of his hands and place it on my cheek. "I'm pretty damn pleased with you too."

That just made me warm and fluttery all over.

Made me rise up into Lance's mouth and gush anew.

Jeff quickly straightened and grasped those fingers I'd been sucking on in one hand to pull them free while he fed me his cock with the other. "Get back to it." It was another bossy command but I saw the smile in his eyes. "Let's see how much I can take."

He kept possession of my hand, lacing our fingers and anchoring them against his thigh.

The room soon saturated itself with our moans, with the scents of sex and sounds of longing. Jeff had gotten his wish—it was difficult to concentrate. Really difficult. Especially when there was so much sensation to savor: the velvet skin of his shaft sliding over my tongue, Lance's hands flexing on my thighs and dipping inward, his lips at my core, teeth tugging on one side of my labia and *sucking it into his mouth.*

Which prompted me to suck harder on Jeff.

And had him swearing like a salty sailor.

"Hold up, baby." In contrast to the string of profanities he'd just peppered through the air, Jeff tenderly pinched the sides of my mouth with the hand not holding mine, opening my jaw and easing his cock out. "Lance?"

The man between my legs slid his tongue over his fleshy captive before releasing it to answer. "Ready, man."

Strong hands soothed my quivering thighs but Lance's mouth stayed away. Far, far away.

I whimpered at the lack, my body thrumming more intently every second.

"Where do you keep the KY?" Jeff asked, interrupting my haze of near orgasmic euphoria.

"The K-what?" I repeated blankly, my lips feeling swollen and aroused, too big for my mouth.

"The sex juice. Lubrication. Easy Glyde."

His question registered. KY Jelly.

"Where is it?" I stalled. Oh darn.

Darn. Darn! I knew he wasn't going to like this so I arched up to lick his shaft, hoping it might in some way make amends. My hand tightened in his. "I don't...don't..."

"You don't have any, goddammit." This time he wasn't as easygoing over the lack of supplies as he had been about the condoms. *"You don't have any!?"*

Even as my body screamed at me for the delay, my mind scrambled for a solution. "Uh, baby oil? Butter?"

I heard a faint snap. "I know just the thing." The confidence Lance exuded doused Jeff's growing ire. "Never fear," Lance assured. "We're covered." His hands abandoned my thighs as his weight left the bed.

I didn't give a second's thought to where Lance might be going or what he was after. All I cared about was the familiar—at least in the bedroom—feeling of failure that threatened to swamp all my wonderful progress. I was determined not to let it. "Jeff, I'm sorry. Really. It's my fault. I should—"

"Hey, hey." He used his knees to backpedal down my body until our eyes met. Releasing my hand, he stroked one finger across my lips. "None of that, sweet Care. I'm not mad. Just impatient." Giving me a self-deprecating smile, he added, "See what you do to me? If anyone's to blame, it's me. I should've mailed a tube of that too."

I nearly giggled in relief. He was being so *nice*. "But—"

"No guilt, remember?"

I did. I nodded beneath his touch. My palms skimmed over the firm, satiny muscles of his back and shoulders, holding on, holding him near. "Speaking of my gift, we—"

"Got it!" Lance sang as he entered. "Chocolate sauce to the rescue."

Holding the pan by the handle, he tapped the underside twice before placing it on my night-stand within easy reach. "It's cooled." He dunked one finger and brought it to his mouth. "Mmm, delicious."

"Condoms," I croaked out. The divinely heavy weight of Jeff and the solid presence of his body —and erection—blanketed me. That, combined with the erotic sight of Lance sucking on his chocolate-covered finger, nearly floated me to heaven.

Jeff caught on. "Where are they?"

"Bathroom. Cab'net." My words garbled out because instead of moving off to get them, Jeff swirled several fingers in the pan and propped himself up on one arm to slide his chocolate-coated fingers over my breast.

"Lance." It was a one-word order.

"Fine," the other man grumped, "but the next time I enter this room, I ain't leaving till I get my rocks off."

ELEVEN

When He Finally Makes Her Scream

"HE THINKS HE'S SO DEBONAIR." Jeff indicated the door with his elbow. "Then he spouts off with something like that. *Get his rocks off*," Jeff mocked. "Ignore the grumbling goofball."

I wanted to smile but couldn't, not with Jeff staring into my eyes, dragging his body lower until his lips hovered over my nipple. Hovered but made no move to lick. Instead, he asked quietly, "Where do you want me tonight?"

"Hmm?" My gaze had dropped to my cocoa-topped nipple. Knotted into a pained point, it strained upward toward his mouth. Probably aided by my back as it arched off the bed.

One hand to my shoulder, he kept me in place, even gave me a little shake. My eyes flicked from my chest, now smelling divinely of the Hershey's factory, to his planes-and-angles expression. The one that portrayed both tenderness and urgency. "My cock, darlin'. Do you want it here"—his chocolate-smeared hand dove between my legs where he pressed one knuckle just inside the puffy lips—"or do you want me here?" He withdrew that taunting touch in order to slide his entire hand between me and the mattress. Grasping one butt cheek.

Gulp. I swallowed hard. Tried to appear unconcerned even as my virgin ass gave a little quiver.

At the same time? I wanted to ask but it would ruin the cosmopolitan act I was trying to pull off. I was a woman of the sexual world, I reminded myself. No guilt.

"And we...are..." Lance returned, brandishing the condoms like a minion serving his king. He'd ripped the top flap entirely off, making the foil packets super accessible. He bowed and let the box slide from his palm onto the nightstand. "*All set.* For the rest of the night."

"Carolina?" Jeff's tone was implacable. So was the fierce way he dug his blunt fingernails into my buttock.

It was time to get cookin' or get out of the kitchen. And I definitely wanted to taste what these two marvelous studs had on the menu.

"Facing me. I want you facing me," I whispered, and when he nodded and bent to lick my breast, I wasn't sure if I imagined the flash of pride in his gaze or not.

"Yee-haw! That means I get tails." Lance sounded overjoyed by the prospect.

"Don't be crude," Jeff said between lip-and-tongue licks. Da-*ang* it felt tremendous, having my bosom provide such a treat—and being eaten in such a way.

"But she's been giving you *head*."

"Head*sss*," I snickered.

"You!" Finished devouring the delicacy off my chest, Jeff skewered me with a glare. "When did you get all sassy? I can't decide if I like it or if I should put that mouth to better use."

I opened wide and wagged my tongue.

When Jeff growled, "Lance, you want some of this?" I decided to stop baiting him. So I smiled as coyly as a Disney Princess, all powdery pinkness and fluff.

But my window of redemption had long passed. *Long* being the operative word as Lance was coating his cock, painting his penis in chocolate sauce and aiming it toward my face. "Carolina's the only one who hasn't had a taste."

"By all means." Jeff maneuvered to my side and propped my head on one of his powerful hands, guiding me toward Lance's waiting, dripping, chocolate-covered cock.

I closed my eyes to the sight of the dark dribbles dotting my sheet and swooped my tongue up the underside, catching all I could.

Lance groaned.

I did too. As the first taste of sweet, sweet syrup and *this* strong, aroused male burst over my tongue and exploded on my senses. In a daze I swallowed and returned for more. The goal of cleaning off his shaft, of pleasing him, paled as the rich, silky flavors blended together, better than ever, and spread like magic from my mouth to my head.

I was dizzy, drugged on sugar and sex. Without conscious thought, I found myself sucking the column of his cock into my mouth. No finesse, no real intent to please; mindless passion guided me now.

They'd been prepping me since the moment I opened the door: Jeff's possessive glimmers, the ones I could pretend he really meant, especially when he stroked his hand down the back of my head and gentled me when I became a bit overzealous in my actions, causing his friend to grunt; Lance's spontaneous striptease and willingness to please. How very attracted I was to them both. How very attractive they both made me feel.

When I moaned deep in my throat, ready for the two cocks I'd taken in my mouth to take me somewhere else, Lance sped the vigorous pumping motion of his hips.

"Easy now, Lance," Jeff cautioned, "she's already got you so clean you squeak."

The support behind my head changed and I was no longer ferociously sucking but allowing the shaft and crown to slide free as Jeff ea sed me onto the mattress.

"Race you to the start line." Lance issued that odd challenge and I blinked open lust-crazed eyes to see the men in a competition—who could put on a condom the fastest.

Jeff finished first and practically strutted around to the other side of the bed. "That'll teach you. Here, hand me that."

Lowering himself to the mattress, Jeff indicated the pan.

"Nuh-uh." Lance refused, but as he did so, he helped roll me over into Jeff's waiting arms. "You mocked it earlier. I get the rest."

At a near growl from Jeff, who'd brought me high in his arms and was framing my face and raining kisses over me, Lance tacked on, "What do *you* need it for? Trust me. She's wet enough."

My ears were suddenly muffled when Jeff held me by the side of the head and whispered something that sounded suspiciously like "Who's sharing the most here?"

To which—I thought—Lance replied, "You've got the woman. I'm keeping the chocolate."

Whether I had heard the exchange correctly or not didn't matter. My body responded anyway. I squirmed in his arms and sought Jeff's mouth. He met me halfway. His lips raged over my face while his hands roved all along my back and thighs, spiking my desire through the roof.

He rolled to his back, taking me with him so that I reclined on his body.

Kissing his way to my ear, he murmured, so softly I could've imagined it except for the heat of his words—and what they did to me inside. "Anything you don't like, you just pinch my ear and we'll stop, okay? No hesitation."

I nodded and *kissed* his ear instead. Halt this? Stop this magical night of discovery? Never!

"Good girl."

At the first deliberate prod of his cock between my legs, I spread my thighs and lifted to my knees, rubbing over his erection until I had it positioned *just so*. The tip of his shaft nudged against my cleft. Made my body weep harder, zinged sparks from the point of contact all through my abdomen. I tilted my hips, increasing the pressure.

When a wet finger painted down the seam of my backside, I jumped.

Lance. How could I have forgotten him? For even a moment?

The second finger-drenched glide had me arching my back and pushing my butt high in the air. "What you're doing feels so dang good."

"That's my cue for more," Jeff said, satisfaction turning his whiskey-smooth voice a tad strained.

Clasping my back tightly with one hand, he reached between us with the other and placed the crown of his cock at my cleft. He held it there, upright, and allowed the advance and retreat my pelvis made riding the gentle, massaging strokes Lance delivered to bring us into closer contact.

"How's it coming?" Jeff asked Lance, his ragged breathing telling me he wasn't as calm as I'd thought. "Certain, uh, *parts* are gettin' mighty impatient."

"Whoops. Sorry." The languid journey of Lance's fingers traveling the crease and mounds of my buttocks skidded to a halt. "I got a little sidetracked, thinking how she'd taste." He shifted behind me. "So why don't I just find out?"

Something wetter and warmer than before slid over my butt. The melted chocolate?

Rolling into the decadent caress, my internal muscles tensed. Then bloomed.

I wanted to take them inside. Both of them. And I wanted it *now*.

As though he sensed my response, experienced the naughty thrill himself, Jeff groaned and his cock jerked beneath me. I widened my legs, lowering my body to trap him there. On the fringes, not quite where I craved him, I paused. "Wait. I think... I think Lance is—" *No thinking about it!* "Lance is pushing his tongue in my ass," I confessed to Jeff as though I wasn't sure if I liked it or thought penance was imminent. "Down my crack! Ah, *mmm*."

He did it again, twice more, licking sauce off with nibbles of teeth and forays of tongue, lingering directly over and in my ass. And I was sure. I liked it. I definitely liked it.

As though I'd been born to it, I sank down on Jeff's shaft, taking him deep, feeling every glorious, thick inch of his erection spearing through me. My inner muscles clamped and squeezed a trail up his cock as I lifted high into the hedonistic attentions of Lance who loudly and lustily continued licking chocolate sauce off my butt.

Then he touched my anus again and "Deeper!" exploded out of me.

Jeff thrust up hard. The same instant Lance moved his tongue in favor of a finger.

"Mmmm."

On Jeff's next surge, Lance rimmed the tiny opening, readying to push inside. More syrupy wetness drizzled over my crack and down, through the virgin territory.

"Oh, yeah," Lance praised. "Just like that, Jeff." Timing his pressure with the rise and fall of the rhythm Jeff created, Lance pushed his finger fully inside. "Hold it steady now." His throat made a sexy-needy sound. "What. A. Sight." The pressure changed as he added a second finger. "Carolina, ever had a chocolate-dipped dick?"

His fingers twisted and scissored, opening that impossibly snug tunnel. "Or maybe, instead of a chocolate-dipped cone, I should call it a *dick* cone."

I slammed into Jeff's groin and circled him, getting some abrasion on my clit from his fine pubic hairs. Hmm, *yeah.*

"Carolina?" Jeff seemed to ask. He anchored one hand behind my head and guided me to look at him. The other he wedged between us to seek out my clit.

The thought of Lance's condom-encased cock, decorated in my homemade chocolate sauce, coming inside my body? Plowing through my ass and filling me even more than his wicked fingers?

"Bring it on." I whispered the words but my eyes told Jeff *Hurry!*

"She's ready." Jeff gave me a tense smile and shifted beneath me, bridging his thighs so that my butt was elevated several inches.

"You are a sweet treat indeed," Lance praised. His fingers withdrew, then came immediately back, rubbing silky chocolate all over, all *in…*

And then I felt it, the unmistakable probe of his cock. At my anus.

Relax, I told myself. Open.

Chocolate sauce.

Lance's cock.

Jeff.

Like cotton candy on your tongue, I melted and Lance easily slipped past the narrow opening. "That was the hard part, sweetheart. From here, it just gets better."

At first I thought that was Lance, praising me, complimenting me, but then I realized the voice was Jeff's rumbling beneath me, Jeff, clutching me. I ducked my head to kiss his neck and he hugged me to him while his friend forged the rest of the way in.

Holy nerve endings, Batman!

Fiery sensations detonated in my depths. It hurt but in a fulfilling, I-was-brave way. It felt good, in a finally-scratching-that-persistent-inch way.

It felt as though the heavens had opened up and were raining nirvana down on me. And when both men began to move? One easing out as the other slid deep?

Holy fucking hallelujah!

My little voice was back. But I strangled her off on a sigh of dreamy contentment.

.   .   .

IN...AND...OUT. In and out. In, out. In-out. In...and...

They moved like this, over and over, their hands supporting me, words encouraging me. Their strong cocks, the ones *I'd* sucked to steel, pleasuring me.

The longer it went on, the more I liked it. The crazier I became.

My body was so unbelievably full, the tactile sensations so new, bordering on the edge of ecstasy and pain.

I started to quiver, to vibrate and go numb from the inside out. My hips tried to move faster, my pelvis to swing wilder. Jointly, they refused to let me.

Some silly, girly-girl whine came out of me.

"Carolina? Let it go, baby. Let go."

Who wanted to let go? I wanted to feel this way forever!

But my body had other notions.

When Lance leaned over me, the musky heat of him blanketing my bottom and back as the pressure and angle of his penetration changed, I fought to gulp air, fought to make it last.

When Jeff praised me yet again and slid his hand from my clit to graze one breast, his fingers stimulating my nipple by just being *there*, touching me without deliberate motions, allowing the pummeling I received to do all the moving for us, my vaginal walls tried to swallow his entire erection, take him so far inside me I never had to let go.

A buzzing started in my brain. Or maybe that was in their balls. Either way, their smooth, controlled give-and-take turned almost vicious as they jackhammered into me so hard, so fast, and so fiercely I collapsed, fell on top of Jeff and let them take me where they would. I didn't even worry about whether I came or not. I'd been fighting off another climax for so long, I just gave myself over to their care. Their cocks.

"Oh-God-oh-God! Jeff, man, I can't hold back."

"Then come, dammit! I'm about to blow a geyser!"

"Uh-uh-uh-uh— Uh-ah! *Ahhhhhh.* Fucking-a, that's what I'm talkin' about!"

"Hold on, Care. Lance—goddammit—don't move! Not—*ah*—yet! God. Care! *Mmmm-mm.* Shit. I came hard. Sweetheart? Sweetheart!"

"Carolina?!"

"Well, damn us both to hell and the penalty box. We made her faint."

"Are you sure that's all—*oh, God*—it is? Hold on, I'll pull—oh-god*damn*-motherfuc*ker!*"

"Would you keep it down! And get it out!"

"But she's so tight. Feels incredible…"

"Lance!"

"Right. I'm trying—uhhh! Ummm. Okay, let me check. Yeah, she's breathing all right. Shallow but breathing, thank our lucky stars. Hell, Jeff, how come we didn't notice?"

"'Cause we're fuckin' bastards, too busy fucking her to pay attention. Damn me!"

"Damn us both. *Ahmmm.*"

"Hell, Lance, don't go and ya-*awwn.*"

"Want me to help roll her over? Move her off you?"

"No. I'm just gonna hold her awhile. How long do we have? I can't see my watch. She's lying on my arm."

"Coach said he'd have our asses on a platter if we aren't back by midnight. That gives us two *ahmmm*-hours-*mm.*"

"I said stop ya-awning! Fuckin' things are contagious."

"Man, you're a bed hog. You'd think this mattress-in-a-jungle would be big enough for the three of us, but shit, Jeff, you're taking your third down the middle."

"Shut up and sleep."

"Yeah, and I know what happened last time. Coach reamed your ass from here to eternity for missing the plane."

"Rest easy. I'm not *sleeping* this time, jackwipe, just holding her. I still can't believe we made her pass out."

But I hadn't. My stamina had cratered, my muscles keeled and my body collapsed. But lying there, stretched out atop Jeff, with his broad hands petting over my head and hair, down my back to my bottom, with the rise and fall of his chest lifting me in time to his steady breaths, I finally caught mine.

So I might not have finished the session with another climax, but my body buzzed as though I'd chugged back a herd of Jell-O shots and topped them off with a Kamikaze chaser. In short, I felt magnificent. Blitzed on sex but miraculously phenomenal. That and exhausted.

With my cheek pressed to Jeff's chest, hearing his heartbeat, sensing its echo in his shaft where it'd come to rest between my legs, I drifted off.

With a smile on my face.

"OKAY, the mountain lions and bobcats I recognize. And I think this one's a Canadian lynx." I nodded to indicate he had the right of it.

Leaving a sleeping Lance, Jeff and I had relocated to the kitchen where I'd heated up yesterday's spaghetti and some leftover homemade cornbread. He was staring at my refrigerator and pointing with his fork. "But that one has me stumped."

He may call me "sweet" but this adorable man hadn't moved a muscle until I'd stirred. I was half convinced he would've stayed there all night, my very own studly, yummilicious body pillow, if I hadn't done the—regretfully—thoughtful thing and let him know I'd returned to the land of the living.

Jeff, wearing nothing but jeans, sat at my kitchen table, a solid oak monstrosity that didn't fit the style of the apartment at all. It was the one thing from my grandmother's house I'd chosen to keep when she passed on. In the sturdy chair next to him, I fiddled with the sash of my robe, a silky, satiny number in a rich shade of eggplant I'd grabbed off my closet door. It could have been sackcloth and ashes for all the notice he'd given it.

Which was okay, really. Just sitting here, hanging out together, casually chatting the last thirty minutes while he downed two servings of spaghetti and was working on his third piece of cornbread had been fun in a relaxed, friendly sort of way.

And now he wanted to know more about my wildcats? Color me delighted. "That's Simon, he's a caracal. They're native to the Middle East and Africa and my very favorite cat, if you were wondering. Simon has the distinction of being my first baby, the first one I adopted."

"I like those tufts on his ears. He looks like a badass." Jeff shifted on his seat and returned to polishing off his midnight dinner.

"He is. Twice the sanctuary has tried to give him a buddy, a cagemate and both times he goes in for the kill. I guess he's a loner."

I stood to refill our water glasses, congratulating myself when I successfully converted the moan I couldn't stifle into a plausible cough. My upper legs and the regions between felt as though I'd ridden bareback across Jupiter—and I'd never even sat atop a horse. Having no appetite to eat, my body still zinging and zapping all over the place, the sheer excitement and exhaustion of earlier had given way to a deep-seated lassitude that nevertheless kept me wired and energized. If walking stiffly.

"It costs thousands of dollars a month to run the place," I informed Jeff, busying myself at the sink. "The food bill alone is several thousand. A lot of people would say just put them to sleep but these animals didn't ask for their fate. All of them were bred in captivity for the sole purpose of either being skinned or to be sold as pets. It's disgusting, what some people will do for a buck."

Hearing myself run on at the mouth brought my impassioned speech to a halt. In silence, I returned to the table and placed my derrière so gingerly, so cautiously, upon the hard oak seat that I was reminded of a coworker who'd had hemorrhoid surgery and had used that blow-up donut thing every time he sat. This time, at least, I avoided grimacing. I gave Jeff a rueful look. "And there I go, blathering on about something that, in the overall scheme of things, isn't as important as—"

"Stop right there." Finished with his last bite, Jeff scooted the plate to the side and reached for my hand. "I like that you care."

"But it's just *cats*. My grandmother always said people need my help more than dumb animals." Maybe that was why helping those who, due to human interference, were unable to help themselves meant so much to me. Now that I no longer lived with her negativity and nitpicking ways, it'd become a source of joy every time I mailed the rescue sanctuary a check.

"Then I'll just have to disagree with your grandmother. Too bad Tulsa's team isn't the Caracals. I wouldn't mind having that on my jersey. It'd be a fair sight better than the swirling gray windstorm we sport now."

"But then all your girls would want one." Had that just come out of my mouth?

Jeff pushed back from the table. The chair legs scraping across the tile sounded extra loud. He stood and drew me into his arms. "*All* my girls?"

My gaze slid right, then left, then up and back down, around and around like a spinning Ferris wheel that couldn't find a point to land. I settled on his chin. Where I noticed a single, tiny whisker his razor had missed.

"Carolina?"

The imperfection somehow made him seem more real, more reachable. "I'd want one," I admitted, still staring at the rebel whisker. "Your jersey. With a caracal."

Blather on, ducks. You aren't making it any better.

But Jeff did, when he said, "And I just might want to give you one."

He threaded both hands through my hair behind my ears and tilted my head until I was looking directly at him. Sans glasses, his eyes shone clear and hot.

Trying to find some neutral footing before we said goodbye, I questioned, "And what about you, goalie Jeff? What do you do when you aren't blocking pucks?"

His fingers tightened ever so slightly on my scalp. "Like you, whether I'm with them all the time or not, I'm tied to family. My mom's raising my sister's three kids, which is a lot for any woman. But for a woman who thought she was done with child rearing ten years ago when my brother graduated and who runs her own business... Well, it's been a tough adjustment on her and Dad."

He paused and I thought he was done, wanted to ask why his sister or her husband wasn't raising the kids. But I wasn't sure I should pry.

He brought it up, my braver side reminded, *ask away.*

I was still debating internally, still staring into his eyes, when he said, "An impaired driver slammed into my brother-in-law's car, killing him on contact. My sister died a week later from injuries she'd sustained. So, if there's anything I'm passionate about, it's educating idiots who get behind the wheel when they shouldn't."

I was stunned. Both by what he'd revealed and that he'd told me. *Me.* His Cinci puck bunny.

Although, when Kathi first told me the term, I'd insisted it shouldn't apply since I certainly wasn't a hockey groupie. *But still.*

My hands found their way to Jeff's waist, partially on denim and partially on skin. I held on tight. My voice was subdued when I asked, "What do you mean by impaired?"

For some reason, I got the feeling this hadn't been an alcohol-related incident, not the way he'd worded it.

His jaw clenched and a tiny muscle ticked near his eye. "The bastard was on three prescriptions, two of them cautioned about driving or operating machinery. But like most folks, he didn't heed the warnings. Didn't have to pay for it either, just my sister and her husband did. With their lives. And their kids...who'll...never..."

Unable to witness the pain he was sharing, afraid of where this might be going, I hugged him fiercely and tucked my face into his chest. The hands he'd molded to my scalp slid to my shoulders. His breath exhaled in a loud hiss. "Now listen to *me* go on." He chuckled derisively. "You're just so easy to be with, I guess I forgot myself. It happened not that long ago, and I'm obviously not ready to talk about it yet. I'm sorry."

"No need," I assured on a whisper. "No need to apologize."

I just stood there, cradled against this hard, amazing body that belonged to an even more amazing man, rocking gently back and forth in his arms, soaking him in, granting him time. His gut-wrenching revelation explained his seize-the-day attitude and no-guilt philosophy. Because he'd lost someone special in a freak accident, Jeff recognized more than most how fragile life was and how vital to take joy wherever you could find it.

It was a hard reminder that life wasn't fair, wasn't intended to be, and the best each of us could do was make the most of what ever we were given. I thanked my lucky stars that the sizable commercial property sale I'd been working on for ages had chosen *that* particular day to go through, with all parties signing off on the final paperwork and prompting my need to celebrate, and that I'd acted on Kathi's idea of how to do it in style. The event that had sent me, fixed-up and feeling horny for once, into that classy bar looking for a one-night stand.

Because I'd gotten that and so much more.

I don't know how long Jeff and I stayed that way, locked in the embrace. I know I closed my eyes, content on so many levels, and neither of us seemed in any hurry to move.

It wasn't until someone honked in the parking lot that we eased apart and my eyelids reluctantly blinked open.

Jeff instantly lightened the mood. "So tell me, Miss Carolina"—he nudged my chin up to meet his gaze—"what do you do for a paycheck around here? This is a pretty nice apartment."

"My job, you mean? I'm a realtor. Commercial properties, mainly."

"So you stay pretty busy and out of trouble? That's good to hear."

I made a viable spitting noise. "Like everything, it comes and goes. Some years are busier than others." Willing to go along with the change of topic, and more than a little interested in the answer, I queried, "And yourself? What kind of plans do you have after hockey?"

"*After* hockey? You wound me! I'll be playing till I'm back in diapers, and even then probably nudging the puck around with my walker."

"That's not funny!" But the image was so ludicrous he had me laughing.

"Then there's always the family business." His hands came up to my arms where he rubbed them over the satiny robe. The cool, silky fabric I'd never really noticed much beyond its color, seemed to stroke me everywhere as a result. I noticed how it cascaded lightly over my bottom, how the matching belt cinched at my waist seemed entirely too tight. I was reminded how quickly and quietly we'd left my bedroom and a sleeping Lance. How I'd thrown it on without bothering to find panties. "I'll probably join in."

Join in? Had we been talking? Because now my attention was on his nude chest and muscular arms, on his proximity. On my attire. And lack of underwear.

"Care?"

Uh… "Family business?" *Think*, Carolina. "You plan on helping your mom out with perms and color?"

"Who said anything about my mom?"

Had he deliberately spread open the lapels of my robe? Or had it gaped on its own? Exposing the barely perceptible inner swells of my breasts and snagging on my nipples? "Okay, then. What does your dad do?"

And was that really me closing the few, meager inches separating us and pressing my chest to his? Swiveling my hips ever so slightly, like a talented belly dancer, to sway against his gorgeous body? To use the contact to widen that gap in my robe?

"My father?" Jeff's fingers tightened on skin now, inside the collar of my robe, and he paused so long I wasn't sure whether he would answer me or kiss me or throw me to the floor and jump me.

I'm for all three!

"He manages a sporting goods store in Houston and I see I missed a spot." Letting me know he'd been aware all along of how my robe had parted, Jeff licked one finger and scrubbed it over my left breast. He bent his head and tongued the area, then stripped the loose-fitting sleeves down my arms. Once I was exposed from the waist up, the robe hanging by its tie around my waist, he grasped my butt and pulled me solidly into his groin. Rocking back and forth, he groaned. "Oh, I could so get it up again. Think I'm mostly there already but we're not going there. Not now."

"We're not?"

"No, definitely not. Not after that pounding we just gave you." With his semi-hard erection that felt absolutely hard to me, he halted the arousing motion and stayed still, snugged deeply into my lower body. "You think I haven't noticed how carefully you're moving around? How many times you've cringed?"

Darn it! I thought I'd hid that. "But I... I—"

"It's okay, sweet Care. I don't expect you to fly through hoops and do acrobatics all night long just because I showed up. Unannounced and with an extra player."

I wanted to do acrobatics—for him! "But I want—"

"Some time to recover." On each of my butt cheeks, his fingers splayed wide and dug in, nails scuffing over the fleshy area. Through my thin robe, the contact was torture. Absolute, erotic torture. "I understand."

"Jeff!"

"Really, I do." Instead of continuing that divine scratching action with his nails, he allowed his hands to inch inward until his fingertips met at the juncture of my thighs. My hyperaware body responded, wanting him again. Needing him. After all, I'd sacrificed an orgasm earlier for the sake of sheer exhaustion. Didn't he owe me one? "I know you need to rest," he said with the patience of a saint. When all I wanted was to sin again. "Aren't up for another round. And in case you're wondering…"

"Jeff." It was a ragged cry this time as every speck of skin hollered for more. More silky strokes. More of his body bared for my viewing, and touching, pleasure. More of him.

Don't forget—more satisfaction! You gypped yourself out of that last orgasm, ducks. Demand he give you another!

Darn straight!

"Wondering what?" I moaned, my breath coming faster in direct opposition to his languid seduction.

He placed his mouth at my ear and wiggled his fingers, pushing that silky robe into my damp heat. "This is just a tiny, tiny taste of your own medicine."

My own medicine? Clueless about anything but the inferno he'd raged so swiftly into being, I cried, "Put it out!"

"*Pull* it out? But, honey, it's not in."

Somehow he'd taken hold of two sections of fabric which he sawed between the swollen halves of my body. My pelvis tilted until the too-light friction was just on the edge of my clit. I grabbed his upper arms, hoping for balance, praying for deliverance. "Jeff! Put it in!"

"Put what in?"

The darn rat sounded truly baffled. What a crock! "Your cock!" I almost screamed it. But stopped myself just in time. The neighbors were sleeping. Lance was too.

"Whose cock?" *Seesaw, seesaw* went the robe. *Spike!* went my temperature.

"Yours!" I was yelling now, self-moderating totally beyond me. "You fiend, put out the fire!"

He angled his head to kiss a wet trail up my neck. In contrast to my shriek, his voice was a mere breeze. "Maybe I like the thought of you burning—for me."

"Jeff." Nothing but a whimper. Oh, I was weak. So very weak.

"Hmmm?" He just kept kissing me, kept sawing the stupid robe over and into my flesh.

I didn't know. I couldn't speak. Couldn't think anymore. Could only reach for him, digging my nails into his biceps, pleading for him.

"Sweet Care?" The kisses slowed to a stop. So did the silky stimulation. Jeff nuzzled my cheek with his. "Trust me when I say I'll regret this, but I'm gonna go wake Lance. We've got to get a move on. Should've left hours ago."

"J-Jeff?" I took solace in the fact that while he said he was about to leave, he didn't move. Not away.

"But before I go…"

"Yes?" He'd ease the ache, squelch the fire, I knew it.

"I just want you to know…" He twisted his hips, dragging his unmistakable erection firmly against my stomach. "I burn for you too."

It took several seconds for that to sink in. It took several more to realize he'd actually abandoned me. Turned on a dime and strolled from my kitchen, left me standing there, trembling and so worked up. So expectant.

Two more seconds to really realize what it meant—his walking out.

No more orgasms for you! Not tonight.

Another four seconds of trying to breathe. Of telling my body it'd done without sex for so many years, why couldn't it just be satisfied already?

Because he's spoiled you! Spoiled you for hot, hockey lovin'.

After that, it only took a microsecond for me to find my voice. "JEFF WHATEVER-YOUR-LAST-NAME-IS! GET YOUR ASS BACK IN HERE!!!"

TWELVE

When He Makes Her a Promise

IT WAS the rawness scraping my throat, the way the floor shook beneath me and the light fixture shimmied above, that told me I'd screamed like a horny banshee. Like an unpaid hooker. Like a rhinoceros in heat with a stubbed toe.

"JEFF!" Okay, so maybe I didn't know him well enough to play with his perineum, to tongue his frenulum, but this was cruel and unusual punishment.

This was downright mean. Rouse me up and leave me hanging?

"Jeff?" It was a croak this time, pathetic and lonely.

"Be right there!"

Grumbling to myself and griping at the universe, I righted my robe, still in awe at how quickly that man could flame my fire. More in awe of how much the last few minutes with him had touched me: his emotional confession, interest over my fridge décor, how much fun he was in the sack and out (the recent sexual torture not withstanding). Had I ever clicked so seamlessly with any man?

Coming to a decision, I reached for what I'd stashed earlier in a corner on the counter. I didn't have to share it. Could keep it easily concealed in my palm—unless I decided to brave it out.

And just in time too, because after only a second's warning both men came waltzing into the kitchen, looking none the worse for wear. In fact, Jeff was grinning like a hound dog with a belly full of kibble, his shirt back on, darn it. "It's Stanton, darlin', Timothy Jeff Stanton. I'm so proud of you."

"Proud?" Huh?

Lance chuckled as he swept over to the sink and bent to rinse his mouth and drink directly from the raised faucet. When he straightened, Jeff tossed him a kitchen towel—making himself awfully at home in my kitchen, wasn't he?

"Thank you, Carolina, for a fabulous evening." Lance came over and gave me a swift hug. "I appreciate you letting me be a part of it."

I nodded when he released me, softened by his unexpected consideration.

Lance pointed to Jeff. "And Bozo here is proud because he finally got you to scream. Least that's what he said in the bedroom when your howl nearly landed me on the floor."

"I also told him it didn't count," Jeff grated out, looking pained at the disclosure, "because I wasn't *in* you at the time."

After winking at me as I sputtered, Lance walked past Jeff. "I'll wait for you out in the car. Keys?"

"Yeah. Thanks." Jeff tossed a key toward Lance, then spun to me, giving me his full attention. He reached into his pocket and stepped toward me. "Here. I want you to have—"

"Holy hell!" Lance came tearing in before he'd fully left. "Do you know what time it is? Coach is going to skin our hides!"

As though the phrase made him think of my wildcats, Jeff looked over his shoulder at my refrigerator before turning back to Lance. "In the overall scheme of things, us being an hour or two late is no big deal. It's not like we're missing a game. Or a plane. Go get it running. I'll be there in five."

"Better make it two. God, Jeff. You said you were going to wake me!"

"And I did, and the sooner you quit bitchin' and clear your sorry carcass out of here, the sooner I'll meet you at the car."

Stopping in front of me, Lance tried to erase the scowl creasing his forehead. "I know you can't help it, but don't tempt him. We should've been out of here two hours ago."

Flattered, all I could do was fake a commiserating smile. "He'll be down in a jiff."

"Sure he will." Groaning to himself, Lance headed out.

Knowing Jeff really did need to leave, I started following, leading him toward the door. "Come on, big guy. Sounds like I'm getting you in trouble twice in a row."

"You don't hear me complaining do you?"

We reached the entryway where Lance had left the door wide open. Stopping just this side of Rupert, I stepped back, making the way clear for Jeff to hit the stairs and keep on running. "I bet your coach makes up for it."

He stopped shy of the doorway, his feet firmly planted *inside* my apartment. "He does. But his bark only chews off my ears. Being with you makes me happy all over."

"Well, sheesh, Timothy J. Stanton, how can I say anything to that?"

"Don't talk. Just take this." I looked down to see what he'd pulled from his pocket. A slip of yellow paper from one of my sticky pads. Complete with his cell number.

Oh. Wow.

"I know you didn't use it last time, so I'm giving it to you again." When I didn't make any move to take the paper, Jeff folded it in half and raised his arm to weave the yellow rectangle in Herbert's hanging basket. "Don't forget it's there now."

"I won't." Heck, I'd probably tuck it in my underwear drawer too. What I'd snatched from the kitchen counter burned my hand.

"We'll be waiting for your call."

Running my fingertip over the edge, I questioned, "We?"

His rumbling voice carrying up the stairway, Lance hollered out the time which he immediately followed with, "We need to get a move on!"

"In a minute!" Jeff called over his shoulder just as loud. Turning back to me and lowering his volume, he clarified, "Me and Rurik. The ol' clock-watcher out there too, I'm sure."

"My three studs," I murmured. At Jeff's raised eyebrow, I clarified. "You three. You're starting to sound like my very own hockey-player posse."

He laughed. "That has a ring to it."

So jingle his bell!

"You'll call, then?" He sounded hopeful.

Which helped make me more certain. "I won't need to. I, ah, I really debated this"—you have no idea how much—"but I want you to have this."

I was so nervous. Holding out my business card, with my full name and professional contact information was one thing; knowing that on the back, I'd penned my personal cell number and email made me feel vulnerable in a way getting naked with him hadn't.

You've showered with the man for Pete's sake! Seen his peter!

True but he hadn't mentioned wanting my number again, not since he'd first asked weeks ago.

Man up and grow a pair! He gave you his!

Shut up! I ordered my annoying, reckless side. Grow a pair? *Tell that to my chest!*

Jeff reached for the card and my hand jerked back without permission. "You don't have to take it. I mean, you may not even want—"

He snagged my wrist and pried my fingers open in order to see what all the fuss was about. His eyes widened when he saw what he held. His lips did too when he noticed the writing on the back. "Oh, I want," he assured me, retrieving his wallet from his jeans and sliding my card right in front. "Why would you think I didn't?"

"Jeff!" Lance shouted. "Shit, man, it's almost two! Our asses are going to be *fried*!"

"Hold your horses, dammit!"

"Giddy-up!" Lance responded without missing a beat.

Smiling at their antics, I explained, talking fast. "Because I'm a realist. I know you and Rurik, and Lance too, all have girls in every rink and—"

"Hold up." Jeff tucked his wallet away and captured both my arms, slipping his hands down until he grasped my fingers. "A girl in every rink? As in ice rink? What's that? The hockey players' sailor equivalency?"

I nodded, feeling crummy. "Well, yeah."

His arms started swinging our hands, outward and inward, knocking them together gently when they met in the middle. As if we had all the time in the world. "I jumped ship a while back, remember?"

My face heated at the reminder. And at the soft way he delivered it. "Tell Rurik I'm sorry about his grandfather."

Jeff slowed the swinging until our arms came to a subtle stop. He rubbed his thumbs over the back of my knuckles. "I will. I know he's sorry he missed you. He really was looking forward to seeing you again."

"You don't have to say that."

"It's true or I wouldn't have. He's mentioned you more than once, his 'little, shy American'. I think he's taken with you." As though he didn't want to give me the wrong impression, Jeff reluctantly admitted, "But that doesn't stop him from taking others."

"I expected that." Oh, how I'd expected that. These guys were *players*, right?

Jeff nodded once and his fingers tightened. "I just wanted to make sure *you* knew the score."

My hands started to sweat. "I-I don't know how to answer you." More than that, I was surprised at how much it didn't bother me. Learning about Rurik, that was. Why should it? I'd known him for an hour, if that. Now the thought of Jeff— *Whoa! Don't go there!*

"Hey. I didn't mean it as a question. Wasn't saying it to be nice. I was simply stating a fact. Now me? I'm not taking others."

"You're not?" That was the second time in as many minutes he'd indicated as much. *Only this time he'd point-blank said it!*

He shook his head and advanced, drawing my arms up to curve around his neck. "Nope. I'm spending my nights alone. Thinking up things to do with you. Ways to seduce and surprise you."

I could get dangerously used to this. "You are, huh? Is *that* a fact?"

"Hell yeah, sweet Care. A fact and a promise," Jeff whispered, lowering his head and ignoring Lance who yelled out the time again. "Have you forgotten already? I'm not stopping until you scratch my back. And scream my name. *When it counts.*"

"Not stopping, hmm?" I breathed against his lips, my head and body in a tailspin. Did that mean what I thought it did? More hockey studs? More sex? More time with Jeff? "Is that a promise?"

"You bet it is."

Score one for the home team!

His answer was almost lost as his mouth took possession of mine.

And I was lost, to anything and everything he wanted from me.

Author Note

THANKS FOR READING *Her Hockey Studs*. The story started out as a simple "sex with strangers" challenge, with Rurik as the Hero. Shocked me to the core when he got Carolina to his hotel room and his roommate joined in!

As a pantster (a writer who flies by the seat of their pants instead of using a detailed story outline), I had absolutely *no idea* Jeff even existed until he opened that bathroom door.

I love being surprised by my characters and wasn't ready to let this trio go quite yet. The surprises kept coming as Jeff's starting to feel possessive sooner than Carolina—or I—ever expected.

Next up will be *The Stud Takes a Stand*. For now, though, I hope you're enjoying the sexual journey he's taking her on. If you have a chance to write a review, it's always appreciated. Reviews and word-of-mouth are the best things you can do for authors you like.

JOIN my newsletter to learn about future releases. Meanwhile, laugh every day and savor some chocolate for me whenever you get a chance. ;)

About Larissa

A lifelong Texan, Larissa writes sexy contemporaries and steamy regencies, blending heartfelt emotion with doses of laugh-out-loud humor. Her heroes are strong men with a weakness for the right woman.

Avoiding housework one word at a time (thanks in part to her super-helpful herd of cats >^..^<), Larissa adores brownies, James Bond, and her husband. She's been a clown, a tax analyst, and a pig castrator (!) but nothing satisfies quite like seeing the entertaining voices in her head come to life on the page.

Writing around some health challenges and computer limitations, it's a while between releases, but stick with her...she's working on the next one.

Learn more by visiting LarissaLynx.com.

instagram.com/larissa_lyons_author

amazon.com/author/larissa-lynx

bookbub.com/authors/larissa-lynx

goodreads.com/larissalynx

facebook.com/AuthorLarissaLyons

www.ingramcontent.com/pod-product-compliance
Lightning Source LLC
Chambersburg PA
CBHW070733190726
48292CB00002B/242